Love Forever, Live Forever
Annette Mori

Love Forever, Live Forever

Annette Mori

Affinity
eBook Press
NZ
2015

Love Forever, Live Forever

© by Annette Mori 2015

Affinity E-Book Press NZ LTD
Canterbury, New Zealand

1st Edition

ISBN: 978-1-927328-59-0

Editor: Nat Burns
Proof Editor: Alexis Smith
Cover Design: Irish Dragon Designs

Acknowledgments

Probably the most important person to acknowledge, besides my wife, is Erin, because without her gentle and kind guidance this book would never have made it to the eBook market. Erin spent numerous hours teaching me, encouraging me, and helping to transform a jumbled story into something I hope is worth reading. She took a chance with a novice writer and I think may have on occasion even neglected her other duties to respond to all my questions. I pestered her every night and without fail, she would review and promptly respond to my attempts to correct issues with the book. It was truly an honor to work with her, and have her mentor and guide me.

What can I say about Affinity eBook Press that hasn't already been said a million times, but without their encouragement and willingness to work with new writers, people like me would never have their words published—thanks to Erin, Nancy and Julie. They are an incredible group of women and the best publishing company out there—no exaggeration.

Thanks to Kay for her methodical and patient beta edit to polish the book even further. Thanks to Nat for her final edit, Alexis for the proof edit, and Robin for her relentless promotion of the book. Finally, thanks for Nancy for her incredible cover.

On my journey, I elicited the feedback from my older sister, Val, who gave me valuable feedback that helped shape the final version of the story. It was good to know that even though my sister is straight, she appreciated a nice little lesbian romance. My other family members were also very supportive, including my nephew, Aaron and his wife, Chelsea, my wife's nephew, Chad and my little sister, Kim. Finally, my wife, Jody, was supportive from the very start. She kept telling me that I could do anything I put my mind to. Even though she's a scientist and never reads romance novels, she encouraged me to write and fulfill my dream. She finally read the book before it actually hit the market.

Dedication

For my wife and her belief in me and for Erin who makes me laugh and helps me be a better writer.

Table of Contents

Also by Annette Mori

The Incredibly True Adventure of Two Elves in Love
(Affinity 2014 Christmas Collection)

The True Story of Valentine's Day

Prologue

It had been five years since I'd seen her, yet there she was standing in front of me. My Sara. How my heart ached for her. She was my first—first kiss, first date, first lover, my everything.

I am with Annie now. Sweet Annie, who has shown me such love and passion that I know she is who I want to spend eternity with— forever wrapped in her arms.

Yet I can still feel the pull of Sara and seeing her again only intensifies those feelings.

I feel Annie squeezing my hand and I know she is telling me that it is all right—that she is with me. I suspect Annie knows there's a story here, but to her credit, she won't ask anything not now, nor later when we're alone. She'll let me tell my story in my own time. God, I love that about her. I love everything about her. She is my soul mate.

How did it come to this? How did my small town farm girl world bring me to this stage in my life—to this abyss, which I'm now standing over so precariously?

To understand, I will have to tell you, the reader, the story of my life up until this very moment. Maybe Annie will read this journal and she will understand. I'm not much of a linear thinker and I ramble quite a bit, so forgive me for my need to add running commentary here and there.

I'm eighteen years old and just starting college when my story begins....

Chapter One

It's the summer of nineteen ninety-eight and it's unseasonably hot for late August in Seattle. I'm sweating so bad that I have big armpit stains on my tank top as I scrutinize the old brick building. Students are bustling about resembling ants in front of an anthill. The old brick building is their anthill.

My dad is pulling books and CDs out of the back of the Honda.

My mom is squinting in the sunshine, politely taking it all in and I can tell that she doesn't like what she sees. The building is old. The rooms are small and there is a decidedly musty smell to the place. Mercer hall appears to be the oldest, most run down dormitory that the University of Washington offers to their freshmen students. Of course, they assign that dorm to me. I'm a reluctant student, but I'm not really given an option.

All the Jorgeson girls will go to college whether they want to or not. Getting a full ride scholarship sure doesn't help my cause. Dad doesn't see the humor in blowing off my scholarship and traveling around Europe until I can see myself as a college student.

I don't give the building much thought one way or another. My attention is hijacked as soon as I glance down the hall and notice the hot red head casually leaning against the wall. My parents don't know about my preference for women. The red head catches me staring and winks. I'm not sure who she's winking at, so I turn my head around looking for who this hottie can be winking at. There is no one else in the hallway and I start blushing as I realize the wink is intended for me. I can't let my parents see me staring, so I look away and focus on my family who are all loaded up with my belongings as they enter the narrow hallway.

"Hey, Nicky, which room is yours? This junk is heavy," my sister calls out to me.

"Don't get your panties in a bunch. Its right here, room two ten. Who asked you to come here anyway?"

I act like I don't want my sister here seeing me off to college, but I really do. My younger sister, Tess, is my best friend. We are only one year apart in age and we always hang out together. I'm really going to miss her, but I can't admit that to her.

"Nicky, be nice. You know you are going to miss Tess, so stop acting like you're all tough." For some reason my mom feels compelled to point this out.

"Well, this building has a certain amount of old world charm," my dad, the eternal optimist, remarks.

"You gotta be shitting me. This is the oldest dorm on campus and it's not some historical landmark, Dad, it's just old and worn down."

I can't help being a little snarky. Remember I want to travel the world, not live in some old musty building with a bunch of silly freshman girls who are looking to find some hot guy to shack up with.

"For such an intelligent young woman, you sure find it hard to resist using profanity. Really, Nicky, I thought we taught you better than that." My mom seems to forget her colorful language when she's pissed at my dad.

I just want them all to drop my shit off and leave me to get settled. I also want to find the red headed hottie. If I'm lucky, she lives in the worn down rat hole I'm about to spend the next year of my life in.

"You know the drive back to Oregon is going to be really long if you don't head back pretty soon. I got it from here. Let me just get the last box from the car and you can be on your way."

"Are you sure you don't need any help setting up your room?" My dad wrinkles his forehead and gives me that concerned parent look.

"Not from you, Dad. You don't know a Phillip's from a flathead screw driver and don't even get me started on your propensity to smash your fingers, or worse, mine, whenever you wield a hammer." I'm not trying to be mean when I tell my dad this because everyone in my family knows this about my dad.

"What about dinner? Will you be able to get a chance to eat tonight? Are you sure you don't want us to take you to dinner before we leave?" I suspect Mom throws this out there as a final attempt to delay their inevitable departure.

It's always about the food for my mom. Mom's way to show love is to ensure we are well fed and it's a miracle I'm not three hundred pounds. I barely escape high school with only an extra ten pounds and I'm a little nervous about what my freshman year will bring. I've heard about the freshman ten, which will make me a disgusting twenty pounds overweight.

"I've got some granola and other snacks for tonight. So, really, you guys should head out so you can get home at a reasonable hour."

The waterworks begin and my mom predictably starts crying. "Oh, all right. I suppose we should get going soon. I can't believe my baby is in college."

I notice that Dad is trying not to let it show, but I see a tear escape from his eye. I even see Tess get a little choked up. It's mass hysteria and I catch it from my family. I can't help getting misty eyed, too. It isn't my fault that my eyes start watering with my whole damned family starting a crying jamboree.

†

I finally manage to send them on their way and I'm blissfully alone in my room. I'm fortunate because my roommate isn't here. I notice her girly stuff strewn all over the right side and she has enough make up and nail polish to stock the downtown

4

Nordstrom's. Two hours pass quickly and I manage to get most of the room set up. Dorm rooms aren't really all that big, so I don't have much to unpack and set up. I get my stereo placed and stock my mini fridge.

My music is blaring when Lisa the lemon shows up with her entourage. I call her Lisa the lemon because when she opens the door to the room her first expression resembles a person sucking on a lemon. I don't think she's happy that I'm her new roommate. Her prissy friends follow her into the room and give me the once over. I'm guessing they are not impressed. It doesn't take a rocket scientist to peg them as future sorority sisters.

"Don't worry, Lisa, you won't have to live here very long. As soon as we pledge with the Tri Delts, we can go live at the sorority house."

"Damn, I was hoping we could be fuck buddies, but I'm allergic to sorority girls." I'm going for shock value here, because the little prissy bitch just pisses me off with her snarky comment.

"Huh? You don't look like a lesbian." Lisa the lemon narrows her gaze and is scrutinizing me now.

I have to give her props for this comment. She doesn't appear shocked by my comment. I readjust my first impression and think maybe her lemon reaction's related to the musty old rat hole we've both been assigned to and not to me.

"What exactly does a lesbian look like?" I genuinely want to know the answer to this question because I don't have gaydar like every other hot-blooded lesbian.

"Oh sorry, that sounded kind of rude. I'm your roommate, Lisa, and don't mind these two. They're not as bad as they sound. You're like smoking hot, so I guess I didn't expect you to be a lesbian. Personally, I couldn't care less, but I don't think we'll be fuck buddies. Sorry, I don't swing that way."

Okay, I definitely misjudge my new roommate. Her entourage I don't misjudge. They don't say a word the whole time they are in the room. They just sit there watching us, like they're watching some tennis match. They do serve a useful purpose when I end up using them as my own personal whipping post whenever I get pissed or frustrated. Don't feel too sorry for them because, if I'm a bitch, they are both the queen of bitches. Compared to them, I don't even register on the bitch meter.

"That's cool, sorry for being a bitch earlier. I'm Nicky, your smoking hot lesbian roommate. Um, I'm not really out yet to my parents so if you could just ignore my snarky initial introduction, I would be ever so grateful."

"Hey, no problem. I probably looked like I was sucking on a lemon, but it's not you, honest. I'm just kind of disappointed that I got assigned to this shit hole of a dorm."

Funny you should say that, Lisa the lemon. I really should rewind my thoughts because I think she might be kind of fun to have around. She seems not to take offense easily and this might work to my advantage. I certainly need a roommate who lets my bitchy moods roll off her back.

"Amen, sister. I thought the same thing. I think we might get along just fine. Welcome to rat hole heaven." I grin at my new roommate hoping to show that I won't be a problem for her.

"Hey, did you see that hot red head who lives down the hall? I think she plays for your team."

"Whoa. First, how do you know that and, second, are you sure you're not gay?"

"Oh, that. Well, my best friend at home is a big ole dyke— her words, not mine. She kind of taught me the gaydar thing. I'm pretty much never wrong now, although I sure didn't peg you for a lesbian."

"You could be really handy to have around. I'm not so good at the gaydar thing. Go figure. It's damned inconvenient, you know. However, I did notice the red head. She was pretty hard to miss because I think she winked at me."

"No shit. She's definitely fuck buddy material if you really are after that."

Lisa's pretty cool and her comment cements our relationship.

†

Sometimes it's painful to remember my old roommate, Lisa. She became a good friend, one that I had all through college. I've missed Lisa and her easygoing manner. She was super funny sometimes and managed to keep me from falling into the abyss several years later. I was grateful for her love and support. Besides family, she was the only one I missed.

Well, that's not really true. I missed Sara, the red head that Lisa nicknamed Red. In fact, I never stopped missing her. I didn't forget her in the thirteen long years since I had talked to her. I didn't think of her every day, but I did obsess over her for at least two years after she left.

I rarely think of Sara since I met Annie. I'd like to think I'm going to get a second chance with Annie and she'll read this journal of mine and know she is the only one I dream about.

Chapter Two

Lisa and her minions exit the room and head out to their snooty sorority function. It's rush week on campus and there seems to be a shitload of activity happening all around me. I have zero interest.

"Hey, you, Red, stop skulking around in the hallway and go down and meet my roommate."

I close the door and cringe, as I realize Lisa has projected her voice loud enough for the whole dorm to hear. I come to love that about Lisa. She always cuts to the chase and has a way of sorting through all the bullshit. I asked her once why she wants to join a sorority since she doesn't seem like the type.

Lisa gives me her dime store philosophy. "Well, Nicky, someone has to add some spice to what they believe is a big old container of sugar."

She never does leave the dorm room to live at the sorority house. "I'm happy to be the spice, but I'm not living with those half-wit priss pots. Besides, you're too entertaining and far too dangerous to leave to your own devices," she told me.

I'm a little amazed that Lisa's philosophy on sororities is similar to mine, but what the hell, I'm just glad she stays my roommate.

"I think if I had to live there, I might kill myself. Sororities are kind of like Stepford sisters and I'm definitely no Stepford anything," Lisa continues.

✝

I sigh as I take a break from my journal and think back on my time with Lisa and Sara. Lisa ended up rooming with Sara and me after that first year of imprisonment in the dorm. From the first day Lisa laid eyes on Sara, she called her Red. I never called her that and I don't know why. Red is a decent nickname. I mean who wouldn't want to be associated with the word red. It's a good connotation. Red hot was how Lisa described her and she was definitely that. Sara was more than the color red. She was more than her outside appearance. I didn't even realize how much more until many years later.

✝

I'm hiding out in my room trying to quell my embarrassment after Lisa's loud proclamation. The knock on the door is tentative. *Shit, shit, shit, what do I do now?* I gather my bravado to yank the door open.

You probably think I have all this experience with women. Well, I don't. I know I like girls, but that's as far as it goes. I lived in a small town in Oregon where we're not supposed to have *those kinds of girls*. I'm not a cheerleader, pom pom girl, or prom queen, but I always had a bunch of guys buzzing around me like bees to honey. I never gave them the time of the day. It didn't discourage them and they were, frankly, a big pain in my ass. I wouldn't know if there were any girls interested, because remember, I have no gaydar. Lisa tells me I'm so oblivious, and if she hadn't stepped in to get Red to meet me, I might still be a virgin.

When I open the door, there she is—the hottie who winked at me. She's just standing there smirking at me. I don't know how to react, so I fall back on my go-to reaction.

"What the fuck are you looking at?"

She throws her head back and laughs. It's not a chuckle—it's a full belly laugh.

I guess she sees through my bravado. What the hell, I motion for her to come in. I still don't know how to react, so I blurt something. "Did you wink at me earlier?"

She is smiling now and I swear I melt right on the spot. I'm a big puddle at her feet.

"Yes, I most certainly did."

"Why?"

"If your eyes had the capability to swing it, I would be naked right now."

"Oh." That shuts me right up. I'm not yet versed in the art of flirting. After Sara, I became a master, but I'm still pretty naïve at this point.

"I'm the RA, Resident Assistant, on the floor. My name is Sara."

"Nicky." Oh, yeah, I'm a superb conversationalist at this point.

Sara smiles at me again and this time I smile back.

"Come on, Nicky, let's go get something to eat. I'm starving and it's my treat."

"Is this...uh... is this like a date or something?" I stutter.

"Do you want it to be a date?"

"Um, no... I mean... yes... um, I don't know."

"Nicky, have you ever been on a date with a woman?" She gets this soft look on her face.

I flush bright red.

Yep, you know what I'm about to do. I lie to her. I tell her the biggest fucking lie ever.

"What? What the hell makes you think I haven't ever been on a date with a girl? Of course I have. I'm between girlfriends right now because of this college thing."

"Okay, let's go hot stuff. I'm really starving." She is laughing again.

I follow her like a little puppy. My insides are doing the Macarena.

†

When we get to the pizza place, she orders a large, and I get to see first-hand how much Sara can eat. She orders the meat lovers special and eats three fourths of the pizza herself. I can't understand where she puts it all. She's really tall, but there's not an ounce of fat on her. I'm the one with the love handles. I think to myself I better get going on some kind of regular workout routine so when I do finally get naked with her, I won't embarrass myself. I really want to be naked with her.

Sara is everything I'm not. She's genuinely nice and comfortable in her skin. I find out she's a business major in her senior year. She's here on a full ride scholarship, too, so she's no dummy. I think she's surprised, but pleased to learn I have a full ride academic scholarship. Sometimes I present myself as someone who is a little rough around the edges because of my constant use of profanity and less than intelligent comments. I'm not entirely sure I'm worthy of her interest, but I'm wildly attracted to everything about her.

Her eyes mesmerize me. They are golden, or amber, with little green flecks. She has these perfect white teeth. When Sara smiles, her face is radiant. The feature most people see right away on Sara is her hair. It's not a crazy Irish red like I suppose most people imagine, it's more similar to copper. It reminds me of a beautiful sunrise. It's shiny and thick and I want to run my hands through it so badly, I can think of nothing else.

She has a way of looking at me as if I'm the most important person in the world and I start to lose some of my nervousness. She reaches deep inside and pulls me away from my false bravado. I don't know it yet, but I'm already starting to fall in love with her.

I'm pretty comfortable talking with her now. We're laughing and talking like old friends and suddenly she makes a sneak attack.

"Nicky, why did you lie earlier and tell me you've had a lot of girlfriends."

"I wanted you to think I wasn't just some dumb freshman. I wanted to be worthy of a date." I blurt this out before I can censor my response. This is the start of what I call my no filter tendencies.

"Oh, Nicky, you are definitely worthy. I don't think I've met anyone quite like you. How can you possibly be so oblivious to how utterly stunning you are? You must have had everyone falling all over themselves to get you to notice them." She smiles again.

I melt again. I'm sure I'm now blushing and I don't know how to respond, but I forge ahead anyway. "The guys were just a big pain in my ass and if a girl was interested, I wouldn't know. I don't possess gaydar and I didn't want to be tarred and feathered for going after the wrong girl in high school."

"Surely someone would have approached you."

"Um, don't you remember my first words to you, *what the fuck are you looking at*? I'm not the easiest person to cuddle up to. You would have an easier time trying to get close to a porcupine."

"Good thing I think porcupines are adorable."

I love this girl. Wait. I didn't say that out loud, did I? Whew. No I didn't.

I smile back at her and she says something about loving my dimples and my smile gets wider. I want so badly for her to like me. I don't have the foggiest idea what I'm doing, but I want her to kiss me, and a bunch of other things I've only read about in those smutty romance novels. What? They're good. I swear they are better than magazines. Guys can keep their magazines to masturbate to. I'll take a smutty book any day.

I'm in the middle of a full-fledged fantasy starring Sara and me on a fluffy white bear skin rug in front of a roaring fire, when she wrestles me from my astral traveling.

"Nicky. Hello. Earth to Nicky. Are you ready to head back to the dorm yet?"

Am I ready? Fuck, yes, if we can find a fire and a bearskin rug. Oops, back to Earth.

"Sure. Uh, thanks for the pizza. I had a really nice time."

Oh brother did I just say something as inane as I really had a nice time.

She doesn't seem to notice what a moron I am.

†

We walk back to the dorm and I'm thinking, *what should I do now*? The whole way back, I'm trying to think of some clever thing to say to get her to kiss me, or at least come into my room so the evening doesn't end. I'm disappointed when she walks me to the door. It's clear this marks the end of our evening.

"I've got to meet some of the other new freshman, but I'm sure I'll be seeing you again soon."

Well, sure, she'll see me again soon. I live two doors down from her, for fuck's sake. It's not the type of goodbye I'm hoping for. I'm not sure it was even a date. She never answers my question. For all I know she takes the entire freshman class out for pizza. I think she must see the look of disappointment in my eyes.

"Yes, Nicky, it was a date and when I say I'll be seeing you soon, I mean I'd like a second date. Is that all right with you?"

"Fuck, yes, that's all right with me. Name the time and place and I'll be there. It can be my treat next time."

She chuckles as she waves goodbye to me.

As she saunters down the hall, I can't help myself. I check out her ass. She has a great ass. Sara turns her head as she looks over her shoulder at me. She waives her finger and mouths, *ah, ah, ah, I caught you.*

I laugh and shut my door. Maybe college won't be so bad after all. I jump on my bed, pull out my latest trashy novel, and hope my roommate won't be back for a while as I slip my hand into my pants. Good thing I wore my baggy jeans tonight.

Chapter Three

Lisa bangs the door open and is thankfully free from her two minions. I'm lounging on my bed both hands visible because my hand is no longer in my pants. She's been gone for four hours leaving me plenty of time with my trashy novel. She grins at me with what I fear is an expectant look on her face.

"So," Lisa asks.

"So what?"

I'm pretty sure I know what she wants to hear about, but I'm playing dumb because I don't really want to fill her in. I don't know her. Even though she impressed me earlier, I'm not about to gossip with her about my date.

"Oh come on. Red was hovering in the hall just waiting for you to be alone. I know you two hooked up. I want details," Lisa presses.

"Even if we *hooked up* as you put it, I'm not about to give you any details. I barely know you."

"We're going to be roommates for a long time. We should dig right into the good stuff. I promise I'll tell you all about my hookups when I have them."

"What makes you think I'm remotely interested in you and some horny dude getting down at some stupid frat party?" I'm back to my bitchy self again.

"You are going to be a really tough nut to crack." Lisa gives me what I judge to be an overly dramatic sigh. "Look, I can tell by that shit eating grin on your face that something happened. You might as well tell me now or I'll bug the living shit out of you until you do. I'm like a dog with a bone. I never let it go."

"Fine. Whatever. We went out for pizza and she's really nice. I like her and I think she might have asked me out again, but we have no specific plans."

"See now that wasn't so hard. How old is she?"

"She's a senior and she's our resident assistant."

"Ooh, an older woman. That's hot. Maybe she can teach you a few things."

"What makes you think I need to be taught anything?"

"Seriously? You look like you just got here from the farm. You have that wholesome girl next door meets model look. Besides, whenever someone puts out as much bravado as you do, that means they have absolutely no experience on the love train."

"Shit. Why is it all the women in my life have to be so goddamned insightful? Fine, I've never dated a woman. I'm a virgin, and just because I'm not mortally embarrassed enough about my lack of worldly experience, I'll admit I have no fucking idea what I'm doing. I'm kinda scared shitless. She was so cool. I really want her to like me."

"Relax. You're totally hot and if I was a lesbian, I would do you. Hey, has anyone ever told you that you have the most amazing eyes. I don't think I have ever seen that color on anyone before. I swear they're like the exact color of the Caribbean Sea. My God, you must have had guys and girls falling all over themselves to have a shot at you."

At this point, I'm softening toward her. She doesn't seem to have any filter and I notice she just says what pops in her head. This is another thing I love that about her. I decide that I can do much worse in the roommate pool.

†

I often think about how unlikely it was for Lisa and me to become such good friends.

15

We became the dyke and the prom queen. Yeah, Lisa was the prom queen at her high school. No one could figure out what we had in common that allowed us to get along so well. I always thought it was because we were both such smart asses all the time. I appreciated that trait in her and I suppose she liked that about me. Lisa didn't ever appear to give a shit about what others thought. I decided if she could accept me for being a big *mo*—you know homo—I could accept her and her sorority sisters.

†

"So what happened to Tweedle Dee and Tweedle Dum?" I ask.

"You mean Missy and Amanda?"

"I mean the two prissy chicks that were here earlier. They looked at me like I was a piece of gum that got stuck on the bottom of their shoe and they couldn't wait to get it off."

"Oh they're not that bad. They can't help the fact that they have led a sheltered life. They're my fall quarter project. I'm making it my mission this quarter to broaden their horizons. I told them they both need to sleep with a woman at least once so they can be sure they're straight."

"You've slept with a woman before?" This surprises me after her insistence that she's straight.

"Sure," Lisa says. "Even though I pretty much know I like guys. I just wanted to be sure, you know. It was a pretty amazing night, but the girl kinda freaked out afterward."

"Well, I don't think I'll need to sleep with a guy. I've known since I was five that I like girls." I'm adamant about this.

"Oh, don't worry. I'm not one of those who will try to get you to sleep with a guy. I have a kind of opposite philosophy in this. Who would want to choose to be gay and deal with all the hassle? I don't think anyone is a closeted heterosexual, but I think there are a lot of closeted gay people. That's why I think that anyone who thinks they're straight ought to just sleep with both sexes—just to be sure."

"Huh? I guess that makes sense in a distorted kind of way. I guess it's a good thing your best friend at home is a *big ole dyke*. She broke you in for me."

"I loved hearing about her escapades, so you're her replacement. I will expect frequent updates of your time with Red."

"Okay, okay. I get it. Really, there was not much to report tonight. I didn't even get a good night kiss. I'm sorry to disappoint you."

"Why the hell not?"

"I don't know. I kinda wanted the date to extend a little longer, but she ran off saying something about needing to meet the other freshmen. She did make sure I knew it was a date and that she wanted another one. So, I guess it wasn't a total bust. Do you think I should wait for her to make the first move?"

"Hmm, let me think on that a bit. I think she might like your innocent farm girl shtick."

I'm about to get bitchy again, when Lisa holds up her hand, and this effectively interrupts what I'm about to say.

"Oh, don't get your panties in a wad. I know you aren't trying to scam her or anything. You really are an innocent. I say let her be the older, wiser, more experienced one that leads you down the pleasure path." Lisa laughs.

"Now that I know a girl is interested in me, I'm not sure I can wait much longer. If she doesn't kiss me next time, I'm losing the farm girl aura and making the first move. I don't care if I don't know anything. I've been learning a lot from my smutty books. I'll figure it out."

"Oh, you go, girl."

Chapter Four

I guess Sara is pretty busy being our RA, because I don't see her for the next couple of days. I'm beginning to wonder if she is still interested in having that second date.

I become unbearable to share the same space with. Lisa comes right out and tells me to quit falling back into bitch mode. I'm feeling bad about taking out my depression on Lisa. I bring back comfort food for me and a peace offering for her.

I still don't understand how Lisa can be so patient with me. I'm not giving her any reason to be nice.

✝

I close my eyes and summon up my memories of Lisa's support. All through our college years, she was always there for me. I sure didn't deserve her friendship. Maybe she saw something in me that I didn't see in myself. I guess I was a good friend sometimes.

One time Sara and I spent the night in the infirmary with her when she contracted pneumonia and her parents weren't able to get there until the weekend. They gave her multiple drugs that night, and I think she had some kind of reaction, because she sort of freaked out. Miracle of miracles, I'm the one who calmed her down. She told me I was a big softy and I told her to shut the fuck up and go to sleep.

I suppose I was also there for her when she learned about her mom. Sara was there for her too. We were her rock. I didn't figure anything out at the time, but I did notice that something was amiss with Sara. I wondered if the horrible thing Lisa was going through with her family affected Sara in some way. Denial is a powerful thing.

✝

I'm coming back from a trip to the campus bookstore and there she is, casually leaning on the wall waiting for me at my dorm room. I'm a little hacked off that she didn't come by earlier. I don't think about how she might have been waiting for me to go see her and that maybe she's irritated with me. Yeah, I'm pissed, so I barely acknowledge her as I nod and then close the door behind me leaving her hanging in the hall. It doesn't take long for her to knock lightly on the door. I open it and try to act all cool.

"Oh, hey, Sara. Sorry I didn't realize you wanted to talk to me. I thought you were just hovering in the hall making sure the naïve little freshmen are behaving themselves."

"Who pissed in your cornflakes?"

"Got a mirror?"

"Did I do something to upset you?"

"You think? How about, when I say I'll be seeing you soon, I mean I'd like a second date." I mimic her words.

She starts laughing. Now I'm really pissed.

I scowl at her and am just about to slam the door in her face, when Lisa pops up and invites her in.

"Oh, hey, Red. Thank God you finally came by. I don't think Nicky can even stand to be around herself anymore, she's being a total bitch to everyone."

"Shut the fuck up, Lisa. This is none of your damned business."

19

Lisa throws her hands in the air and plops back on her bed. I've seen her do this before—she is done with me for the day.

"Come on, Nicky, you're coming with me. I'm sorry if you got the wrong impression." Sara grabs my arm and pulls me into the hallway.

Now I'm beyond pissed, I'm devastated. I think she's not interested and maybe she's not even gay. I can't help it, a tear escapes and I hate myself for getting my hopes up.

Sara gently wipes the tear with her finger. "I had to go home. There was a family emergency requiring my attention, otherwise I would have come by a long time ago. I'm sorry if you misread my absence as disinterest—nothing could be further from the truth."

I hear her rush to explain this all to me. I see that the look on her face is sincere. Perhaps there is a hint of trepidation that I might not believe her.

"Oh." I don't know how to respond at this point.

"How about we get some coffee? Your treat, remember?"

Now I'm smiling, a genuine happy smile—the first one in two days. "That sounds perfect. I'm sorry I reacted the way I did. I was pissed because I thought you were playing with me. I was looking forward to seeing you again."

"I was looking forward to our second date, too. Do you think your roommate will still be in your room when we get back?"

"Yeah, probably. Why?" I miss the clue train.

"Never mind. Starbucks awaits."

†

We walk down to the University District and she takes my hand. It's really sweet and I don't mind. The U-District is a liberal place and nobody seems to care if two women are walking around hand in hand. I like that about Seattle. It's different from the small town I come from. I start to notice other women who glance at us and give us an approving nod. I think I'm starting to develop some gaydar. It comes in handy several years later.

"Hey, Kelly, what's up? Can I get a vanilla latte with cinnamon on top?" Sara says to the barista. She glances at me. "Nicky, what's your pleasure?"

I think, *a vanilla Sara with whipped cream on top of her luscious tits*, but at this point, I still have some filter. "I'll take the same, but can you use skim milk instead." I still have those ten pounds of extra baby fat to lose. I pull out a twenty from my pocket and hand it to the barista.

Kelly winks at Sara and takes my twenty.

I wonder if Sara and Kelly have some kind of history. I get a little jealous. "So, like do you know her or something?"

"Who? Oh, Kelly, sure I know her."

"Um, how do you know her? Did you date her or something?"

"Yeah, something like that. Old news, don't worry."

"Um, it doesn't quite look that old to her. I think she might still have a thing for you."

"Nah. She has a super nice girlfriend now. She's just a big flirt and I think the wink was intended to show how impressed she is with you. You do know how gorgeous you are?"

"Okay, you are forgiven for not coming around for two days and you are so getting some today." Instead of causing her to flush with embarrassment, I turn beat red.

"Really. Now?" She raises her eyebrow. "I guess it's back to my room then, because it sounds like your roomie might make it a bit awkward for us, unless you like someone to watch."

Oh, shit, I'll take your flirtatious comment and raise you a blatant sexual innuendo.

Kelly saves me when she hands me my change and points to the end of the counter where our drinks are waiting. I stuff a few dollars into the tip jar and hurry to retrieve my beverage.

Sara is chuckling behind me as she picks up her coffee. "So, in all seriousness, I was hoping you might want to come back to my room when we get back to the dorm. Being the RA has its advantages. I have a single room."

"Um, sure, yeah, I'd like that."

Now I'm tempted to chug my coffee and drag her back to the dorm like some sort of cave girl. But I force myself to calm down and sit and enjoy my latte in a cozy corner of the coffee shop.

"So, are you all ready for classes to start next week?" I think Sara takes pity on me by making small talk devoid of sexual innuendo.

"Yeah, I think so. I just picked up all my books. I can't believe how expensive they are."

"They'll look nice stacked next to your lesbian romance novels." Sara starts laughing again.

"You snooped."

"No, I saw the book on your bed. Don't worry, I have a few of my own. I particularly like the supernatural ones about vampires and shape-shifters."

"Oh, yeah, I like those too. I pretty much like anything with hot sex involved. Oh, God, there I go again. I guess being an eighteen year old virgin leads to a one track mind."

"You know I'm not in a race to deflower you."

"Why not? I want to be de-flowered. I'm sure I'm the only virgin on campus."

"I seriously doubt that, but even if that were true, it's all part of your incredible charm. I like that you are still innocent."

"Oh, trust me, I'm not at all innocent. I just have the misfortune of living in some backwater town with limited choice of sexual partners. If anyone had offered, I'd have definitely taken them up on it."

"I'm sure you would have had offers if only those high school girls knew they had a chance."

"Not that I'm happy I waited, but I'm glad you're my RA. Hey, are there any rules about RAs dating their dorm mates?"

"Well, no, but I don't think they jump for joy when it happens. Conflicts occur sometimes and then they have to move us. I'm willing to take the chance. You're definitely worth it."

"So, are you planning on spending your life with that coffee, or can we take it and head back to the dorm?"

"Anxious to be alone are we?"

"Fuck, yes. Not only am I a virgin, I've yet to get my first kiss from a woman." Okay, so maybe my filter is already gone. I slap my hand over my mouth. "I can't believe I just said that. Can I be any more pathetic? I'm sure you just can't wait to spend more time with me."

"Nicky, your honesty is refreshing and absolutely adorable." Sara chuckles. "However, I don't intend to take you to bed just yet. We are going to do this right. I'm going to court you and you are going to court me right back. I expect to be lavished with attention and I plan to spoil you rotten."

"Okay, I can live with that, but can we re-negotiate the terms of my deflowering?"

Sara laughs so hard I think she might wet her pants. "Come on, Nicky, let's head back, I can already see I'm going to have my hands full with you."

She grabs my hand and pulls me to my feet.

"Oh, I know where you can fill up your hands." I point to my chest and give her the biggest shit-eating grin I can manage to spread across my face.

Chapter Five

I drop by my room just to let Lisa know I'll be with Sara for a little longer. Lisa is such a mom sometimes because she always wants to know where I'm going and when I'll be back so she doesn't worry. For some reason, she thinks I'm vulnerable and naïve.

I'm convinced I can talk Sara into going a little farther than she thinks we should. I'm a ball of sexual tension ready to unravel before her very eyes.

We enter her room and it's so neat and orderly. I wonder where she hides her sex toys. Just kidding. I don't think she really has sex toys, I just hope she does. I have some semblance of restraint and don't ask her where she's hiding them. I plop down on her bed and try to look sexy—I don't even come close. I probably just look desperate, but I hope my honest, open approach still intrigues her.

She grins at me and sits on the bed next to me. She brings her hand up to my face and brushes one of my errant strands of hair back.

Her touch is so intimate and so electric that I can feel the tingle of energy. I'm no longer brave because I'm scared shitless. I want her to kiss me so badly that I can hardly breathe and I start shaking in anticipation. This is not a figure of speech. I'm shaking as if I'm out in subzero weather and my body won't stop shaking from the cold. I don't feel cold. I feel hot—burning up hot—like I imagine women going through menopause might feel. I'm pretty sure I'm not going through menopause at eighteen, but I know what a hot flash must feel like.

She leans in and pauses one inch from my face. She is two seconds away from what I'm sure will be an epic first kiss and then the terrible noise starts.

Beep…beep…beep…beep.

I jump so high I bang my head against some part of her body. I'm not even sure what part.

"Is that the fire alarm?"

"Shit. Yes, it is. I'm so sorry, Nicky, I have to go and see what's going on and if we have to evacuate. It's always a prank. I'll be right back."

She leaves the room in a rush, and I'm pretty sure that not only will I die a virgin, but I'll die never having experienced my first kiss with a woman.

Can my night get any worse? Lisa, it seems, decides that as long as the alarm is blaring she should come visit and get an update and barges into Sara's room uninvited.

This irritates me.

"Hey, roomie. Still a virgin?"

"Yes. So just turn back around and leave us alone, will ya?"

"Aw, did you two kiss and make up after your bitchy reception earlier. I'll leave, but I want a minute by minute rehash when you get back."

"Shh, the alarm just turned off and I think she's coming back. Please, Lisa, I'm begging you. Will you please get the hell out?"

"Oh, all right. You don't have to be so touchy. Jeez, I can't wait for you to finally lose it. Maybe you won't be wound so tight and then you'll stop acting like you're in the middle of menopause."

The door slams behind her.

Hmm, funny you should compare me to a woman in menopause.

Sara opens the door to her room and arches one of her eyebrows. "Was that Lisa I just saw leaving?"

"Um, yeah, she was just checking to make sure I was okay."

"Yeah, sure. She wants to hear all about our night, doesn't she?"

"Well, so far there is not much to tell. Can we change that?"

Sara sits back down on the bed, takes my hands in hers and leans in to kiss me.

At least I think that is what is about to happen, but someone knocks on the door. "Oh, for fuck's sake. Can you please ignore that?" I growl.

Sara moves toward the door.

I decide fuck that and pull her to me. My lips meet hers in an act of desperation. It's not how I envision my first kiss, but her lips are so soft and full that I moan because it feels so good. She starts kissing me back and I even start to feel her tongue come out. I think maybe I have a chance tonight and then I hear the knock again.

She pulls away from me and I think I see a look of apology, or maybe it's frustration. She goes to the door, opens it, and the other RA assigned to the dorm is standing there.

"Um, hi, Sara, sorry to bug you but one of the freshman is kind of freaked by the alarm. She doesn't understand why we didn't evacuate."

"Can you talk to her, Dani? Explain that this happens all the time the first week when the sororities and fraternities are rushing and need to play their little pranks. I'll owe you."

"Okay. Is Nicky in there with you?"

Sara nods.

"Have fun," Dani says.

I'm just waiting for her with my hands propping me up on her bed.

Sara closes the door, takes two quick steps into the room, and gently pushes me down on the bed until I'm lying on my back. She climbs on the bed, turns on her side, and looks at me.

I feel like I'm little red riding hood and she's the big bad wolf. Nevertheless, I turn on my side and face her.

Sara takes one of her hands and slowly strokes my arm, then down my hip, deftly avoiding the side of my breast where I so desperately want her to go. She leans in to kiss me.

This time the kiss is slow and sensuous. I'm sure my insides are going to burst open. I start shaking again and I feel my excitement begin to grow. I reach for her and manage to move my hand under her shirt as I caress the side of her breast over her sports bra. I imagine her letting me take off her shirt and bra. I can't wait to put one of her nipples into my mouth. I don't think she's going to let me do that tonight, because it won't stop there and I remember Sara saying that she was going to court me. I decide this is enough for tonight.

Then she surprises me and cups my breasts rubbing my nipples.

My nipples become rock hard. She's still kissing me and things really start heating up. I'm ready to rip our clothes off. I want us both to be naked.

She pulls her hands away before gently kissing my lips.

I feel the loss of her hands immediately.

"Nicky, we have to stop, or I won't be able to control myself. You are entirely too irresistible."

"Willpower is overrated," I insist.

I tell myself next time I'm not wearing a bra or panties so she can have easy access to where I most want her hands or mouth.

"I really want us to take the time to do this right. I don't want a one night stand with you."

I sigh and roll over, completely frustrated. "Okay, ball park number, how many dates do I have to wait?"

She bursts into laughter. "You'll live. I promise not to make you wait too long. Will you stay tonight, even if you don't get your way?"

I take a few deep breaths to calm down a little. "Yeah, sure, I'd like that, but can we kiss some more if I promise to keep my hands above your shirt?"

"Yep, I think we need to make sure you get the full experience of making out since you missed that in high school."

We make out in her room for several hours and I don't tell her that I have had a tiny orgasm fully clothed as I squirm around on top of her. I feel like an adolescent who can't control her hormones. Does it count if you still have your clothes on? I wonder if I've technically lost my virginity.

Sara wraps her arms around me and I fall into a deep, blissful sleep.

It feels so good sleeping in Sara's arms. I'm convinced that I'm madly in love with her and we will be together forever.

†

The next morning we are startled awake by loud knocking on Sara's door.

"Tell them to go away. We don't want anything they're selling," I mumble.

"Very funny. You know I have to answer the door."

"No, you don't. Just pretend you went for an early morning run."

We hear Lisa's voice on the other side of the door. "Hey, you two lovebirds, open up. Let's get breakfast. You're buying, Nicky."

"See, you can tell them to go away after all. No big emergency, it's just my nosy roommate," I argue.

"You know she's not going to go away until she gets the scoop."

"I don't kiss and tell." I'm proud of my stance on this.

"It's not like there's much to tell anyway. You're still a virgin."

"Yeah, well...um...about that. Does it count if I, uh, you know...fully clothed." Oh God, I feel like a teenage boy confessing to premature ejaculation.

"You did? Really? I couldn't tell. Wow, you are going to be so easy. All I'll have to do is blow on you and you'll come."

"Not helping. So am I still a virgin or not?" I turn beet red as I ask this in all seriousness.

"I suppose it depends on your perspective and how you define losing your virginity."

I think about that for a little bit, and then decide I should wait and compare my experience when I'm naked.

Bang bang bang.

"Come on guys, open the door. I'm bored and you guys are gonna be my entertainment."

I can't help but be amused with Lisa.

Sara gets up and opens the door.

Lisa is grinning at us. "Shit, you both are already dressed. Disappointing. I thought I might catch some titillating lesbian nakedness. I may not be a carpet muncher, but who wouldn't like to see you two hotties naked in the middle of some girl on girl action."

"Sorry to disappoint you. My only purpose in life is to entertain my new completely inappropriate roommate. Hey, have you ever been tested for Asperger's?" I ask with sarcasm.

"Ha, ha, very funny. You will grow to appreciate my direct approach to life. Now let's get going, I'm starved and you're buying me breakfast."

"Why am I buying you breakfast?"

"Because, I ran interference for you two lovebirds and kept our dorm mates from knocking on the door last night," Lisa explains.

"You missed one. Dani came by. I'm deducting your beverage from the breakfast. You get to pay for that on your own." My argument makes perfect sense to me.

"Deal. Let's go already. I haven't even made a dent in the freshman ten I'm supposed to gain this year. Besides, I can't wait to hear all about your night. You don't look like someone who's been shagging all night long."

"Shagging?" I've never heard this term before.

"Yeah, I just love the English term for fucking. Sounds so much nicer, doesn't it?"

"Um, yeah, I guess so. All the info you're getting is we had a nice evening, so no more questions. Okay?" I'm hoping she will stop being so nosy.

"Not okay, but I'll leave it for now."

Sara is just watching us with an amused smile on her face.

I slap her on the arm. "Stop encouraging her."

"What? How am I encouraging her?" Sara asks.

"It doesn't take much with Lisa. Smile at her and she thinks that all her nosy questions are completely legit."

"Hey, anyone who refers to me as a lesbian hottie gets a certain degree of latitude." Sara smiles.

"See, Red doesn't care. I only want what's best for you two. As far as lesbian couples go, you two are perfect together. I wanna be the lesbian equivalent of a fag hag. How about a dyke diva? I'm a diva who hangs with dykes." Lisa laughs at her own joke.

"Oh, brother, you're more like a dyke dumbass." I glance down at my wrinkled clothes and consider running back to my room to change, but then I decide what the hell.

Sara whips her shirt off right in front of Lisa and puts a new one on.

Lisa's eyes get wide and she looks away when she sees Sara change.

We head out to breakfast and Lisa manages to weasel out of paying for her own beverage.

Chapter Six

The hustle and bustle of the new school term starts as we all settle into our routines with classes, studying, and with our pitiful university work-study jobs. I end up applying to work in the school cafeteria—with a specific assignment to the dish room.

I can't even begin to describe the disgusting art projects students can conjure up with various cafeteria food items. Rush hour in the cafeteria results in scraping off the dishes with our bare hands—depositing the food into the regurgitated water sprayer. I'm not exaggerating here. The sink has a perpetual waterfall where we scrape the dishes. After about five minutes, the water starts spewing salad, peas, and any other solid food item as the water recycles itself. It's so disgusting, that we think what the hell—it's just easier to use our hands because we're getting food all over ourselves anyway. Not everyone gets a job so I suppose I can't complain too much. At least I'll have some spending money to go on dates and pay my fair share of the pizza and beer tab.

Six weeks go by without us realizing how time is flying and I'm still a virgin. Our nighttime make out sessions are super steamy at times, but Sara still refuses to take it any further. If I had balls, they would be blue.

I spend every night sleeping next to Sara. It's nice, but I'm ready to take the next step. I need to find a way to convince Sara of that. I think that maybe it's because being eighteen just sounds so young to her.

31

My birthday is coming up and I can't think of a better present, so I broach the subject with Sara one night. "Hey, Sara, not that I want you to get me a gift or anything, but I was hoping we might be able to do something special on Saturday cause it's my birthday. I turn nineteen. You know, beyond the jail bait age."

Sara laughs.

I never get tired of hearing her laugh. I know this sounds corny, but it truly is music to my ears.

"Yes, I know it's your birthday. We get the inside information on everyone on our floor. Since you brought this up, I'm afraid I'll have to ruin the surprise just a little. I was planning on taking you somewhere special."

"You're not on call or anything are you?" I have an ulterior motive for asking this question. I want to make sure no one interrupts us like when we first kissed.

"No, why?"

"So if the fire alarm goes off, or there's some freshman emergency, you won't have to answer your door then?"

"Well, no. If I'm here in the building, I'm expected to respond."

"So if you're not in the building?"

"I can't respond if I'm not here to respond."

"Perfect, then my birthday present to myself is a night without interruptions even if that means I have to take you to a bed and breakfast or hotel or something."

"Oh, I can't let you do that, but don't worry I have that all taken care of. My family sort of has access to these remote cabins in the mountains. Are you game?"

"Oh, yes, that would be perfect. Thank you so much. Remember, I'm turning nineteen, a really good age to engage in some really adult behavior." I lean over and kiss her.

"Message received. We'll see, Nicky." She pulls me back to her and gently kisses me.

The kiss turns especially passionate and I get a feeling that there will be more of that on Saturday. I'm getting my hopes up that Saturday will be the night I finally get to lose my virginity. I hope the wait is worth it.

†

I don't have a car and I wonder if Sara is keeping her cards close to her vest regarding where we are heading on Saturday for a reason.

She tells me to pack warm clothes and comfortable shoes.

We end up leaving on Friday so that we can spend the whole weekend at the cabin. I'm so nervous, but I'm trying not to show it. I pack enough clothes in my duffel bag for a month long excursion into the Himalayas.

I struggle with lifting and placing my massive bag in the back of her Honda civic.

She chuckles at me. "What the hell do you have in there? You know we're only going to be gone two days."

"I know, but you know the Pacific Northwest, blink once and the weather changes. I wanted to be prepared for any kind of weather."

"I thought you were angling for getting me naked and keeping me that way for the whole weekend. So in that case, you won't need any clothes."

"Is that a possibility?"

"No. You will at least need to pull something out of that duffel—which seems to contain your entire wardrobe—for dinner on Saturday night."

"But the rest of the time...."

"No, this weekend is not intended to be a fuckfest."

"Damn. I can expect some fucking though, right?"

"Nope. We will not be fucking, but I hold open the possibility that we will make love."

"Deal. I'll take that. No reneging on that promise."

"I did not make a promise. I just said I hold open the possibility...."

"You're killing me, Sara."

33

"I seriously doubt that, but I don't think you will be disappointed."

I grin at her and fold myself into the passenger seat. I'm more than hopeful about the weekend.

We get a late start and end up stuck in rush hour traffic. Seattle traffic sucks. The drive over the pass to the cabin is uneventful and since it's so late, I can't even enjoy the scenery. It doesn't matter though, because I'm so excited to be alone with Sara for the whole weekend.

I make myself a solemn promise that I will not remain a virgin after the weekend. I'm so fixated on losing my virginity that I can barely think of anything else. I'm the definition of a one-track mind.

†

We get to the cabin about three and a half hours later. The full moon shines a soft glow over the massive evergreens.

Once Sara unlocks the cabin door and opens it, I'm amazed to see a robust fire crackling in the fireplace—a real fire.

The silence is broken with the howling of what must be a huge pack of wolves. I look at Sara.

Sara is frowning.

I think that maybe the fire is not supposed to be going. I get nervous that someone is going to interrupt our weekend. I swear I have the worst luck.

Sara glances at the fire and smiles. "Oh, thank God, Ting built us a fire."

"Ting?"

"Yeah. Ting is a good friend of mine. I asked her to set up the cabin for us."

"Ting is an unusual name. Um, she's not going to be staying with us for the weekend, is she?"

"No, silly. I asked her to start the fire because I knew it would be really cold and I didn't want to struggle with getting the place heated up after the long drive."

"She must live close by. I didn't see any tire tracks."

"Yeah, it's something like that. Come on, let's pull our stuff out of the car and get settled. I think there might be some food to munch on so is it okay if we don't have a big fancy dinner tonight?"

"Of course. Hey, if you expected the fire, why do I get the impression something was wrong when we first got here."

"Oh, it's nothing really. I just didn't like hearing the wolf pack."

I get the sense that Sara is being evasive but my obsessive focus on losing my virginity keeps me from thinking anymore about it.

"Oh, okay. We're still on for the naked sex Olympics, right?'

"God, Nicky, you really do have a one-track mind." Sara starts laughing. "Come on let's just get settled and maybe get some good sleep, because our day will be pretty full tomorrow. There are really great trails to explore."

"Hiking? Really? I mean not that hiking is bad or anything, but I was envisioning a whole different set of exercises."

"One-track mind." Sara shakes her head as she goes to the car to retrieve our bags.

I jog after her and manage to wrestle my overstuffed duffle bag to the ground and sort of drag it along into the cabin.

†

Thankfully, there is only one bed, but I suspect even if there were two there wouldn't be any awkwardness on where people are sleeping, because I've been crashing in her room every night. Unfortunately, when I say Sara and I are sleeping together, I mean we are literally sleeping together and not the euphemistic sleeping.

Sara tosses her bag into the bedroom and heads to the small kitchen. "Let's see what snacks Ting left for us." She opens the refrigerator and pulls out a tray of sushi.

I'm not very worldly but I know what sushi is. I'm not however, worldly enough to have ever tried sushi and I crinkle up my nose in disgust. "Um, thanks, but no thanks to the raw fish."

"Have you ever had sushi?"

"Nope, and never wanted to either."

"I think you should at least try it. I'm taking off my shirt and putting a piece on my stomach. Your reward for trying sushi will be to retrieve your piece from on my stomach."

Sara carries the tray over to the rug in front of the fireplace and gets comfortable. She removes her shirt and places the slimy little piece of fish on her stomach.

I start laughing, but her little ploy works, because I dive right in and give her stomach a little lick for good measure—after I grab the piece of sushi.

"That was one of my favorites, fatty tuna," Sara tells me before I have a chance to really taste the morsel in my mouth.

Fatty tuna, now that sounds appetizing.

I was prepared to hold my nose and quickly swallow when I find myself enjoying both the taste and texture. It's really delicate and melts into my mouth like a really tender piece of meat.

"Okay, you win, that was pretty good. Can I try another?"

"Here, try this." She offers me a piece with some kind of teriyaki sauce.

I lick the sauce off her fingers as she feeds it to me. It's got a kind of sweet, delicate taste. I really like this one, but choke when she tells me what it is.

"Congratulations, Nicky, you just ate your first piece of eel." Sara giggles.

I'm about to spit it out, when I think, *what the hell?* I really like it. "Maybe you ought to just give me stuff to try without telling me what it is."

"No way. You need to know what you like and what you don't when I take you to a sushi restaurant in the future."

"Fine. I'll let you broaden my horizons with different ethnic foods, if you also broaden my sexual horizons. Since I'm a total neophyte, you have a lot of broadening to do with both food and sex. Hey, I bet we can even combine the two."

She laughs again and gives me a relatively chaste kiss.

We finish eating our sushi and have some Japanese type ice cream dessert wrapped like a burrito in some kind of sweet rice-based shell. It's really good too. There are three or four flavors including green tea and red bean. By the time we're finished, I'm extremely full and have managed to try most of the different fish. My least favorite is the red snapper, but I admit to really liking everything else.

Since we sort of played a bit with the sushi and dessert—getting a little creative with the how we fed it to one another—I'm a little wound up, but it's getting late.

Sara drove the whole way through the shitty Seattle traffic and I can tell she's really tired. I figure we have the whole weekend, so I suggest we get ready for bed and let her know that it's okay to get a good night's rest. I think Sara is relieved that I don't expect her to fulfill all my fantasies tonight.

We take turns in the bathroom and both end up wearing tank tops and boxers.

I'm standing in the middle of the bedroom lost in my own thoughts when Sara closes the gap and gives me a gentle kiss before she leads me to the bed.

I feel protected as she wraps her arms around my back and shoulders. I lay my head on her shoulder and can't think of any place I would rather be than sleeping in her arms. Her steady breathing lulls me to sleep in less than a minute.

Sometime in the night, we shift and she ends up spooning me as I turn over to my side. Her arm drapes casually over my stomach. We sleep like that undisturbed until the early morning sun rays dance across our faces.

†

I'm not much of an outdoors type person, but I enjoy our time in the mountains. The fresh air, sunshine, and interesting flora

37

suck me in, and before I know it I'm thinking, *yeah, I could do the camping thing.*

Sara shows me the secret place where mushrooms grow and where you can find huckleberries.

Sara is pointing at this ugly little mushroom. "Nicky, this is one of the culinary delights of the Northwest, a chanterelle mushroom."

I crinkle up my nose in disgust. "Yuck, fungus."

'Don't be so judgmental. You didn't think you'd like sushi either."

"I'd eat anything if you put it on top of your stomach.'

Sara shakes her he= d and points to a bush with small dark red berries. "Nicky, we just hit the mother lode here. I can't believe we just found the elusive huckleberry."

I pick one of the berries and pop it into my mouth. "Yum, this is really good. You don't need to put these on your body, but it might be fun licking one of these little gems from your navel."

"You have no idea what we've found here today. Both of these Northwest delicacies are rare to find. We are so lucky to just stumble on this spot. I know some people who take their harvesting spots very seriously. You aren't supposed to ever reveal where they are to anyone. I've even heard of fist fights erupting over encroachment of harvesting spots."

"Oh, I'm shaking in my boots now. The berry and mushroom mafia will surely come after us."

Sara smiles at me. "Joke about this all you want to, but I'd suggest you keep this location a secret."

I smile now as I recall that, a few years later, I discovered that people really were crazy about protecting their harvesting spots in the Northwest.

†

We get back to the cabin around four o'clock and I try to get her to take a shower with me before dinner. She declines, but promises me an evening I won't forget. She keeps her promise.

I get distracted from my story and mull over how this night affected me. I never forgot that evening. It comes back to haunt me many times over the years. I always set it aside and put it in a special place. I'm finally able to place everything in the right perspective and cherish the memory without diminishing my love for Annie.

I need to try to capture some of those feelings of that night here in my journal. I hope that Annie reads and understands this.

I think it's important to note that someone once told me the way to be more empathetic is to always ask, *why would a reasonable, rational, person do this*? Sometimes I remember to do this, most times I don't. Annie always remembers this. I'm sure she is the most empathetic person on the planet.

†

Sara takes me to a quaint little restaurant surrounded by trees. Only locals know about this place. It doesn't look like much from the outside—or from the inside for that matter—but the food is better than any upscale restaurant I've ever been to.

The tables and chairs are all different styles and look like they just arrived from the thrift store. The plates and silverware are just as mismatched and I doubt the tables have ever seen a tablecloth.

Mary, the cook, owner, and waitress, knows Sara. Big surprise there.

She saunters over and winks at Sara. "Hey, girlfriend, who's your friend?"

If Mary wasn't twenty years older with a lot more than my extra pounds on her, I might be jealous, but she greets Sara like a favored aunt might greet her niece. She pulls her into a big bear hug.

"Hey, Mary. Meet Nicky. She's a very special person in my life right now."

Mary arches her eyebrows. "Really? Hello, Nicky. You must really be special. Sara never brings her girlfriends here. I have to learn about them through the gossip mill."

I blush. I'm so pleased to hear this that I jump up and grab Mary and I give her my warmest hug. "I'm so happy to meet you."

"I like this girl already." Mary grins and winks at Sara again. "Don't be a stranger now. I expect more frequent visits with this one in tow."

Mary saunters away to cook our special meal.

After dinner, we take a leisurely stroll through the woods and eventually arrive at the cabin. It's still early and the sunset creates a spectacular backdrop.

I open the door and find a rose petal path to the bed. Lavender candles fill the air with their sweet scent. The fireplace creates a hazy glow that softens the edges around the room. It is the most romantic thing I can imagine.

"Ting?" I ask.

"She owes me. I asked her to set things up while we're at dinner. She did a good job, don't you think?" Sara looks at me and her slow sexy grin reaches the corners of her mouth—her very kissable mouth.

I start to cry, just a little. I'm so happy she thinks I'm worth going to all this trouble. "Oh, my God. Yes! Sara, you are so amazing."

We both shrug out of our coats and Sara leads me to the couch where a bottle of white wine is chilling. She fills up both of the glasses that are conveniently located next to the bottle. I notice a small jewelry box sitting next to the glasses and Sara reaches for it and hands it to me. In the box is a beautiful necklace with an unusual blue stone. The stone is nestled into a rose gold setting and the back of the pendant has an inscription. *All My Love, Sara.*

"Happy birthday, Nicky. The stone is called a larimar and it's a rare blue variety of pectolite found in the Dominican Republic. The color and location of the stone reminded me of the color of

40

your eyes—like the Caribbean Sea." She picks up her wine glass and lifts it in the air.

I lift my own glass and touch it to her glass.

"Cheers," she says as our glasses clink together.

I'm overwhelmed with emotion, but manage to say *cheers* back and we both take a sip of wine.

I'm not a wine connoisseur or anything, but I like the taste. I know instinctively this is one of the better quality wines.

"Will you help me put this on?" I hold up the necklace.

"Of course. I can't wait to see how it will bring out your eyes—not that they need it—because they're kinda like Elizabeth Taylor eyes, only blue."

Sara gently brushes my hair aside as she fastens the necklace in the back.

The electricity from her touch sends shivers down my spine. I lean in to her and she caresses my neck and moves closer as her lips barely touch me.

I'm halfway to losing complete control.

She places my hand in hers and leads me to the bed—the wine forgotten.

I'm tempted to rip off our clothes, but I get the impression that we will be taking our time as she slowly lifts my shirt up above my head.

Her hands stroke up both sides of my arms as she removes the shirt and tosses it aside. She kisses my neck again and then places a gentle kiss on my lips. As her hand strokes down my back, she releases my breasts from my bra. She removes my bra and her feather light touch moves over the sides of each of my breasts.

I can barely breathe because I'm so wound up. I reach for her shirt because I can't wait to see her naked, but she beats me to it as she removes her shirt in one swift movement. I don't sense any desperation in the move. It's the most sensual thing I've ever witnessed.

She's not wearing a bra and I get my first look at her breasts. They are perfectly round, and even though the room is warm, her nipples are erect as if they are standing at attention, awaiting my orders.

We embrace and are finally skin to skin. I can't believe it's finally going to happen.

She whispers in my ear and her soft breath tickles the bottom lobe. "You are so beautiful."

I'm in awe of her, but I can't think of anything to say back so I just tell her she is, too.

We tumble on the bed together and I can't remember how we get fully undressed, but all of a sudden, Sara lays next to me completely naked.

She reaches over to the side table and retrieves a feather. She begins to brush the feather over my hypersensitive body.

It is a feeling unlike anything I've experienced before. All the nerve endings in my body are on high alert. As the feather begins its journey down my stomach, my arousal reaches an uncomfortable peak. I'm so ready for her to touch me, to taste me, to enter me. I've been dreaming of this since I met Sara. I reach for her, because I also want to touch every part of her.

She gently pushes my arms down. "Ah, ah, ah, not yet. Just relax and enjoy the sensations."

There is no doubt I'm enjoying the sensations when I moan and make several other pleasure noises.

She does not let up on her teasing approach. "You're killing me here, Sara."

She whispers in my ear as she kisses my neck. "I seriously doubt that, Nicky."

The kiss sends a new set of shivers down my body.

She continues the expedition with hands and feather.

I feel her mouth travel down my body and I can't help myself. I cry out. "Oh, my God, yes, right there, please don't stop."

She lingers occasionally on various parts of my body and I barely hear her soft response to my desperate plea.

"I have no intention of stopping my worship of your beautiful body," she whispers.

Her touch feels so reverent. I wonder if she wants to make sure she is being considerate. At this point, a considerate touch is the last thing I'm praying for.

She delicately parts my legs as she continues her migration to my pulsing vagina. Her tongue sets a direct course inside as her hands part my hair and find my sensitive bud.

I gasp in a pleasure I cannot imagine even exists. I'm on the edge and try to get her to increase the pressure by gyrating my hips. My pleasure intensifies even further as my clitoris swells in response to her touch. Finally, I propel over the cliff as wave after wave of bliss overwhelms me in the most powerful climax I've ever experienced.

"Oh, my God, Sara, I'm so in love with you." I blurt this out before I have the good sense to censor my response—it doesn't matter.

She pulls me into her arms and tightens her hold. "God help me, I love you, too."

I think I feel a tear on my cheek. I hope it's because the experience is just as powerful for her, but a niggling sense of uneasiness washes over me. It takes me a few minutes to recover, but I'm eager to try out what I think I've learned from my research. My research consists of reading hundreds of lesbian romance and erotica books.

Lisa had stuffed lotion and a strap on contraption in my duffel bag, claiming them as my birthday presents and that I had better make good use of them this weekend. I don't want to leave the comfort of her arms, so I end up leaving the toys in my bag for now. I make good use of them later in the weekend.

My hands begin their pilgrimage down her body as I find her most sensitive spots. Thankfully, Sara is very responsive to every one of my touches. I know this because she is dripping wet and I marvel at the knowledge that I'm the one responsible for her state of arousal.

I'm naïve and tentative in my approach, but Sara never says anything that makes me feel inadequate. She does not stop my slow exploration of her body. I'm not really sure what I'm doing so when she moves her hand over mine, I take this as a sign of encouragement to continue. I find the response I'm eagerly looking for. Her breathing begins to quicken and her hips are moving. I can feel her responding to my touch and it doesn't take long for her to cry out.

"Oh, yes, right there. Yes, touch me just like that. You can go inside, deep inside."

I push two fingers deep inside and begin an in and out motion that sends her over the edge.

Her reaction startles me. She makes this quiet, *woo woo* type sound—like a forlorn wolf howling. I take that as a good sign and wrap my arms around her.

Now I know I feel tears and I'm worried. "Oh shit, did I do something wrong? What happened? I'm so sorry. I should have asked what to do. I'm so stupid. I thought I could kind of wing it and let things happen and I would know what to do."

"Shh, shh, you were perfect. I'm not crying because you did anything wrong—these are happy tears. I've never felt this way before. I promise. Everything is perfect."

I smile at the memory of that night. It was perfect. I never forgot my first experience. Even after Annie and I made love for the first time, I didn't forget that night with Sara. No one ever forgets their first time, especially if it's with someone you love. I hope if Annie reads this, she will understand because it doesn't in any way diminish the depth of my feelings, when I first made love with her.

We don't get much sleep that night. The floodgates have opened and I'm bound and determined to try out everything I can think of that sounded so good in my smut novels.

Sara is game for anything and she teaches me a few new things I haven't read about yet. I tell her again that I love her.

This time she jokes back and says I probably just lust her.

I turn her face to mine and make her look at me—really look at me. "I may be young and naïve, but I know what I feel and it's love," I tell her in all seriousness.

She nods at me. "I love you, too."

I believe her even though she has what I think is a really sad look on her face. From somewhere deep inside me, I know she isn't lying....

Chapter Seven

As I write in my journal about my first time with Sara, I can't help but take a side trip down memory lane. I can't help thinking about Annie and how we met and fell in love. I know I should finish my story about Sara, my early days in college, and how my life took such an unusual turn, but I can't ignore these vivid memories of Annie. I have to write them down.

I'm not proud of the fact that my propensity for one-night stands keeps me from having any meaningful relationships with others. It suits me until the night I meet Annie and I'm forever changed.

Although I don't deserve to have wonderful women come into my life at just the right moments to help me through the rough spots—that is what usually happens. Cass, my best friend, is one of those people. Six months ago, they sent her to me and even though she's been a bit of a tight ass, she's taught me so much. Cass has her own demons to deal with. Maybe the fates brought us together because we were destined to meet Annie and Vic. Vic is Cass's salvation every bit as much as Annie is mine.

I meet Annie one night when I drag Cass out to a quaint lesbian bar. I love music and I know The Orchid is supposed to have live music on Friday nights.

Vic is also there with Annie and this leads to Cass's reconnection with her. When Cass first sees Vic, she gasps and I wonder what that's all about—I think that maybe she recognizes her from somewhere. I am convinced that both of us feel a deep sense of gratitude at our good fortune on that fateful night.

Before we even enter the bar, I hear Annie's sweet, soulful voice. Annie captivates me the minute I glance at the stage and see her. There is something about her that causes me to abandon all my fears. For the first time since Sara, I know I'm ready to let someone in again.

Annie is simply stunning. She's about my height at around five foot six and has the most exquisite blue eyes that I've ever seen. They remind me of a sunny day in Seattle. You know, the line from the television show, *Here Comes the Brides—the bluest skies you've ever seen in Seattle*. Seattle really does have the bluest skies.

I don't really know how lucky I am that Annie lets me in until three months later when I'm talking with her best friend, Vic.

"I'm really surprised how Annie reacts to you" Vic tells me. "I've known Annie since grade school and she always shies away from everyone except me. I was shocked that she let you touch her the first night you met. Even before that night, she would try to melt into the background wherever she went. You know, she used to wear these hideous black glasses until she met you and began wearing her contacts. I think she always tried to hide behind her glasses. You're lucky she's let you in and you'd better not hurt her."

"I would never hurt her. I love her more than I ever thought possible," I respond.

Too bad I'm not able to keep my promise to Vic, but I never wanted to hurt Annie.

I don't know why, but Annie opens up to me and she's like a completely new person when we all get together. Even though Annie is painfully shy, her wicked sense of humor comes through.

I've never had so much fun on dates as I do with Annie. We do so many different things and I pester Cass all the time to help me so I can spend time with Annie in the sunshine. Annie loves to bike and sail, so we spend a lot of time on bike trails and boating. I make Cass buy us a big powerboat before the second date we have with Vic and Annie and later Annie and I explore the waters of Puget Sound.

Friday nights are movie nights and Vic, Cass, Annie and I cuddle up and usually watch a romantic comedy. Our first Friday night we convince Annie to let us watch the movie that is based on one of her books. She blushes and protests a little at first because I think attention embarrasses her, but we prevail. All I can say is, wow! I run right out the next day and buy the book.

Every day with Annie is a joy, no matter what we choose to do. Even though Annie is shy and reserved, she seems to blossom around me and I take that as a sign that we are truly meant for one another.

People say that opposites attract. I guess that's really true for Annie and me. She is so gentle and sweet and I'm, well, you know how I am. I hope that I bring out the best in her and I know she brings out the best in me. If I lose her, I will lose that part of myself that is good and right. If Annie goes on without me, I fear she will crawl back into her shell. Vic told me how bad it was for Annie after her assault and I don't want to be the one responsible for setting her back.

I know that this journey down memory lane is an interruption in my story about Sara, but I just had to write it down while the memory is fresh in my mind. Anyway, back to my story....

Chapter Eight

A year passes and I'm still one hundred percent head over heels in love with Sara. I believe she feels the same about me.

Lisa is a good friend to both of us, so at the end of our freshman year we decide to move out of the dorm and rent a small house together.

Sara graduates and turns down a graduate assistant position at the University of Berkeley, but manages to get a graduate assistant position at the UW. I'm thrilled that she passes up her opportunity to move to California, because I know I have at least two more years before we have to consider our future together. We both know it's not the best idea to complete graduate work at the same school where you were an undergraduate, but neither of us can even imagine being apart for the next two years.

Sara, of course, is getting her MBA. She's so brilliant and I have no doubt that she will have a bright future. Leaving school and taking a job is two years off for her and I don't want to think that far ahead.

We find a cute two-bedroom house to rent that is not in a completely dilapidated neighborhood and the three of us settle into our new place. The house is probably a little more than I can realistically afford, but Sara assures me that it's no problem for her to help subsidize my share. She mentions that her family is well off and she doesn't even need scholarships or graduate assistantships. She tells me that she just feels better doing some things on her own.

I still haven't met her family, but I don't give it too much thought. I wonder if maybe her family doesn't know about us and she's afraid they will cut her off financially.

I haven't told my parents yet either, but I'm determined to change that soon. She's met my family, but I didn't introduce her as my girlfriend.

My sister, Tess, figures it out and tries to tell me that she's pretty sure mom and dad know, but they are just waiting for me to tell them. She tells me it's pretty hard to miss because of the way we look at one another.

I grill her about this comment one night.

"You look like you are ready to fuck each other on mom's dining room table," Tess tells me.

"I promise I'll tell them soon. I'm just not ready yet," I tell her.

My sister doesn't know that I still haven't figured out what I want to major in and that I don't have a clue what I'll be good at— besides fucking my girlfriend. I think I'm pretty good at that, because we get a lot of practice. Sara still does that howling thing and I don't think it is remotely strange anymore. Tess doesn't need to know that either.

†

After we'd been living in the house for a few months, the three of us are lounging in the family room watching some inane sitcom. I don't even remember what show it was because what unfolds in the next few short minutes is so devastating it overshadows all of my other memories of that awful night.

The phone seems unusually loud as it rings.

I'm closest to the phone, so I reach over and answer it. "Hello."

"Hey, Nicky, is Lisa there?" I recognize her dad's voice on the other end of the phone. He sounds different tonight, like he has a cold or something.

"Oh, hey, Mr. Schultz. Sounds like you have a really bad cold. Let me get Lisa, she's right here." I hand the phone over to Lisa.

She motions at us as she puts the phone to her ear and I understand that she wants one of us to turn the television down.

"Hey, Dad, what's up?" Lisa listens for a few minutes.

I'm watching her expression and I start to get concerned that something is wrong.

Lisa is always cheerful and smiling. I never see her in a bad mood and I've never seen her cry.

Tears well up in her eyes, and she sounds like she's choking on her words as she responds to her dad. "Okay, Dad, I'll be there in an hour."

I look over at Sara. She looks at me with what I imagine is the same question in her eyes.

"What's going on, Lisa?" I ask.

Lisa is sobbing now as she answers. "It's…it's… my…mom."

We both flank her sides and take her hands in ours. We're trying to get the rest of the story and comfort her at the same time.

"What's wrong with your mom?" Sara asks.

"She has cancer," Lisa blurts out through her tears.

Neither of us say anything. We both just hug her and because I don't have experience with this sort of thing, I don't know what to say. I don't know if Sara has any experience either since she remains silent too.

"It's stage four pancreatic cancer and it's already spread to her liver, stomach, and bones. The doctor's say they can't do anything more for her and they give her three to six months." Lisa's voice is monotone.

"Shit." It's the only thing I can think of to say.

"I have to go home now. I'll figure out later what I want to do about school. I know Mom will insist I remain in school." Lisa begins to sob again. "I don't know what to do now but I don't think I can stay."

"What can we do for you? Do you want us to come with you?" Sara asks.

"No. I'll be fine." Lisa continues to sob uncontrollably.

"Lisa, let us drive you at least. We can come pick you up whenever you're ready, but I don't think you should drive by yourself right now." Sara's tone is insistent.

Lisa nods and seems to accept our support. She heads to her bedroom to grab some clothes and other travel items.

I look at Sara. I'm hoping she will know what to do for our friend. "Shit. Life is so fucking fickle. I hate that this is happening. God, Mrs. Shultz can't be much more than forty and she looked so healthy when we saw her."

Sara looks over at me and she seems so sad and gets this faraway look in her eyes.

"Yeah, unfortunately human life is so fragile," Sara remarks.

"I can't even imagine how hard this would be if it were my mom. I suppose it's even worse when it happens to your child. I used to volunteer at the hospital in the children's ward, and it is just so heartbreaking to see the parents with children who are dying."

✝

I stretch and think about my volunteer work and the eventual road I ended up on. I know, surprising that I volunteered at hospitals, isn't it? At one point, I thought I wanted to be a nurse, but I ended up getting my masters in counseling and thinking my career path would be something with hospice patients or grief counseling.

Remembering that time, I feel a lone tear trickle down my cheek. I have such fond memories of Lisa's family. I used to spend as much time with her family as I did with my own. Sara and I ended up spending a lot of time with them because they always had the best holiday parties and were geographically closer than my family.

Life, however, took me on a road with many twists and turns and I ended up being a product of my experience. The exposure to Lisa's tragedy with her mom certainly had an impact, but it was a much bigger twist in my life that led me down a different path.

†

The forty-five minutes it takes to get to the Schultz's is eerily quiet. It is one of the few times we are not joking and teasing one another. We are so comfortable with one another that up until now no topic is off limits. The drive is so somber and I imagine that none of us knows quite how to respond to this change in events.

We all get out of the car and it seems to me that we're acting as if we're going to our own funerals. I suppose we are reluctant to face the reality of what we'll encounter beyond the front door.

Mr. Schultz opens the door to greet us and he tries to present us with a smile. It looks like a sad smile to me. I'm pretty sure we all recognize that his heart is breaking.

"Sara, Nicky, thank you for driving Lisa. Will you come in for a minute?" He opens the door and I understand that he is trying to wave us in.

"No, thanks, Mr. Schultz, but we'll be back whenever Lisa needs us to come get her. I don't really think her professors will care too much if she misses her classes tomorrow, but I'll go see them and tell them what's up." I look over to Lisa. "You can let me know what you decide and I'll take care of everything, Lisa. Don't worry about a thing," I offer.

"Thanks, girls. I really appreciate you helping Lisa out."

Lisa goes into the house but Mr. Schultz remains outside as he shuts the door.

I wonder if he is closing the door so he can have a word with us without Lisa overhearing.

"Can you girls do me a favor?" he asks.

"Of course," I state.

"Whatever you need," Sara adds.

"I know Lisa and she won't be thinking clearly. She'll want to drop out of school but we don't want her to do that. I know we can figure out a way for her to visit often without dropping out. It's what her mother wants for her."

I notice that his eyes begin to water.

"I have to honor that. She has to honor that. Will you help her through the grief?" he asks.

I step up to answer this grieving man. "Mr. Schultz, if you're asking us to convince Lisa to do something that may not be the right choice for her then I'm afraid we can't do that, but we can promise you we'll be there to help her determine what she can live with. She may come to the realization that she wants to honor her mom's wishes, but you have to let her decide. It's not too far from the college to your home, so we can all figure what to do together if that's what she wants. I promise we will be there for her every step of the way."

I may not have many brilliant moments in my life, but I'd like to think this is one of them.

Mr. Schultz nods at us, gives us both a hug, and goes back into his home.

I suspect they have a lot to figure out as a family. I believe we play a big supporting role, but it's time for the main players to sort things out.

✝

I'm off again on another tangent and stop writing. I can't help thinking about how Mr. and Mrs. Schultz treated us like their own daughters. They knew all along about our relationship and never once treated us any different from Lisa's straight friends. I recall making a promise to myself that night. The next time I visit my parents I am going to tell them that I am gay. I remembered thinking that life is too short not to be open with them. The Schultz's knew more about me than my own family and I vowed to change that. I didn't want the precious moments with my family to bypass me and forever regret my time with them. I didn't know then how profound this was as my time with my family was already starting to tick away—the hourglass was out of sand.

†

Before we get in the car, Sara reaches out and hugs me frantically and I can feel her desperation. I react the same way to the somberness of the evening.

As we are driving, I break the silence. "Sara, I don't know if you're out with your family, because you don't really talk about them. I guess I assume there's a reason for that. I'm thinking it's time I told my family." I look at her, because I want to see how she will react. "Are you okay with that?"

She's driving, but takes her eyes off the road for a second and glances over at me. "Yes, of course. I think they may already know and I get the feeling they're just waiting for you to make it official. I really like your parents so I'm hoping they won't be unhappy."

"Yeah, that's what my sister said. I'm pretty sure they like you too. They seem to think you've had a good influence on me. I was gonna tell them all about the influence you've had, but I thought they might not appreciate me telling them all about our fuckfests."

"I told you, we never fuck, we make love." She mock glares at me but then starts to chuckle.

"Yeah, I suppose most of the time, but I think we do actually fuck sometimes."

"Yeah, it's probably good to keep a few things to yourself."

"I love you, you know that right?" I smile for the first time that evening.

"Yeah, I do. I love you too. No matter what, I hope you'll never forget that?"

"Never."

The clue train speeds by again.

55

Chapter Nine

Lisa decides to stay in school and we all settle into a routine. I get assignments and notes for her classes on Monday and Friday. Sara drives her home on Thursday evening and I pick her up on Monday night and sometimes we go there on the weekends and hang out with her family.

Lisa puts on what I assume is her brave face and sometimes I get her to laugh and joke with me just like old times. Sara is her genuinely warm and nurturing self and I provide the comic relief when things start to get too sad.

Her mom is a beautiful woman who turns into a skeleton right before our eyes. It's shocking to see the transformation and I think there are times that it's more than Lisa can handle. It's during those times I'm the only one Lisa will talk to. Maybe she opens up to me because we started out being blunt and honest with one another and I believe she knows nothing she says will shock me.

I have a front row seat to what I view as Lisa working out her anger over the disease and her guilt for staying in school while her mother is dying.

"God, Nicky, I don't know if I'm hiding my reactions well at all. My mom caught me looking at her the other day and she started crying and saying, *I know I look so ugly right now.* Then she kind of joked and said, *well, I always wanted to be model thin, but perhaps I've taken it a bit too far.* I think I choked out something like, *Mom, you will always be gorgeous.* I lied to my mom, Nicky. You know what she looks like. She is like a holocaust victim and my heart breaks every time I see her."

"Oh, Lisa, it's okay. I think this little white lie to your mom will not result in a direct path to hell. I, on the other hand, have secured my place in hell with my evil lesbian ways."

"I'm so afraid no one will be there when she passes. I don't want her to die alone." Lisa begins to cry quietly again.

I put my arms around her. "She won't die alone because we'll all be there. I promise."

"Do you think there's an afterlife?'

"I don't know, Lisa. I've never been very religious, but then again a lot of strange things happen and who's to say what's on the other side. Death is pretty scary, so if it gives people comfort to believe there's something more, than who am I to say there isn't. The important question is, do you? Does your mother?"

"I think I do. I also think that if there is ever someone deserving of a better life after death, it's my mom. I'd like to think she'll be somewhere looking fondly on all of us, even you, despite your sinful ways."

"That sounds perfect to me. I need all the looking after I can get."

"I'm worried about my dad. He's still so young. I think he's going to worry about what I'll think about him dating. Honestly, Mom can never be replaced, but I don't want my dad to be lonely. I want him to find someone. Is that awful of me to think like that? My God, my mom isn't even dead yet."

"I think it's gonna be a while before your dad will even consider dating. You know, the heart is a muscle and just like all our other muscles, sometimes it gets damaged, but when it repairs itself, it's much stronger. You gotta keep exercising it—so it gets stronger. Sometimes the exercise itself breaks it down, but a little time and distance from the exercise and boom it's stronger than before. I think we have the capacity to love more than once in our lifetime and I think it's okay for you to imagine that your dad will find love again."

"Wow, Nicky, that's kind of profound. I didn't know you had it in you to be so philosophical. So you don't think there's only one true love in life? How about for you and Sara? Don't you think she's your one true love?"

"Yeah, I do. So, I hope I don't have to feel the same loss as your dad, but everyone says that time heals all wounds. I don't think your dad will ever forget your mom, but that doesn't mean he won't have the capacity to become whole again."

"You know, it's times like these that make me glad I'm not in a serious relationship. I can't even imagine what my dad must be going through. It seems like all love does is create heart wrenching pain."

Sara steps inside Lisa's bedroom. "Sometimes, Lisa, you just can't stop it. It's like two magnets coming together. No matter the consequences, you allow yourself to fall because to stop falling is impossible."

"Hey, babe, I didn't hear you come in." I smile up at Sara.

The phone starts ringing and our discussion comes to an abrupt halt.

I know the time is near and at any moment Lisa will get the call.

Lisa rushes to answer the phone.

"Hi, Dad... Okay... Yeah we're on our way."

Lisa hangs up the phone and tears are streaming down her cheeks. "My dad said the hospice nurse told him mom won't make it through the night."

I know it's finally time to say our goodbyes.

Both Sara and I have told her many times that when the time comes, we will be there for her, so Lisa knows she doesn't even have to ask. No matter what is happening in our lives, it can wait. This has top priority. We all have overnight bags packed. We nod to one another and grab our bags.

†

We make it to the house in record time. I don't care that Sara speeds the whole way there.

Lisa bounds up the stairs, beckoning to us with her hand and we follow her up to the bedroom. We hang back a little as Lisa sits beside her mother on the bed then leans over and kisses her mother's forehead.

Lisa's dad is sitting in a chair on the other side gently holding her mom's hand.

Her mom's breath is labored and I notice how much effort it takes for her to acknowledge her daughter. "Lisa, how are you?"

"Oh, Mom." Lisa starts to cry. "I love you so much, Mom. I don't know what I will do without you."

"I will always be there for you no matter where I am."

Those are the last words Lisa's mother speaks.

Sara and I stand off to the side like quiet sentinels watching over our friend in her hour of need. Sara starts to cry and I grab her hand to lead her out of the room. I want to let the family say their final goodbyes in private.

I rarely see Sara cry. I guess there is more to her distress than watching Mrs. Schultz in her final moments on this earth.

"This reminds me so much of my dad," Sara says quietly.

Sara never talks about her family, so I'm particularly intrigued by this impromptu confession.

"Sara, you've never talked about your family. Is your dad seriously ill?"

Sara nods and begins crying again. "Remember the family emergency when we first met and you were so pissed because you thought I was blowing you off? Dad took a turn for the worse, but then he rallied. He's doing okay now, but there are times when he doesn't do so well and then I worry about my mom."

I feel blessed that Sara is letting me into her world a little more. I never push the issue of family with her because I think she has her reasons for not sharing and I respect those. I believe that when she is ready, she will introduce me to them.

"Sara, you know I'm always here for you—no matter what. You just have to let me know what you need and when you need it and I'll be there."

She nods but doesn't say anything more. The conversation is over. Done. The little turkey thermometer pops up to signify there will be no more talk of her family.

I don't say anything more.

†

Sara and I are quietly talking in the hall, waiting for Lisa. We are waiting to be her calm place in this raging emotional storm. I think I know Sara well enough now to assume that she will be there with me to provide the calm.

Lisa gets her wish—the wish she told me about during one of our long talks. Her mom dies, not alone, but with her family surrounding her as she takes her final breath.

Lisa comes out of the bedroom and sobs quietly. She glances over to us, then nods, signifying that her mother has died.

I know Mrs. Shultz's struggle is over and I believe she is at peace and doesn't feel pain anymore. I'm relieved. Sometimes death is a blessing and, perhaps, doubly so for Mrs. Schultz. I want to try to help Lisa understand this, but I imagine her loss is too raw now and I remain silent. Sara and I just put our protective arms around her and let her cry on our shoulders.

I surmise her dad is too distraught to help her at this moment, so the support must come from us. I don't mind. I love Lisa and there isn't any other place I'd rather be than by her side.

The next several days are a complete daze for me and probably for Sara and Lisa, as well. We help her dad make arrangements for the service. We help him pick out the urn, hire the caterers, and call all their family and friends letting them know Mrs. Schultz is finally at peace.

After Lisa's aunt and uncle arrive, we take Lisa to a hotel and book two rooms so that she doesn't have to be constantly

60

reminded of her loss. More family is coming from out of town and I assume that the house isn't big enough for everyone.

Sara takes care of the bill. No one argues with her because at this point, we are used to Sara quietly taking care of things for us. I instinctively believe that this is the way Sara likes to show her support. This is something she often does throughout our relationship.

Of course, it's not the only way she supports us. Sara is so empathetic that I think she misses her calling by getting an MBA. I wonder why she never goes into counseling or a helping profession, but when asked she tells me that her parents expect her to carry on the family business and I never question this.

Chapter Ten

Two more years fly by. We still live in the little house by the university district.

Lisa and I are about to start our senior year of college and Sara is taking extra classes, so we get a reprieve on our future. I know she's applying for jobs around Seattle and I'm encouraged by her efforts to remain in the area.

We're sitting on the couch, again watching some ridiculous sitcom, when the phone rings. Once again, I don't remember the sitcom.

Lisa answers the phone and hands it to Sara. "Sara, it's your mom."

I don't know how I know this, but I know it's bad news because Sara's mom hardly ever calls. After two years together, I still haven't met her family and I don't know why.

†

It's funny the things you remember after the fact. I saw a picture of her mom and dad one day. It fell out of a book that Sara was reading as I was putting it away. I studied the picture and noticed the resemblance right away. Sara's mom looked just like her.

I thought that maybe Sara was embarrassed, because it was clear to me that her dad was a lot older than her mom. I wondered if maybe he was her step dad, but then I saw that Sara had his eyes. The picture must have been old, because her mom looked so young. I understood then how her dad's health had declined if the picture was any indication of his age.

†

"Hi, Mom." Sara cradled the phone to her ear. "Okay... I understand... Yes, I'll take the first flight out... What? Are you sure? Okay, I'll ask her...Yes, I'll ask Lisa too...all right, bye, Mom, I'll see you soon."

Sara is now crying again. It's only the third or fourth time I've ever seen her cry.

I cross the room quickly to embrace her, because somehow I know without asking that it's about her dad. I look her in the eyes and I hope that she can see that I know.

She hangs on to me and it feels so desperate that I don't know how to make it better.

"It's my dad," she finally says through a cascade of tears. "He isn't expected to last the night so I need to get a flight out right away. Mom asked me if you and Lisa might want to come with me."

I'm so shocked by this recent turn of events that I don't say anything for a few seconds. I think that maybe she misinterprets my hesitation.

"It's okay, you don't need to come with me. I'll be okay. I told mom I would ask, but...."

"Oh, my God, Sara, no, I want to come. I'm sorry I hesitated for even one second. I'm just so shocked that your mom wants us to come."

"Sara, I want to come too," Lisa jumps into the conversation. "I want to be there for you, like you were there for me. I don't care if it means missing the first week of classes. Whatever you need is so much more important."

I finally find more of my voice. I'm ready to do whatever it takes to support her. "Sara, you know there is nowhere I would rather be than by your side. I have some savings, so book whatever flights you can."

"Ditto," Lisa adds.

Sara waives her hand at us. "No, I will take care of all of the costs. It's a small drop in the bucket to our family. Mom would not even hear of you paying for yourselves. I'll book us in a hotel, because family will surely overrun the house. I can get us a rental car and we can head straight to the hospital. Is that okay with you?"

"Of course," we both agree.

The three of us jump into action as we hastily pull clothes together. We throw various items into our bags. I don't care if I'm forgetting something, because I can always pick up anything I need in California.

I just want us to be ready to leave as soon as we can, so that we can get Sara to the hospital before her dad passes. I know how important closure is. I know she will never forgive herself if she is not able to say goodbye.

Sara is able to book us a flight scheduled to leave in three hours.

†

We make it to the airport with just enough time to get through security before our departure time.

I've never been to California, but I'm not thinking of this trip as some kind of vacation, or holiday trip. I only care about how I can support Sara.

Sara is drumming her fingers on the counter at the car rental place. I have never seen her so agitated. A sound comes out of her throat that sounds like an animal growl.

I don't think much about it at the time, because everyone's nerves are raw.

I place my hand over Sara's to quiet her drumming—because it's annoying and not helping.

The young girl behind the counter appears nervous and afraid.

I think that Sara's drumming just makes her take longer to do the paperwork.

I glance over at Lisa and give her a silent signal to take Sara for a walk while I handle the car rental paperwork.

I don't let Sara drive, because I see how wound up she is. I'm afraid she won't be safe. She has a sullen expression as she sits in the passenger seat and her legs bounce up and down in a nervous fashion. Sara is never surly with either of us, so I don't take offense.

"Can't you drive any faster?"

"I would rather not take the chance of getting pulled over for speeding or driving recklessly. I'm already doing ten over the speed limit. That's all the chance I think we should take," I explain patiently.

"What if we don't make it on time?" She begins to cry.

This, I believe, is her biggest fear. I have to admit, there may be some reality to her admission of alarm.

I stop caring about being pulled over and step on the gas. I drive more recklessly than I have ever driven in my life, but I don't care. I only want to get Sara to the hospital in time to say goodbye.

✝

We screech to a halt in front of the main entrance at the University of California Medical Center. Sara jumps out and briefly glances at me.

I don't know if she is asking for permission to run in without us, or sending an apology.

I don't give her the time to explain. "Go. We'll park the car and meet you at his room."

Sara nods her head and manages a small smile. "My dad is in the intensive care unit. I'll meet you there."

The University of California Medical Center is a huge hospital and we get lost trying to find our way to the room. One of the nurses passes us in the hall as we are looking for the room and I think she takes pity on us. She shows us to the intensive care unit where Sara's dad is dying. I'm not really sure whether we should go in or not, so we hover just outside of the room.

Sara is leaning over the bed rail sobbing as she holds her dad's frail hand.

Nothing prepares me for the scene that unfolds. Her dad looks like he's one hundred years old. I think it has to be the illness that is making him look older than he is. I glance up at the beautiful woman on the other side of the bed holding his other hand. She is looking down at him with an expression I can only describe as soul wrenching love. I cannot put this picture into perspective.

The woman looks so young, that she can't possibly be Sara's mom. I know Sara doesn't have a sister and the expression on the woman's face is the love of a wife—not a daughter.

The beautiful woman looks up and smiles at me. She gracefully exits the room and extends her hand. "Hello, you must be Nicky. My daughter's description does not capture your beauty, but then I do not believe words would be able to do justice to your loveliness. I am Claire, Sara's mother. It is a pleasure to finally meet you. I have heard a lot about you."

Her introduction stuns me. I want to say to her, *I can't say the same about you since Sara rarely talks about her family,* but for once, I don't blurt out what I'm thinking.

I say something appropriate, "Hello, Mrs. Duncan. Thank you for inviting us. I'm pleased to meet you, but I'm sorry it's under these sad circumstances. I can't think of anywhere else I'd rather be than by Sara's side."

Lisa steps forward and extends her hand. "Hello, Mrs. Duncan, I'm Lisa, Sara's other roommate. Ditto on what Nicky said."

Mrs. Duncan takes both Lisa and me by the arm and begins to lead us farther into the hallway. "Come on, girls, let's go get a coffee and leave Sara with her dad for a few minutes."

Before we get too far from the room, I glance back at Sara who bends over her dad whispering something to him.

Although he is barely awake, whatever she says appears to register with him and he nods. He turns his gaze in my direction and stares at me. It gives me the creeps, because I don't really know what it all means.

†

I sit patiently in the family waiting area drinking stale hospital coffee. I don't know what to say. Both of my parents seem so young and healthy compared to Sara's dad. I think back on Lisa's experience with her mom and I feel guilty for the luck I have had with my parents.

Sara's mom interrupts my thoughts. "I had to see for myself. Sara explained her love for you and I have to ask if you do...feel the same, that is?"

I wonder if her question is disproval of our relationship or something else. I'm usually good at reading people, but I can't read her.

I get a little irritated by the question, because I don't know what her intentions are. "Excuse me?"

"I apologize. I mean no disrespect. You may have misunderstood. I do not disapprove of gay relationships. I am just worried about the consequences of you and my daughter staying together. It is a very challenging road. A road I myself have traveled."

"No, no, I'm sorry. I jumped to a conclusion. My parents have been really great about me and Sara, so I don't have any experience yet with the ugly side of society. I don't think you have to worry about that. I do love Sara very much."

"Mmm, I don't doubt that. My daughter is a far better person than I am. I have been selfish with love in my life—consequences be damned. You seem to be a survivor and I am glad to see that."

"Thank you." I respond and begin to relax.

I remember now, that at the time, I thought she was giving her approval. I didn't realize until many years later that she was trying to tell me something very different.

Sara comes out of the room swiping her hand across her cheek to remove the tears.

I stand up and put my arms around her hoping she will feel all the love and support I'm desperately trying to convey to her.

Lisa pats her shoulder and I think she is trying to say we're here and we're not going anywhere.

Sara kisses the top of my head. It is such a sweet gesture.

She pulls away from our embrace and turns to her mom. "Mom, can I talk to you for a moment?"

Sara and her mom move away from the group and I watch their very animated discussion.

I can't really hear anything, but I see a look of anguish on Sara's face. I assume they are talking about her dad. I think I see Sara mouth the words, *I know, I know,* but I don't understand what it all means.

Sara walks back to us. "The nurse said it won't be long now and we are heading back to his room."

I give her a hug. "We will be right here if you need us."

†

Less than two hours later, Sara's dad dies with his wife and daughter by his side.

Sara finally comes out of the room. "His passing was peaceful. I'm so glad I was able to get here in time." She nods at us and then waves her hand.

I assume she wants us to follow her and we do.

We leave the hospital and head to the hotel.

I notice that Sara has been crying. She seems at peace with the loss of her dad, but there is a melancholy about her that lingers for the remainder of the time we're together.

I remember thinking that grief is different for everyone and she certainly has a right to be sad for however long it takes to process her dad's death.

The California sun is shining brightly on the freshly dug grave. It's in stark comparison to the somber mood that seems to lie over the attendees like a blanket of dense fog. The weather in California doesn't get the memo about the solemn occasion. I suppose there are some families that choose to celebrate a person's life after their death, but I definitely get the impression this is not the case with Sara's family.

There are hundreds of people at the funeral, but we don't really meet too many of the family. I assume they are all family and friends but they all seem to be close to our age or older. I remember thinking how odd it is that there doesn't appear to be anyone at the funeral over the age of forty. Sometimes I'd catch a wary gaze and there is more than one person that seems to look at me with curiosity. I try to ignore the looks, especially the ones that don't even try to mask what I perceive as hostility.

I think I understand why Sara never talks about her family and I wonder if her mom is the only one who approves of our relationship. I don't talk with Sara about my observations. I figure if she wants to talk about her family, she will.

"Lisa, do you think it's odd that no one appears to be older than forty?"

Lisa shrugs and doesn't really answer me.

I wonder if Sara's grandparents or great aunts and uncles are all dead. I even have a horrible thought that maybe there are hereditary issues and all of her family dies young. Then I remember her father and how old he looked lying there in that bed.

Sara doesn't spend any time with family and friends and, except for a few people, she doesn't take the time to introduce us. Sara does a quick introduction to Ting, her friend that set up the cabin on my birthday.

"Are you okay?" I ask Sara.

She just nods.

She looks so sad to me. I feel so powerless. I want to know what to do to take away her grief but it seems there is nothing I can do.

✝

Three days later, we head back to Seattle and attempt to resume our lives.

My birthday is coming up again and Sara tells me she would like to take me back to the cabin.

I readily agree. I desperately want to see her smile again and I hope some rest and relaxation at the cabin, where we have so many fond memories, will help. I'm looking forward to our mini-vacation.

Chapter Eleven

I'm so excited to go back to the cabin where Sara and I first made love. It is a magical place to me.

It doesn't matter that the gray clouds seem to smother the early sunshine. I don't remember feeling uneasy about anything or wondering if this was some kind of premonition of things to come.

Sara still seems grief stricken and I don't know what to do to cheer her up. I offer to drive to the cabin so she doesn't have to deal with the sucky Seattle traffic. Sara just hands me the keys and lets me drive. Normally we would be chatting away to pass the time, but Sara is not saying too much. I decide not to disturb her quiet reflection.

When we arrive at the cabin, I can't believe that even in the midst of her grief, Sara manages to make sure it's ready and the fire is blazing when we get there.

We stand in front of the fire and Sara drapes her arm over my shoulder. She pulls me into a warm embrace.

Her kiss is so sweet and gentle that I really feel how much she loves me.

She pulls away from me and whispers. "I want you to always remember how much I love you. Please never forget that, no matter what happens."

I can barely hear what she says, but something in the way she says this worries me. She sounds so sad.

"Sara, are you okay?"

"Yes, of course." She shakes her head and smiles. "Let's see what Ting left us to eat."

She starts laughing as she looks in the refrigerator. It's the first real laugh I've heard in a week. She pulls out a huge tray of sushi.

I love sushi now. Ever since Sara made me try it on that first birthday weekend at the cabin, I've become a sushi connoisseur.

"Hmm, I wonder where your tray is," she jokes.

"Ha, ha, very funny. You can have the snapper and I'll take the rest."

"No way. Just remember not too long ago, I had to put it on my stomach to entice you to try it. You were a virgin in more ways than one."

"Well, I'm not a virgin anymore, thanks to you, so get your cute ass over here and we can feed one another that delectable tray of sushi."

Sara picks out a fatty tuna cone and hands it over to me.

I dip the cone in some soy sauce and take a bite. "Mmm, my God, this is orgasmic. Where does Ting get this sushi? It's some of the best I've ever had."

"Sushi Zen. It's by far the best Sushi in the state. I know. I can really pound down the sushi and you certainly have come a long way in your ability to put this stuff away too. Ting really outdid herself this time. This tray can easily feed ten people."

"We can always nibble on it throughout the weekend after we work up an appetite. I plan to ensure we qualify for the sex Olympics this weekend. No hikes in the woods this time around, I want us to spend the weekend in bed but I will allow one detour to your friend's restaurant. I still remember the meal we had there and that was three years ago."

"That sounds like the best idea I've heard in a long time."

We eat so much sushi that we roll into bed uncomfortably stuffed. It's been a long day with the drive to the cabin after an emotional week and we both fall asleep tangled in one another's arms.

†

The next morning I feel rested and wake up before Sara.

Sometime in the night, she'd discarded her clothes. Her long red hair fans out over her pillow and her perfect breasts peek out of the sheets. It's too much of a temptation, so I turn over and lightly stroke her naked breasts. The morning light shines on her sleeping form and it's the most beautiful thing I've seen in a long time.

Sara stirs as I begin to caress her. "Mmm, that feels nice." Her amber eyes open slowly as a smile lights up her face. "This is a wonderful way to wake up."

"You are so beautiful. I love you so much. I can't imagine waking up next to anyone else," I declare.

Sara's smile fades, but she kisses me.

I feel her kiss all through my body and truly believe the kiss has all the passion of a woman in love.

"I love you, too, more than you'll ever realize," Sara says.

Something seems off, but I ignore that feeling because Sara shows me through her touch and her kiss how much she loves me. I don't give her strange words another thought.

We end up making love all weekend long, with minor breaks here and there for food. At times, our lovemaking seems frantic.

I wonder if Sara is trying to imprint the memory into her brain. The passion in our lovemaking is so intense and it reminds me of our first time.

I pinch the bridge of my nose as if that will keep me from processing this memory. Like our first time, I will always remember this weekend. It didn't start as a cherished memory, but it settled in like an old shoe.

Out of the gate, the memory was bitter, as my upcoming grief would overshadow everything. The bitterness overtook my senses and I tried to spit it out with angry words. Closure made all the difference in the world, but my peace came with a hefty price. I

73

only pray that Annie will understand how I needed closure and how this need was completely separate from our love.

†

Monday is a busy day for me and I end up spending all day on campus. Lisa also has a full day of classes, but we would usually meet up for lunch and finish our afternoon classes before heading back to our little house. Parking is such a bitch that we always commute together on Mondays.

Sara is still applying for jobs in the Seattle area, so she doesn't meet up with us today. I expect her to be hanging out in the living room when we get home.

I call out to her as I enter the house, "Hey, Sara, we're home. Do you want to order a pizza or something?"

My voice is an echo in the empty house. I know instantly that something is fatally wrong. I see an envelope on the coffee table, but it doesn't register.

I run upstairs to our bedroom and notice how empty the room seems. I'm in a daze as I look in the closet and peer into the bathroom. There is not a trace of Sara anywhere.

I think I'm going out of my mind and I scream in anguish. I don't understand what's happening.

Lisa rushes up the stairs, takes in the scene with one quick scan of the room and gasps.

I wonder if she thinks the same thing as I do. Can the impossible be unfolding right in front of her, too?

I run downstairs then remember the envelope on the coffee table. I think Sara must have had a family emergency, but I don't understand why all her stuff is gone. Her car is still in the driveway, so it doesn't make any sense. I know she'll be back, because her car is still here.

Lisa appears to be in a daze as she follows me down the stairs.

I tear open the envelope and try to scan the contents of the letter addressed to me.

Love Forever, Live Forever

My dearest Nicky:

This is the hardest thing I have ever had to do in my life. I don't know if you will ever understand the choice I had to make. I know you may not believe me, but I made the choice because I love you more than you can ever imagine, and for that reason, it was the only choice I could make. Remember when I said we were like two magnets. I am so sorry. I couldn't help falling in love with you. It took all my strength to leave today, but I just couldn't be selfish anymore. My mom and dad reminded me of the choice I had to make. I wish things were so different. I even considered making a very selfish choice, but in the end, I just couldn't do that to you. I know you won't understand all this and I really wish I could explain more. I just wanted you to know that I will always love you. Please don't try to find me, I don't know how strong I can be if you do. The rent on the house is paid for the next three years, so you don't need to worry about finances. I've transferred my car into your name. I'll try to keep tabs on you from afar so that if you are ever in need, I can find a way to help.

I will love you forever,
Sara

The letter flutters to the ground as I sit in shock. I don't even know what to think or feel. I'm numb. I'm in denial.

I turn to Lisa. "I've got to find her. Lisa, you have to help me find her."

I grab the keys to Sara's car and start for the door.

"Wait. Where are you going?" Lisa asks.

"To the cabin. I can ask her friend, Mary. She'll know where to find her. Maybe there's a clue in the cabin. We need to call every Claire Duncan in Los Angeles. This is a mistake. It's a huge mistake. She loves me. I know she loves me. I can fix this. I know I can fix this—whatever *this* is."

Lisa grabs me and pulls me into a hug. Then the waterfall starts and I turn, sobbing into her shoulder.

"It's okay. We'll figure it out together."

I see Lisa glance at the table. She is still holding me as she speaks. "Nicky, I think this might be another clue to what's going on." She lets go of me as she reaches over and picks up an envelope with her name on it.

I'm leaning on her shoulder as she opens the envelope. I read the letter along with Lisa. It doesn't matter that Sara addressed the letter to Lisa.

Dear Lisa:

Please take care of Nicky for me. Help her understand what a wonderful woman she is. You have been such a good friend to me, please be a good friend to Nicky now. I'll never forget our friendship and I will be watching out for you, as well. Don't let her try to find me. Help her move on. Remind her that her heart will repair and she will be stronger for it.

Love,
Sara

I don't care what Lisa's letter says. I know I can fix everything. I just need to find Sara and talk to her. This is a horrible mistake.

"She must think I don't care, because I never push her for more in-depth information about herself. I don't care what her secrets are or why she feels the need to run. I will love her no matter what. I have to tell her that. It's all my fault. I know this now and I'm ready for action," I tell Lisa.

"Nicky, wait, I don't know what really happened, but I know that something happened when we were in California. You must have sensed this."

"Jesus, Lisa, her dad just died. She's just confused and blinded by her grief. Everything is going to be all right." I walk to the door. "Are you coming or not?"

I don't think Lisa's really convinced this is the right thing to do, but she comes along anyway.

She grabs the keys from me. "I'm driving."

I'll bet she's worried that I'm too keyed up to concentrate on driving us to the cabin and she's probably right.

✝

I manage to get us to Mary's restaurant without taking too many wrong turns.

Mary glances up from her notepad. She doesn't seem surprised to see me. She attempts a smile, but I notice that it doesn't reach her eyes. It seems sad.

"Hello, Nicky. I thought you might come here first."

"Have you seen her? Do you know where she's gone? Do you know what happened, because I sure the fuck don't?" I fire these questions at her hoping she has some answers for me.

Lisa hangs back.

I honestly believe Mary wants to be there for me, but I don't think she quite knows how she can help.

Mary motions me to a private room in the back. The room is comfortable with a well-worn leather couch, a soft ultra suede recliner, and a television. Mary sits on the couch and I sit on the recliner anxious for Mary to fill in the blanks for me.

"I know this is all confusing to you and you don't understand anything. I wish I could give you the answers you need to move on," Mary starts to explain.

I stand up and start pacing the room. I'm really agitated now.

She gets up from the couch, comes over, and hugs me. "Oh, honey, she has her reasons, but you mustn't ever forget that she loves you more than you will ever understand."

"Fuck that. If she loves me so much, why did she leave? You know and you just won't tell me. There is absolutely nothing she can tell me that will change anything for me, I don't care what's happening. It won't change how I feel about her. If you won't tell me where she is—can you at least tell her that? Tell her I'm sorry and she can tell me anything."

"I'll tell her if I see her. I promise. I don't think it will matter and I know you don't understand why, but she did what she thought was best for you."

I start to yell. "She doesn't get to make that decision on her own. Fuck. She already made that decision. You can fucking tell her I want a say in this. She never gave me a chance to explain anything. I deserve to be part of whatever fucked up reasoning she used to make this decision for us both."

"I don't think she believes she had a choice."

"We always have a choice. We just have to prepare for the consequences. She took the chicken shit way out. You can tell her that too. I never took her for a coward."

"Oh, honey, you don't have all the information to say that. Sara is not a coward."

"Oh, yeah? Why don't you enlighten me then and tell me what the fuck is going on."

"I can't."

"Fuck you." I stalk out of the room and grab Lisa. "Come on, time to do some research. I'm gonna track down her mom."

†

I'm typing furiously on the computer searching for any Claire Duncan in Los Angeles or any of the surrounding suburbs. I start dialing all the numbers and asking if this is the Claire Duncan with a daughter, Sara, living in Seattle. Lisa helps me, even though she is more reticent about this being the right thing to do. We spend hours trying to track down Sara's mom, but she ends up being just as elusive as her missing daughter.

In desperation, I track down the funeral parlor that took care of all the arrangements for Sara's dad. I try to wrangle any information I can about how to get in touch with Claire or Sara Duncan. They tell me they don't have any contact information. They thought it odd at the time, but because Mrs. Duncan insisted on paying cash and not providing any personal information, they honored her wishes.

I'm now at a dead end and have to face facts. Sara is gone and she's not coming back.

†

I cry myself to sleep every night for two months.

I call my parents and they come to the house to help console me. Nothing works. I'm seriously considering trying to get a prescription for happy pills, but my parents talk me out of it. I just want the pain to end.

Lisa holds me every night as I cry myself to sleep.

I don't know how I do it, but I manage to continue to go to my classes. My grades suffer, but I make it through the quarter. My professors know something is amiss and they cut me some slack.

Everyone tells me that it's only situational depression and I will survive this. I have my doubts, but I make it through those first two months and things start to get a little easier.

I see a counselor because my parents and Lisa tell me they are worried that I might harm myself. I have to admit the thought does filter through my brain, but I don't really give it serious consideration.

One morning I'm about to make some coffee and all of a sudden I start to think about never seeing Sara again. My heart starts to race. I begin to sweat and I start shaking. I'm having a full blown panic attack. I've heard people describe this to me, but I don't really understand how scary panic attacks are. I don't tell anyone about this, not even Lisa, who I've filleted my soul to. I'm afraid my therapist will send me to the funny farm, so I don't tell her either.

I don't date. I don't do anything socially my senior year in college. Lisa is the only person who manages to get me to go out on occasion.

Sometimes I go home. Sometimes I go to visit my younger sister at the University of Oregon. Most days I just study and take long bike rides.

79

When I'm on my bike, I can sometimes let the sunshine permeate my mind and give me some peace.

Lisa tries to get me to go to the gay bar with her and her best friend from home. It's on one of those weekends that we have a truly nasty argument. I think she's finally had enough of my brooding self.

"Come on, Nicky, come with us."

I shake my head no.

"Shit, it's been six months. It's time for you to move on."

"Shut the fuck up. You don't know anything. I don't fucking want to go out and be surrounded by a bunch of happy lesbians all paired up."

"Trust me, they are not all paired up and it will take you thirty seconds before someone starts chatting you up. You're the hottest lesbian they will ever see," Lisa's friend, Sandy, interjects.

"Been there, done that. Sara was the hottest lesbian they ever saw. Oh, but wait, Sara disappeared. Too bad for them that they don't get to try to cruise on her now. Maybe she took off with another hottie she met at the bar. Maybe you even know who it is that she's shacked up with now."

"Nicky, you know that's not true." Lisa's tone is calm and reasonable.

I'm not listening to reason. "I don't know anything, because she didn't fucking tell me anything."

"Nicky, you know it's not healthy to keep going back over this. I don't believe for one second that Sara intended to hurt you. The Sara I knew was a kind and compassionate human being. If it hadn't been for both you and Sara, I never would have made it through the grief and depression when my mom died. She must have had her reasons for leaving. I know she loved you with all her heart."

"Fuck you, Lisa. As usual, you're making excuses for Sara and taking her side. You don't know a fucking thing. If she loved me so much, she would never have left. Just leave me the fuck alone. I'm not in the mood to meet anyone new," I shout.

"Nicky, there are no sides here. You have so much to offer someone. Even when you're being a total ass—we love you."

"Yeah, well, I must have been too much of an ass for Sara, because she's gone. Why haven't you left too?"

"I'm not giving up. One of these days we're going to get you to come with us and you'll have a good time."

I never go out to the gay bar with Lisa in my senior year of college and my last year is mostly a blur. I barely remember making it through, but I somehow managed to graduate.

Lisa graduates with me and decides to continue her postgraduate work at the UW when the college accepts her into the MBA program.

I decide I want to help people and Lisa convinces me that I'll make a great grief counselor. I apply to graduate school and they accept me into the University of Washington counseling program.

Chapter Twelve

The good thing about the graduate counseling program is that it forces you to take an in-depth look at your life. My life sucks.

I hate my group counseling class. They have us form our own counseling group and everyone gets to take turns on the hot seat. The poor slob we ripped apart this past week had to bare his soul to our un-trained asses and he left the group in a puddle of insecurity.

I almost decide to drop the class, because I'm not about to tell a bunch of dickwads anything about my life. Yeah, sure, my life sucks and I haven't managed to move on, but that doesn't mean a group of neophytes will be able to help me. So I do what I always do, I lie through my teeth. There is no way this group is going to sink their grimy paws into my psyche.

It's ironic that this particular turning point in my life I owe to a girl in the group who runs at the first sign of commitment. I'm oddly attracted to her, probably because I want to figure out why she runs. Then maybe I'll have some insight into Sara.

I pick right up on the fact that she's a player and a lesbian. It doesn't hurt that she's very attractive and bears a small resemblance to Sara. Unfortunately, I also recognize that she's remarkably insightful and sees right through my bullshit. I know she doesn't buy anything I share with the group. I admire that about her.

After class, I'm walking out believing I've convinced everyone that my life doesn't suck.

Sandy follows me out. "Bullshit," she whispers.

"Excuse me?"

"What you just told the class is total bullshit. Your life is not all rainbows and butterflies."

"Rainbows and butterflies? What the fuck do you know about my life?"

"I know someone in relationship hell when I see it."

"Well, for your information, Ms. Smarty-pants, I'm no longer in a relationship and haven't been for a year," I blurt this out before I have a chance to censor myself.

"Yep, I figured that. When I say relationship hell, I mean you've convinced yourself that the only one for you is whomever you were fucking a year ago. Well, let me tell you, they sold you swamp land in Florida. You know, you don't have to love the person you're fucking and it's a whole lot easier to part ways when you don't. I'll bet you haven't been laid since she left."

"Fuck you, Sandy."

"Yep, thought so. Look, you're a beautiful young woman and I hate to see your youth wasted on a broken heart from your first love. You probably never even dated before her. You owe it to yourself to sow your wild oats and in the process you might learn a few things about yourself and what you want in a partner. Lesbians are so predictable sometimes. We date, fuck, get a U-Haul, and marry—all in less than a week. How can you possibly know a person is the one in less than a week? Don't buy into all that crap about love, forever, and soul mates. Live a little, love a lot, and find out a bit more about dating before you settle on one person."

Sandy starts to make sense to me. I've been alone and lonely now for a year. I even find myself attracted to someone for the first time in a year and I consider Sandy safe. I'm pretty sure she doesn't want a relationship and neither do I. Later on, she becomes my occasional fuck buddy but this happens after she reintroduces me to the local lesbian scene. She also becomes my teacher.

†

Sandy drags me to the women's bar in Seattle one night. I haven't been there for more than a year and that night is like an awakening for me. It's like the fog on my glasses suddenly evaporates. I see a lot of single, attractive women and they are looking in our direction. I smile at a pretty blonde and she smiles back and lifts her glass in the air.

A few minutes later, the bartender comes over and sets another beer in front of me.

"Looks like you have a fan," Sandy leans in and whispers.

I blush and look over at the blonde. She smiles again and raises her glass and mouths *cheers*.

I'm an ass sometimes, but my mom did teach me manners. I stroll over to her table to thank her so I can meet her and her friends.

Sandy comes with me and I see her checking out the other women at the table.

"Um, thanks for the beer. I'm Nicky and this is my friend, Sandy."

"Yeah, I know who you are."

"You do?"

"Yeah, you used to be with Sara, but we haven't seen you here in a while and we haven't seen Sara either." The blonde nods at Sandy. "Sandy, your reputation precedes you."

"Why, thank you." Sandy takes a bow.

I'm a little off kilter by her comment about Sara and I begin to stutter. "You...uh...you know Sara?"

"Not really. It's just you two were like a Hollywood couple. You were so beautiful together and always seemed so happy. Where is Sara?"

I almost lose it.

Sandy steps in and takes over the conversation. "Sara and Nicky aren't together anymore. Sara's moved away."

The attractive blonde has a sympathetic look on her face, but I think it's fake when she smiles at me.

"Oh, I'm so sorry, but her loss is my gain. Why don't you and Sandy join us? I'm Dana and this is Jodie and Holly." She points to her two friends.

Sandy starts chatting up Jodie.

I'm nervous, so I start drinking the beer quickly. When Dana puts a shot of tequila in front of me, I don't hesitate to drink it down, even though I don't like tequila. I've been a little tipsy before but never falling down drunk.

I get plastered this evening for the first, but not the last time in my life. I don't remember everything, but I do remember the bathroom.

✝

Dana grabs my hand and starts dragging me into the bathroom. We are both giggling like little schoolgirls. She dips her head to look under each stall. Finding each one empty, she pushes the handicap stall door open.

"More room." She pulls me into the stall and starts kissing me.

Before I even realize what's happening she has her hand down my pants. It's been so long that I can't help my response. I start moving with the same rhythm as her hand.

"That's it, Nicky, just let go—let me fuck you."

"Oh, God, yeah just like that. I'm coming."

It's not the best sex I've ever had. In fact, it's not even as good as any time Sara and I made love, but it's better than sex with myself. I haven't touched another woman in a year and she's right there in front of me ready and willing. I reach out to her and put my hand under her shirt. My touch is gentle and slow.

I find out this is not what she wants.

"Oh, Nicky, you are so sweet, but I don't need you to make love to me. I need you to fuck me. You don't need to be tentative."

I learn how to fuck someone that night. I'm a fast learner and I get really good at it. Before we leave the bathroom, she is screaming out my name.

Sandy winks at me as Dana and I leave the bathroom. Sandy soon becomes a recipient of my quick learning.

†

The next morning I stir as the light comes into the bedroom and it feels like my head is about to explode. I carefully open one of my eyes—big mistake. The light in the room causes my head to pound even more. I think I'm literally going to die from my exploding head. I'm sure I'm having an aneurism. I'm also sure some rodent crawled into my mouth and took up residence, because it feels like I have a mouth full of fur.

All of a sudden, I realize I'm not alone in my bed. I remember Dana's name, as her blonde head turns in my direction and her eyes open.

"Good morning, sexy," Dana purrs.

A scene from the prior evening floats through my alcohol soaked brain and I remember fucking Dana in the bathroom stall. For a split second, I think I have totally fucked up and I believe I just cheated on Sara. Then the fog clears from my brain and I remember Sara is gone and likely never coming back.

"Um, Dana?" I'm pretty sure that's her name but I'm not one hundred percent positive.

"Yeah. Good for you. You remembered my name."

"Um, don't take offense, but there's not a whole lot I remember about last night, except being with you in the bathroom."

"S'okay. We did have an awful lot to drink. I'm glad you at least remembered the bathroom. That was awesome but it's too bad you don't remember the rest. You must have had a lot of pent up sexual energy."

I lift my head and start to get up. I feel dizzy and a wave of nausea almost causes me to toss my cookies right on top of her bare breasts. I run to the bathroom and make it just in time. I'm praying to the porcelain god as Dana calls out that she's gonna make us some coffee. I'm too hung over to protest.

I think Lisa's going be pissed, but Lisa doesn't say a word. She comes into the bathroom, as my head is hanging over the toilet.

She brushes my hair back and gets me a wet washcloth. "Everything purged yet?"

I turn my head to look at her. She's not smirking. She has a concerned look on her face and I know at that moment what a good friend she is. I know she loves me and I appreciate the fact that she isn't giving me a lecture right now.

"Yeah, I think so."

"Do you need any help getting up from your prayer position?" she asks.

Okay, so maybe she can't help that one small jab.

"No. I need to brush my teeth, because I swear something evil crawled in my mouth."

She motions to the glass of water and aspirin on the counter. "Drink the whole glass, Nicky, and then come on down. Dana appears to be making some coffee. She's seems quite comfortable with the morning after routine and is tooling around in the kitchen like she belongs here."

I detect a small note of disgust in her voice.

"I'm sorry, Lisa. I'll be right down."

"Don't worry about it, Nicky. Just be careful. Okay? Let me make you some toast. I promise it will help."

"Thanks, Lisa. I really am sorry."

"It's okay, really. Just promise me you won't replace Sara with that dipshit downstairs making coffee."

"Don't worry, there is absolutely no chance of that. I promise Dana is not a replacement for Sara."

I keep my promise. In fact, I never bring anyone home that becomes a replacement for Sara because any woman I bring home is always a one-time thing. It becomes a ritual and Lisa's always there with water and aspirin.

I'm not sure if Lisa thinks this turn of events is good or not. I'm going out now, but my choice of women is not extraordinary.

I have no expectations of any of the women I see and they have no expectations of me. I have a string of one-night stands and sometimes I drink so much I can't remember the person's name the next morning.

Lisa sits down with me one evening.

I think she's trying to do some kind of intervention because I recognize what it is right away. I'm in the graduate counseling program after all.

"Nicky, can we talk for a few minutes? Maybe you can stay in tonight."

"I don't need a mother, Lisa. I have a perfectly wonderful mother. I also don't need a fucking intervention."

"I'm worried about you, Nicky. You're drinking a lot lately and some of the women you bring home...."

"What the hell happened to, *Nicky, come on, come out with us, it's time you moved on*. I've moved on. What the fuck do you want from me?"

"You know what I meant. I meant move on and start dating, not fucking every woman in Seattle. Please don't do this. Don't be like Sandy. You know she's not happy."

"No shit, Sherlock, but then happiness is overrated. At least I'm getting laid now. I do agree with one thing, it's a bitch waking up with a hangover every morning. I will stop drinking so much. Are you happy now?"

"Well, at least that's something. Just promise me that after you get through this phase, you will consider giving a real relationship a chance. Should I remind you of your wise advice when I was worried about my dad? *The heart is a muscle that can repair and be even stronger after it's been hurt.* You said that to me years ago—so you must believe that."

"Yeah, yeah, okay. Can you just let me sow my wild oats for a little longer?" I give her my best puppy dog eyes.

"Yes, as long as I get to dance at your wedding someday."

Chapter Thirteen

I've just completed graduate school and, although I'm still not interested in any long-term relationship, I've gotten my drinking under control. I promised Lisa that I'd cut down and I do. It's a good thing but instead of using alcohol to numb my pain, I find a new addiction—sex.

I begin cruising the gay bars. I go out just about every night and rarely end up alone. I have a rule that I don't go home with the same person every night—or any night for that matter. The only exception I make is with Sandy, because she knows the score and isn't looking for anything else but sex. I suppose I get a reputation as a player but I don't care really. I just know I'm not ready to be in another relationship. If I wasn't one hundred percent gay, I might have considered giving up women altogether, but I obviously don't choose that path.

Lisa is so worried about me—she starts to join me when I troll the bars. She doesn't come every night, but she's there enough that the patrons begin to think of her as a regular. At first, everyone keeps their distance because they know that Lisa is my straight roommate and I'm very protective of her. Lisa is a knockout and I don't want any of my *acquaintances* pawing all over her.

One night, a striking woman enters the bar. I've never seen her before, so I suspect she doesn't know the scoop when she makes a beeline for our table.

I imagine Lisa thinks she's heading to our table to make a play for me, but she only has eyes for Lisa. Lisa looks up and it kinda looks like she's checking this woman out. I'm a little surprised at the way she's looking at her.

The woman approaches our table.

She doesn't look at me, but instead smiles and motions to the seat next to Lisa. "Hello. Is there anyone sitting there? The bar is kinda crowded and I was hoping I could join you since there seems to be an empty seat."

Oh, brother, that's the lamest pick up line I think I've ever heard. I'm about to step in and tell her to get lost. Even though she's the type I would go after, I'm not about to let some smooth talker cruise on Lisa.

Lisa surprises me when she says, "We'd love for you to join us. I was saving the seat for you." Lisa winks.

What?

"Thanks." The woman sticks out her hand. "I'm Gabrielle, but everyone calls me Gabby."

Lisa takes her hand. "Lisa." Lisa points to me. "This is my roommate, Nicky."

I wonder if I'm imaging the extra long time Lisa hangs onto Gabby's hand.

Gabby and Lisa spend the whole night talking and dancing. I have to admit there is some kind of chemistry there, so I stop being my overprotective self and let nature take its course. I wander off that night and find a willing partner. I don't really think much about Lisa's reaction to Gabby.

When the bar is about to close, I see Gabby lean over to kiss Lisa. I'm not too worried at this point, because it doesn't look at all like Lisa is pulling back from the kiss. I remember thinking, *hmm, I guess Lisa's not so straight, after all.*

Lisa and Gabby become an item after that night and there are several women who will never forgive me for blocking their initial efforts with Lisa, but I don't care. If they really had a serious chance, I'm sure Lisa would have gone for it despite my interference.

Love Forever, Live Forever

✝

I continue my nightly pilgrimage to the bars and sometimes Gabby and Lisa join me, but mostly I go by myself or with Sandy.

One day I'm looking at myself in the mirror and I see bags under my eyes. My face looks bloated. My eyes are so bloodshot, I think I can't really see any other color but red. It's not such a pretty sight. Ha, amazing eyes—not so much anymore.

I've already stopped drinking to the point of praying over the porcelain god. I decide it's time to cut down even more on my drinking and to start running again. I don't like anything about myself anymore. I don't hate who I am, but I don't like what I've become either.

I get back into shape and the clarity in my eyes returns. I've turned a corner and although I still prowl the bars and have numerous one night adventures, I stop bringing them all back to the house. I know Lisa is not pleased that I continue to sleep around, but she is thankful that I'm not drinking to excess anymore.

✝

Lisa and I are crying on the couch, because the end of an era is near. Graduation is tomorrow and she has a job in California for which she's leaving in less than a month and I'm really going to miss her. She's been my rock for the past three years. I love her like a sister and her leaving is as painful as when Sara left.

"Oh, my God, Nicky, I can't believe we won't be living together anymore. Shit, you and I have been living together for a quarter of my entire life. You are my family and I'm gonna miss you so much. Why don't you try to get a counseling job in California?"

"I don't think I can, Lisa. It's just too expensive to live there and besides, I like the Pacific Northwest."

"I can't believe you are passing up an opportunity to see half naked women twelve months out of the year. You know, beaches, swimsuits. California is like a gay Mecca."

"Yeah, well, I kinda feel comfortable here now. Besides, I don't think I could really survive if by some odd circumstance I run into Sara or her mother. If she's anywhere, she's probably in Los Angeles. I know it's an awfully large city, but it would just be my luck to come across her at some gay bar down there. I'll visit you, that I promise. Then I can drink in my fill of California babes."

"Any prospects for a job yet?"

"Yeah, a few. I'm looking into hospice or Bailey-Boushay, the HIV/AIDS house. I've gotten to know a few of the residents and I think I would fit in well. They seem to respond to me."

"You would be perfect, Nicky. Sometimes I think you don't realize what a good heart you have. All that crustiness on the outside hides your big marshmallow inside."

"Shut the fuck up. I'm an asshole and always will be."

"No, you're not, Nicky, and someday someone will help you see that."

"God, I love you, Lisa, but you know not in that way." I wipe the tears from my eyes and give her a big hug.

"I know, ditto."

"I can't believe how far we've come and I can't believe you really had no clue about yourself. I think your exact words to me when we first met were, *I don't swing that way* and, *I like guys*. You were so full of shit. Funny thing is, I believed every word out of my mouth. I'm glad you met Gabby because she's perfect for you and I really wish you the best. You deserve it, roomie."

"You'll find her—you know, the one you're meant to be with. I know you will."

"I'm still young. I have plenty of time, and you know, I'm in a good place right now. I'm happy with my life the way it is—I really am—so stop worrying."

I am happy. I am in a better place. I've made peace with my life and at this point I really don't want a relationship. My last year of graduate school brings fun and joy in my life and Sandy has been a help. She is responsible for my turning point. I'm back to my old self and I have more confidence. Life is good now.

✝

Lisa and Gabby pack up the car and stack boxes neatly into the U-Haul trailer attached to the towing hitch. It's early summer and the sun is shining brightly in front of our house.

I can't help myself—I'm crying. It feels like the bottom is dropping out of my safe and secure world. I'm really happy for them and I know that despite them assuring me they will miss me like crazy, they are excited to start their new life in California.

"Oh, Nicky, don't cry, we'll visit soon. And you promised you would visit," Lisa tells me.

"I know and I expect to be invited to the wedding—or civil ceremony—or whatever the fuck they're calling it now. You know California isn't any more progressive than other states. Don't forget they passed Proposition 22 not that long ago."

"Don't be such a cynic."

"I'm not a cynic—I'm a realist. Fucking moral majority is neither moral nor a majority, but somehow they have an impact."

"We'll call when we get there. Nicky, please take care of yourself. Be good and stop running around and sleeping with every woman who takes a breath."

"Yeah, yeah, Mom."

Gabby, who I've gotten to know a little better, steps up to me.

"She just wants you to be happy," she whispers in my ear. "I think at one point she was either in love with you or Sara. I can't really figure out which one, but I know you mean the world to her. You two were all she talked about when we first met. I think if she sees you with someone special she can relax and we can really get on with our life."

I frown at Gabby and wonder where this is coming from, but I don't give it much thought at the time, even though it was a strange thing for her to say. I shrug and don't respond.

Lisa wipes a tear from her eyes and hugs me. Her hug is constricting and reminds me of the last time I embraced Sara. I consider the possibility that I might never see her again and wonder if she is thinking the same thing.

†

I go back into the house after they drive off. I'm alone with my thoughts and I look around the empty house as my memories with Sara haunt me. I'm all of a sudden completely alone and I feel the loneliness creep into my soul. The bleak sadness threatens to overwhelm me.

Since I don't really want to think about anything too deeply anymore, I call Sandy. She's always up for going out. Lately Sandy has been seeing a woman and I think that finally she's ready to settle down. I'm happy for her.

I think there is hope for me yet if Sandy can settle down and fall in love again. I'm ready to be around people in love and lately I'm feeling good about myself. I want to celebrate life. I'll miss Lisa like crazy, but I'm ready to just have a little fun before following up on my two job prospects.

I have second interviews with two different places and things are really starting to click. I'm ready for a new chapter in my life.

I tell Sandy I'll meet her and her girlfriend at the bar in an hour. I hurry up and take a shower, trying to transform my puffy eyes after my cry fest with Lisa and Gabby.

†

Sandy and her girlfriend are talking quietly in a corner of the bar. Sandy gently kisses her on the lips. It seems like such a sweet gesture and so unlike her, that I think it must be love.

I'm swaying to the music. Several people ask me to dance and I dance with some of them, but I'm more content to listen to the music.

It's getting crowded in the bar and I notice a beautiful woman watching me. She has an air of confidence about her that I find intriguing, but the dancing makes me too hot to pursue her just yet, so I step out onto the outdoor patio.

The breeze is glorious as it brushes across my face. I turn around to go back inside and notice this guy with a penetrating gaze. He has dark features that probably turn both male and female heads. I think maybe he doesn't realize it's ladies night. I can't really tell if he's gay or not, so I'm not even sure he realizes he's in a gay bar. He must have some idea though because the interaction in the bar is pretty obvious.

Something is amiss, but I ignore the hair that rises on my neck and I smile at him. "I haven't seen you here before. You do know the pickings are slim tonight because it's ladies night."

"I was hoping you might be flexible with your choice of company." His velvety voice washes across me.

"Nope, sorry to disappoint you. I only love the ladies. I do love them quite well though," I quip back.

I hope he will just leave without making a scene. I recognize his type. He thinks he can get any woman he wants into bed.

"Have you ever been with a real man? How can you know what you like if you haven't ever been with a man? I know you would not regret it with me. I can be very gentle," he purrs.

I've had enough. I almost tell him to fuck off, but instead I try to be polite in my response. "Thank you, but no thank you."

I don't even have time to react. In a flash, he slices open my shirt with a huge hunting knife. He's pulling roughly on my pants as he manages to undo them, pulling them down along with my panties. Now I'm panicked, I try to fight him off, but he's too strong. I don't get a chance to react before he has his pants undone and penetrates me. I scream out in pain.

Until this point in my life, I'm a gold star lesbian and have never had sex with a man. The viciousness of the act shocks me. I continue to fight and manage to bite down on his arm.

He is pushing my head down on the patio and screams at me. "You fucking bitch. You bit me."

95

I feel a sharp pain in my chest and don't realize what has happened. I glance down at the hunting knife sticking straight up in my chest.

I have a moment of consciousness as I realize I'm about to die. It's true what they say—your life does flash before your eyes. My life with Sara plays like a movie reel. I see my family. I see Lisa and Gabby leaving for California and I even picture Sandy with her new love.

The beautiful woman I saw watching me earlier appears. I think maybe I'm already dead, but I can't imagine the violent scene before my eyes happening in the afterlife. My brief thought that she is the angel of death passes when I see her fangs.

Every vampire movie I've ever seen flashes through my brain and somehow I know this is my only chance for life so I nod at the beautiful woman. I don't really know how she understands what I'm asking, but she does.

It's a strange feeling dancing on the edge of death. The beautiful woman is holding me in her warm embrace and I feel a trickle of something in my throat as she holds her wrist over my mouth. I don't even know how to really describe the sensation of the transition.

It's like a tickle in my whole body. My senses become hyper alert. I can hear several conversations happening in the bar. I don't feel the pain in my chest or the pain in my vagina anymore.

I look down at my chest and the knife is gone but there is a large red stain completely covering my ripped shirt. I look up into the beautiful eyes of my savior not realizing the consequences of that nod yet.

I smile at her. "My God, you are so beautiful."

"Come, little one, we must hurry. I must clean this up before someone finds us, then I will take you to a safe location and will teach you our ways. I am sorry we do not have more time for me to explain."

She is so fast that I don't see everything. Before I know it, the body is gone and she has a new shirt for me to wear. I'm in a daze as I change my shirt and horrified when I see the enormous puddle of blood on the patio. I wonder how she will possibly take care of that.

"I will need the help of the others to thrall so many because the evidence from your wound is too obvious," the beautiful angel explains as she points to the pool of blood.

She leads me back into the bar and I catch Sandy's eye. Sandy arches her eyebrow and gives me a thumbs up as we leave the bar.

"Are you really a vampire?" I ask after we leave the bar.

"Yes, and against all the odds, so are you. Come, we will go to Athena House."

Everything crashes down on me as the stark reality hits and I black out. I don't know how I get to Athena House but I can imagine that the beautiful vampire probably carries me. Maybe we both fog there but I don't learn all about fogging, the preferred means of transportation for a vampire, until later. I don't really remember all the details of that time.

✝

I wake up in a strange bedroom where a healthy fire is roaring in the fireplace.

I feel violated and unclean. I don't feel pain anymore, but I remember him on top of me and recall his stale breath along with the odor of his body as he penetrates me. That moment leaves an indelible memory.

I throw off the covers of the bed and panic. I feel very different. My movements are so fast that I have to concentrate to control my speed of motion. I tilt my head to listen for any sound but don't hear anything. I'm freaking out and think the only safe thought that comes to mind.

This is a nightmare. I wish I was in my own home.

I feel a funny sensation in my stomach—like an elevator dropping too quickly. Suddenly, I'm no longer in the strange bedroom.

✝

I'm standing in the living room of my house. *Thank God, Gabby and Lisa left for California this morning,* I think. I surmise that I can go from one place to the next by concentrating and thinking of where I want to be.

I try an experiment and think about wanting to be in my bedroom. I feel the sensation again and open my eyes to see I'm standing in front of the dresser mirror in my bedroom. I look into the mirror and see my reflection. I think that's odd, because I remember seeing or reading that vampires don't see their own reflection. I begin to wonder what else I need to learn.

I decide I should not tempt the fates and I make a point of not going out into the sunshine the next day. I don't know what will happen, but I'm not about to take the chance of burning up like some crispy marshmallow over a fire.

I look around my bedroom and notice that the colors seem more vibrant. Sound is more vivid and I hear the wind whistling in the trees even though the breeze is light tonight.

I have second thoughts about leaving the beautiful vampire. It's irresponsible of me not to find out more about my new life but I don't know how I will correct this. I make a decision to go out into the night and try to find others like me so they can teach me.

I'm embarrassed about running away, but it's too late now because I don't quite know how to get back to where she took me—it's not a place I'm familiar with. I hope I run across the beautiful vampire later. She seemed kind.

I close all the blinds in the house, because I'm afraid the sun will shine in the next day and do damage to my body.

I think it's a good idea that I didn't turn into a vampire during my drunken days, because I don't want to immortalize that look. Fortunately, I have been working out and running lately and I'm in the best shape of my life the night I become a newling.

It's strange because when I look at myself in the mirror, I look the same, but different. There is a kind of glow about me that I can't really put my finger on.

I test out a number of theories that night and the next day. I pull a beer out of the refrigerator and drink it down. It doesn't repulse me and it tastes a little better than I remember. I guess taste is another sensation enhanced by the vampire blood running in my veins. I wonder if touch, and particularly sex, will be better as a vampire.

I remember seeing the beautiful vampire sucking the blood from my attacker and I wonder if I will have to do that to keep alive. I don't feel any craving for blood, but maybe the cravings come later.

I open the refrigerator and reheat some pizza. I want to know if I can still enjoy food and find that the pizza tastes especially good and I think, so far, this isn't too bad. I can eat and drink, I still look the same—a little better— and I don't see any fangs yet. I can imagine going to a place and *bam,* there I am, transported at super human speeds. Yep, things might be totally cool.

I decide I like being a vampire. I haven't considered any downside yet.

✝

The next day, I don't feel any different. I'm careful to stay inside, and besides being completely bored, I don't feel any ill effects.

As soon as the sun sets, I head out. I don't know what I'm looking for, but for some reason I believe I will find someone who can shed some more light on my changed situation. I decide to visit Sandy to see if she can tell whether there is a difference in me. I knock on her apartment door.

Her girlfriend answers the door and greets me. "Hey, Nicky. The woman you left with last night was smokin' hot," her girlfriend says.

"Hey, I heard that." Sandy comes out of the kitchen. She has two glasses of wine in her hands.

"Oh, hey, I'm sorry to barge in. I didn't realize you guys were having a quiet night in. I thought I might be able to talk you into going out."

"Um, not tonight, Nicky. We're, uh, well, we're celebrating our two month anniversary."

I get a big smile on my face. Sandy looks so cute to me. It seems like she's confessing their relationship to me. "Oh, Sandy, that is so great and I'm so happy for you," I gush.

Sandy's girlfriend takes the wine back into the kitchen and leaves us alone in the living room.

"Hey, you look different—like really good. Something happened to you last night, didn't it?" Sandy is looking me over.

"What? No, nothing happened—same old, same old."

"Nuh, uh, something is definitely different. Did the hottie you left with finally break down your barriers? I'm really glad for you, so don't fuck it up. Okay?"

"Shit, you really are domesticated now if you're telling me not to fuck something up. Two months of playing house and you're already singing a completely different tune."

"It's time, and I really like her, Nicky. I don't want to fuck up a good thing."

"You are older than me. It's time for you to settle down but I don't think I'm quite ready for that yet. That woman I met was really something and I hope to run into her again."

"You don't know her name, do you?"

"No, but for some reason I think we will run into one another again. Hey, I'm gonna take off and leave you two lovebirds alone."

"Are you sure that's okay? I mean, we could go out with you if you want."

"No way. I'm fine. I'll catch you guys later."

†

I arrive at the gay bar and it is beyond crowded. People are dancing and laughing and I find myself getting into the groove of the place. A few acquaintances come up, say hello, and invite me to join their tables. Other women look my way and smile. I feel good tonight.

I turn my head toward the bar and then I sense her presence. A woman glides up to me with long chestnut hair. She is stunning.

Her dark blue eyes penetrate mine as she introduces herself. "Hello, Nicky. I am Faustina. The High Council sent me to answer your questions and help your transition. Sabrina is worried about you. She thinks it might be easier if someone else indoctrinates you since you seem to have fled from her."

I glance in her direction. As I look into her eyes, I feel a sense of calm. I feel bad about leaving so abruptly the night before. *Sabrina must be the beautiful vampire who saved me.*

I want her to know how sorry I am that I ran from her, so I try to apologize. "I'm so sorry I left Sabrina. Will you please tell her I'm sorry? I just kind of freaked and thought of my home then bam, all of a sudden I was in my living room. I didn't know how to get back. Somehow, I knew someone would find me."

"You are smart. I see you did not seek the sun today."

"No, I tested some things out, but I didn't want to take the chance with the sun. For some reason I thought that part of the legend must be true. So, I can't ever be in the sun anymore?"

"Come, let us sit and talk. What can I get you to drink?"

"I think I'll just have a coke tonight. I want to have my full faculties."

"Good choice."

Faustina leaves to get our drinks and I look around the bar. I sense there are others, but I don't know where they are and I sense that maybe Sabrina, my savior, is near.

Faustina sets the drink in front of me and takes a seat across from me. "You will be able to go into the sun, Nicky, but there is something you must do if you are to enjoy the rays of the sunshine. The gift that Sabrina has given to you comes with a set of responsibilities."

I'm now feeling particularly good, because I don't have to give up the sunshine. That would suck if I never got to see the sunrise again or ride my bike on a nice sunny day.

"Okay tell me what I have to do to be out in the sunshine."

Faustina does not sugar coat or hesitate with her next words. She states it in a matter of fact manner. "You must completely drain a human being."

"What? I can't do that. It's murder."

"Was it murder when Sabrina drained your attacker?"

"Well, no. That could be considered self-defense, I guess."

"We are not monsters, Nicky. We only drain those that deserve to be drained. We have a strict code and we will teach you the code if you desire to see the sun."

"What if I don't want to drain someone? Do I still have to kill a human to survive?"

"No, Nicky, you do not need to kill anyone to survive." Faustina chuckles. Her expression looks oddly incongruent with her refined features.

"In fact, you can choose to age naturally. If that is your choice, you never need to take the blood of anyone. You can choose to remain immortal by taking small amounts of blood from human hosts without killing them. The only time you need to drain a host is if you wish to be out in the sunshine the next day."

"Okay, I can live with that. Suppose I want to take a little blood without killing someone. How would I go about doing that?"

"Vampires possess powers of persuasion we refer to as thralling. Humans are drawn to us. Humans are already drawn to you, so it will not be difficult to find very willing hosts, Nicky."

"How do I know how much to take without going too far?"

"It is instinctual to us. We can feel the heartbeat and we know when we are getting too close. Most often, it only takes a very small amount of blood, so it never comes close. We do not feel a need to feed, so it is very easy to stop after taking the required amount."

"Okay, but how do I break the skin? I mean I don't have fangs like Sabrina."

"Oh, but you do. Our fangs emerge when we call upon them to come out. It is a little like thinking about home and transporting there. Once you thrall a host, you simply tell yourself it is time to feed and your fangs appear."

"So, how exactly do you thrall someone?"

"Please pick out a host and I will show you."

I look around the room and I figure as long as I'm not hurting someone I might as well pick out someone attractive. I catch eyes with a stunning blonde who appears to be scrutinizing me. I nod in her direction. "All right, how about the blonde at two o'clock?"

Faustina glances at the blonde and starts laughing. The blonde raises her glass to Faustina and smiles.

"No, I'm sorry but I don't think you will get what you need from Juno."

"She's another vampire, isn't she?"

"Yes, she is. She would like to get to know you, Nicky, but blood exchange is not possible between vampires. However, other bodily exchanges are very possible."

"Hmm, good to know. I'd love to meet her, but I'd better pick someone else and learn this lesson first. How about you pick someone for me?"

Faustina selects a sporty brunette. Before she saunters over to the cute brunette, she gives me instructions. "A thrall comes quite easily to us. First, get the host to look into your eyes. Once you have direct eye contact, all you have to do is concentrate on thinking that whatever orders you give to them they will obey. It is sometimes more difficult to avoid thralling humans but you will find this out soon."

As I am watching Faustina approach the brunette, Juno, the stunning blonde, winks at me and casually strolls over to our table.

"Hi, I'm Juno. Mind if I join you?"

"No. Take a seat."

It doesn't take long for Faustina to bring the brunette over. I'm thinking hard that I want the brunette to make eye contact with me when I shake her hand.

Faustina chuckles to herself as she introduces the brunette. "Nicky, this is Sam. Sam, this is Nicky."

Sam looks into my eyes and I concentrate on having her listen to whatever instructions I give her.

"Hello, Sam, nice to meet you. You are so happy to meet me that you shake your ass like a puppy wagging their tail." I direct her, as I thrall a human for the first time.

Sure enough, Sam is shaking her ass and Faustina and Juno are laughing.

"Sam, I want you to come into the bathroom with me."

Sam shakes her head up and down and follows me into the bathroom. Faustina and Juno join us in the bathroom. Juno is grinning.

Fortunately, for us, the bathroom is clear.

"Sam, I want you to lift up one foot and flap your arms like a chicken."

Sam raises her left foot and starts flapping her arms.

I start laughing. "God, this is so much fun—what a great parlor trick." I'm reacting as if this is a big game.

"As humorous as this little demonstration is, I think you should try to take a small amount of blood. Juno and I will be right here with you to make sure the bathroom remains clear and that you do not harm Sam."

I concentrate on thinking about taking a little blood and I'm a little startled as I feel and see, in the mirror, the fangs that appear in my mouth. "Sam, I need to make a small prick in your neck and take a little blood from you. I promise I won't hurt you."

Sam presents her neck to me.

When I gently pierce her skin, Sam moans. I think I might be hurting her so I pull back.

She pulls me into an embrace. "That feels good, don't stop," she whispers.

I tentatively suck just a little bit and taste her warm and salty blood. It isn't tasty, but it's not disgusting either. I don't feel compelled to continue sucking and I pull my fangs out of her neck. My fangs immediately retract.

Sam sighs in contentment.

Juno brushes her finger over Sam's neck and the two small holes disappear. I turn to Juno with the question in my eyes.

"Yes, Nicky, you can do that too. Just brush your fingers over the puncture and the holes will close leaving no evidence of your feed," Juno answers

"Can I practice that thrall thingy some more?"

Faustina nods her head and Juno just smiles. I can tell Juno and I will definitely get to know one another better.

"Sam, you really have to fart, but you're around a bunch of people, so when you let it rip you crinkle your nose and dramatically look around as if to say, *who's the culprit*. You're trying to throw everyone off the scent. Ha, ha, pun intended."

I'm amazed as a foul smell fills the bathroom and Sam crinkles her nose and wildly looks around the room. Juno is laughing so hard I think she's going to pee her pants. Do vampires ever pee their pants? I wonder.

"Wow, I can thrall someone into a physical response. Hey, does that mean I can thrall someone into an orgasm?"

Juno gets an odd look on her face. It looks to me like she is trying not to smile and I'm pretty sure she must be thinking, *I can't believe she just said that*. Yet, I also get the feeling she's amused—even though she shouldn't be. She nods her head to confirm my question.

"Good to know. Not that I ever need to thrall anyone to get them to come," I boast.

I don't think I amuse Faustina with my antics.

"All right, enough fun and games. You need to tell Sam that she will not remember anything, including meeting you tonight," Faustina directs me.

I look into Sam's eyes again and give her the final command. "Sam, you will not remember meeting me. You will not remember coming into the bathroom, farting, or waving your arms like a chicken. You definitely will not remember my fangs and the small amount of blood I took from you. You will remember having a really nice evening with friends." I look at Faustina for confirmation. "Good enough?"

"Yes, that will suffice. In the future it is not necessary to be so specific in what they will not remember."

"Awesome. I like it. Brevity is good. Except I'm not usually so good with brevity. In fact, sometimes when I get nervous, I kinda ramble. I say whatever stupid shit pops into my brain. Kinda like now, because you probably don't really need to know all this, right?"

Juno smiles again. I think I even see the corners of Faustina's mouth turn up in amusement, but she just nods again.

I can do this. I'm really going to like being a vampire.

†

Juno intrigues me. I definitely want to get to know her a little more intimately. It isn't until two nights later when I'm hanging out with Juno at the gay bar again that I begin to seriously consider draining my first human.

Juno is telling me a little bit about vampire history. She tells me about this vampire, Cassandara, who is like their best crusader. She gets to hang out in the sun all the time because she manages to find and drain a bunch of super bad dudes. Juno tells me it's kind of sad because she never lets anyone get too close to her after losing her lover five hundred years ago.

I think about Sara for a second and wonder if I'm doing the same thing with my brief affairs, but I toss that off as bullshit. No way will I wait five hundred years.

She tells me she likes being a vampire and especially likes tracking down child molesters. She's three hundred years old and her history is rather sad. Her father was a real bastard.

I suspect that's the reason she targets child molesters.

106

I learn that it's really hard to kill a vampire, especially when they are getting a steady supply of blood.

Juno and I practically close the bar and walk confidently into the pitch black night. I'm feeling safe walking the streets of Seattle, because I know it will be hard for anyone to harm me now. I suppose it appears really strange to see two women walking the streets late at night in some questionable parts of town.

I'm not paying attention as we're patrolling the side streets, so I'm not really sure why I hear her whimper before Juno does. I turn to look in the direction of the dark alley where I hear the sound. I also have enhanced eyesight and I see a guy leaning over some woman lying on the ground and it sure doesn't look like he's trying to help her.

Juno notices where I'm looking. "Rapist," she whispers.

"How do you know?"

"I can read his disgusting thoughts."

"Come on. We have to help her." I can ask about the thought reading thingy later.

We appear in front of him and he sneers at us. The woman's clothes are ripped and she looks like she's been beaten.

"You two better get the fuck outta here, unless you want to join the fun," the man growls.

The woman whimpers again. "Help me," she pleads.

What I see enrages me and I yank the guy from the woman. I learn at that moment how strong I am now.

His arm is hanging loosely in a particularly grotesque manner. He screams out in pain as he lunges for Juno.

Juno turns to face him and even I'm a little frightened as her fangs gleam in the moonlight. She looks as scary as the vampires do in those cheesy vampire horror movies. Her beautiful face transforms into something oddly compelling—but clearly deadly.

She pierces his neck and begins to drain him, when she abruptly stops. "Nicky, would you like to see the sun tomorrow?"

I think I know what she's asking me. She's offering to let me drain this piece of shit. The thought of taking another's life in these circumstances doesn't seem so wrong anymore.

I'm not quite ready yet, so I shake my head no in embarrassment.

Her response is gracious. "It's okay, Nicky. I understand. My first kill was difficult, and believe me, he was the definition of a bastard. I saved more lives by taking his life. I know this will be a process for you. The decision to take another life should never be made lightly."

It's still too new to me. I turn away. I cannot look and I walk away as Juno thralls the woman and somehow takes care of the man.

It will be another month before I drain my first human. Through the years, I find there are a surprising number of deserving hosts and I become quite ruthless in my approach.

Chapter Fourteen

I'm not able to count on finding a deserving host to drain every night, so normal counseling jobs are out of the question. As a result, I never make it to the second interview with Seattle Hospice or the Bailey Boushay house.

I'm careful what I tell my family about my life in Seattle and my vagueness seems to concern them. It's even worse with Lisa because she knows me so well. It's a blessing that she and Gabby moved to California. I don't think I'd be able to hide things from her without thralling her. I'm tempted to thrall her and my family to make it easier, but it seems like a violation and I'm not comfortable doing that to the people I love. I know I wouldn't want someone fucking around in my mind—brainwashing me and taking all my control away.

I find other vampires and learn that they are all women—no men. I like that little fact. Apparently, the same universal truths apply in the vampire world, in that only women can give life and, as an added bonus, that life does not require sperm. Creating a newling—a new vampire—is like giving birth and I learn just how precious this gift really is in the vampire world.

I don't meet the two oldest vampires, Cassandara or Helena right away. I only hear stories about them. I meet Helena and the High Council when I get into a little bit of trouble after revealing myself to Annie but I float around for many years before I meet Cass. She becomes my best friend.

The other vampires I meet tell me about the safe houses and I find my way back to Athena House. It becomes one of my favorite hangouts. The vampires give me money and help me out whenever I seem to flounder a little. It's as if they are there, waiting in the wings, watching over me and, whenever I have a need, they materialize.

I learn later that Sabrina is always watching to make sure I'm okay. She feels responsible for me but never quite knows how to tame me. I get the nickname Little Wild One and I become as infamous as Cass and Helena, but for very different reasons.

I uncover the mystery of how Sabrina knew about my desire to become a vampire the night of my assault, when Juno explains how vampires have the ability to read minds. It doesn't take long for me to learn that I'm particularly competent with this special power.

My family keeps pressuring me to come for a visit, but I don't quite know how to manage that. The first few years I'm not as good at finding hosts to drain, so I don't think I can count on being able to spend time in the sun with them. Lisa and Gabby call all the time and beg me to visit. I get the impression that Lisa's convinced something is wrong.

One day she calls me and wakes me from a deep sleep. "Hey, girl. When are you coming to visit? If you don't get your cute ass down here soon, we're coming up to Seattle."

"Um, sorry, Lisa, I know I promised." I'm half-awake, so I mumble my response.

"Oh, hey, sorry, it sounds like I woke you up. It's the middle of the day. Late night?"

"Um, I'm working nights now."

"Really? What kind of counseling job did you get at night?"

"Oh, you know, crisis and grief counseling doesn't just happen during the day."

I feel horrible lying to my best friend, but the alternative is worse.

"Bailey Boushay?"

"Yeah, sometimes the guys wake up at night and need someone to talk to."

"Nicky, you are a saint. Only you would take a night gig that probably no one else wants to work."

"Yeah, that's me, a regular fucking saint," I respond dripping with sarcasm.

"One day, Nicky, you will believe that you are a good person. So any chance you can get away and come visit us? We have some news."

I'm following the news in California and the passage of Assembly Bill 849 is encouraging for gay marriage. However, I think it is very unlikely that Schwarzenegger will sign it into law. I think I know what their news will be. I remember how Lisa is an eternal optimist and I assume that she thinks with the latest news on the Assembly Bill, she and Gabby should get married. I have to figure a way to be there for them without thralling them.

"I know you're excited, but honestly you shouldn't hold your breath, because the governor isn't going to sign it."

"We don't care what our asshole governor decides. It's only a matter of time."

"Okay, you tell me when and where and I'll be there. I would never miss your wedding."

I make this promise to Lisa and I intend to keep it. I will call upon my vampire buddies to see if they can get me some leads on deserving drainees, because I intend to dance at Lisa's wedding.

"I know you won't miss it. We can't wait to see you. It's been more than a year and I already feel like you're slipping away from us."

I hear the tremor in her voice on the other end of the phone and I feel like a total ass for not keeping in touch. Lisa is the one who always calls and makes an effort to stay connected.

I haven't officially told her I no longer live in our house. I called her up one day and told her that she won't be able to reach me on the house phone any longer, but I have a cell phone number for her. Lisa doesn't ask any questions and I believe that she feels that it's too difficult for me to live in the house without her and

Sara. She's partially correct, but the bigger reason is that I've become a nomad and don't really need a place to stay anymore.

"We're shooting for next month. Do you think that will be a problem for you? I mean can you get off in early October. I know it's kind of short notice," Lisa says.

"I'll make it work."

"You can stay with Gabby and me. We don't have a mansion or anything, but our place is big enough to have you stay with us. All you need to do is get the plane ticket. We'll take care of the rest."

Lisa is so sweet. I guess she assumes that I don't have much money. She is partially correct, but whenever I need anything, I don't have any problem getting the money for it, so I tell her not to worry.

✝

I make it to Lisa and Gabby's wedding. I take Juno as my guest and she helps me find drainees.

It's like old times with Lisa and I begin to really think about the consequences of being a vampire. I come to the sudden realization that I won't be able to stay in touch with them forever. At some point, they will figure out I'm not aging.

Some of the vampires tell me of the agony of distancing from their families. Some never had to experience this, because the shorter life expectancy made it unnecessary in ancient times.

I begin to think about how I'm going to handle this. I learn the best way is to fake my death. I'm not ready to do that yet, but I know the time is coming and, all of a sudden, I realize the downside of being a vampire.

✝

Four more years fly by and I force myself to consider the drastic option of faking my own death. I'm visiting my family and my sister, who I've always viewed as particularly observant, notices my appearance.

"God, Nicky, what is your secret? You look the same as when you graduated college. I'll bet everyone thinks I'm the older sister. I want whatever cream you're using."

That comment cements things for me. I know what I have to do, but it breaks my heart to do this to the people I love.

I run into Juno the next week. I wonder about her timing, because she always seems to appear just when I need her. On occasion, Sabrina or Faustina come to my aid, but Juno and I seem to be more compatible. Although I sense Sabrina's care and concern for my welfare, she usually lets Juno answer my call.

"Juno, I need your help. I think it's time."

Juno nods.

Her smile looks rather sad to me and I view this as a telling sign to how hard this is going to be.

"I don't want them to think I killed myself so it needs to look like an accident."

I still have Sara's car even though it's a constant reminder of our life together. It seems appropriate for me to use her car in my staged accident. It's one more thing for me to let go of—one more reminder of my old life.

†

Juno and I stage an accident on a curve in one of the state routes to the mountains. Juno helps me create skid marks and we make it look like I was trying to avoid a deer or some other wildlife.

It's the middle of the night and the overcast sky keeps the moon from shining brightly on the curving blacktop that seemed to slither between the giant majestic pine trees. The highway reminds me of a big black snake—ominous and deadly. It's the perfect night for subterfuge and a snake is a fitting symbol for what we are about to do.

I don't know where she gets the body of a young woman around my age to place in the car. I don't ask. I assume she thralls some medical school lackey or something like that, because I know she doesn't drain women.

We push the car off the cliff with the body inside and Juno manages to ignite the gas tank so the body becomes a crispy critter. Once again, I don't ask how she does it, I just accept that it will work.

Later, I figure out that the vampires have to thrall a whole lot of people, including the highway patrol and a Seattle detective that my family contacts to make sure it's really me in the burned out car. I hear all about how my family has a hard time believing I'm dead.

†

It's surreal going to your own funeral. It's like watching a movie about your life or something.

I think my family is going to cremate my body because, after all, I've given them a huge head start, but they want a gravesite marker to visit. They ship my body, or rather Jane Doe's body, back to Oregon.

I can't help myself and show up at my own funeral. I don a black hoodie and dark sunglasses. I tuck my blonde hair into a baseball cap and, unless you look close, you can't even decipher my gender as I hang back and watch the mourners.

My mom is sobbing. I see how my dad is trying to be strong for her, but he's crying too. My sister, Tess, looks in shock.

I feel horrible.

Then I see them. Lisa and Gabby are there and they are sobbing just as hard as my parents. As I glance farther, I see Sara standing next to Lisa. She is like a ghost to me. I can tell she is crying and she appears to be genuinely heartbroken.

I'm compelled to listen in. I take a few steps closer and hope I don't get close enough for anyone to recognize me.

Lisa turns to Sara. "It's been a long time, Red," she whispers. "It's good to see you again. I hate that I never got to say goodbye. This is my wife, Gabby. I don't think you ever met her because you left before...well, you know, you just left."

Sara is sobbing as she responds. "I'm so sorry. If I knew this would happen to her, I would never have left."

Uh, oh. I've seen that look on Lisa's face before—she's pissed. God, I love that woman.

"Yeah, well, you're too late now. You broke her heart. She was never the same after you disappeared. You did that to her. You might have even done this to her and I can't help holding you responsible."

This comment appears to destroy Sara and I don't think she knows what to say.

Lisa continues to rant. "How did you even know what happened. No one hears a word from you for eight years and here you are now after she's gone. Well, bully for you."

Gabby touches Lisa on the shoulder. "Hon, stop. Can't you see how destroyed she is. I don't know her, but I do know genuine grief."

"God, Red, I'm sorry. I'm just so sorry." Lisa starts crying again. "I'm just really pissed and you're the convenient whipping post for my anger. It's just so unfair. Last time I talked to Nicky she sounded good—like her old self again. You were a good friend to me—every bit as good as Nicky. I missed you too and I was angry, but I got over my anger. Now I'm just so angry that Nicky's gone and I never got to say goodbye to her. It's oddly reminiscent of when you left. I don't like when I don't get closure."

"It's okay, Lisa, I understand. I really did have my reasons for leaving and I'm sorry I can't tell you why. It doesn't matter now. I made the choice I thought best at the time. You are absolutely correct—life really is not fair and if I knew then what I know now, things might have been different. Hindsight is always better than foresight. You must know, I didn't leave because I stopped loving her. I will love her forever and I will never forget her. I didn't get my closure either. I deserve this. It's karma that I didn't get a chance to say goodbye, but it's not your kismet."

When I hear Sara say this to Lisa, I remember feeling especially guilty. Before the accident, I meant to call Lisa, but I didn't know what to say to her. So I didn't call and tell her how much I love her and appreciate all the support she'd given me throughout the years. Yep, I'm a total ass for not calling one last time.

I listen in for a few more minutes and then leave.

"You're not going to disappear again on me, are you? I don't think I can handle that right now," Lisa seems to be pleading with Sara.

Sara pulls Lisa into a hug and shakes her head. "No. I promise to keep in touch—even if it's only by phone."

I guess my absurd thought that maybe Sara and Lisa have been keeping in touch all along is wrong. I leave my first love and my best friend with the memory of them hugging at my funeral branded into my brain. I've had enough.

Before I leave, Sara raises her head as if she's heard something and she glances in my direction. She narrows her gaze at me and a strange expression appears on her face. I get the impression she is trying to figure out a puzzle. Then she shakes her head.

I wonder if she thinks the thought she's having is impossible. I get worried that she recognizes me and I need to do something quick. I've learned how to thrall someone from afar. I concentrate on entering her mind and removing any possibility that she recognizes me. I feel bad about thralling her, but I don't think I have much choice in the matter—she can't know that I'm still alive.

When she turns her attention back to Lisa, I take that as my cue to leave. I slip quickly and quietly away.

I put my pen down and swipe angrily at my tears. I'm done for the night because I can't bear to think about the day of my funeral anymore. I sigh and close my journal—I've completed writing about the first part of my journey.

Chapter Fifteen

It's been five and a half years since my fake death and I don't see Sara again until today. I can't help myself because all those feelings from long ago come rushing back. I still love Sara and wonder, is it possible to love two people at the same time, in the same way? I'm more confused than I've ever been in my whole life. I also wonder if Annie can understand how I'm feeling, yet still believe me when I tell her she is the only one for me.

For the past six months, I've been spending the majority of my time with Cass, Vic, and my sweet Annie. Cass is so much better and not so lonely now that she and Vic have reconnected. Cass hasn't had a lover for more than six hundred years and she's convinced that Vic is her reincarnated fifteenth-century lover—the one she never got over.

Cass has been in so much angst since meeting Vic and she's struggled over what to do about a five hundred year old promise that she made to her fifteenth-century lover. She promised that if she returned, you know, reincarnated, she would offer her the gift of immortality. Unfortunately, it's not so easy to get the gift to stick. Through the centuries, loads of vampires have tried with their lovers, but failed. Ultimately, the result is the death of their lover. It's a good thing that a shape-shifter bit Vic and ended the moral dilemma for Cass

So, at first I thought how cool—Vic is a shape-shifter. I even made some dumb ass joke about her being my pet wolf. Yep, you guessed it, the comment really pissed off Cass—the tight ass. I mean it was just a joke. God, she has no sense of humor.

I was so excited to meet Vic's pack. Yep, she belongs to a pack. How cool is that? I thought we'd get to meet these elusive shape-shifters now and they were especially eager to meet us vamps.

We get there and I'm so excited that I'm practically bouncing off the walls. I scramble out of the car like I'm about ready to meet the President of the United States or something. Just as we're ready to enter this huge lodge, Sara comes strolling around the corner. Out of the corner of my eye, I see a stunning red head and then I realize who it is. I about shit my pants when I see her. I guess she is equally shocked to see me.

Sara gasps as she gets a good look at Vic's entourage and sees me. "Nicky? Oh, my God, Nicky, is it really you? It can't be. You, uh, you're dead. I was at your funeral. You look the same as I remember. Wait...."

I can see the wheels turning in her head as everything clicks into place for her.

"Are you a vampire?"

She's approaching our group really fast. She reaches out to me and is just about to embrace me. Annie is just watching the interaction and I'm terrified about what she must be thinking.

I gotta stop the train wreck. "You keep your big hairy paws to yourself."

I know I'm being a total bitch, but now that you know most of the story, maybe you understand my reaction. I can see the hurt look in her eyes and I admit it softens me just a little. I notice that she can't even speak as a tear escapes before she has a chance to compose herself.

"I'm sorry. I know I'm being a bitch. It's been a long time, Sara. You look good." My voice softens and then I remember Annie is standing right next to me. "Sara, this is my girlfriend, Annie."

Annie steps forward in her adorably shy way. She doesn't usually do very well meeting new people, but her impeccable manners always override her reticence.

"Hello, Sara, it's nice to meet you."

Even though I love Annie and she is my future, I can't help taking a journey down memory lane. Annie's way too good for me. God only knows why she sticks by me.

I spot Cass watching the interaction between Sara and me. I've been around her long enough to know she doesn't miss much. Unlike Annie, who has not said a word, I know Cass won't leave it alone. I'm still her responsibility and I'm convinced she's gonna make damned sure I don't fuck up.

Sara shakes off what I presume is her shock at seeing me and extends her hand to Annie. "Hello, Annie, it's very nice to meet you. Nicky is a very special person and if you are her girlfriend you must be as special as she is. I hope we will have a chance to get to know one another."

Yeah, can you imagine my ex-lover and current lover hanging out and talking about me? No fucking way will I allow that to happen. I glare at Sara. She shrugs her shoulders at me and seems to recover from the shock of seeing me. I can tell by her expression this isn't over and I think she needs to talk to me, as much as I need to talk to her.

Sara turns to me. "Nicky, I know you don't owe me anything, but I was hoping we could get together and talk. I'd like to fill in some blanks. I think we could both benefit from having a conversation."

Inside I'm jumping at the chance to talk to Sara, but instead I shrug as if to say it makes no difference to me one way or another. "Yeah, sure, whatever."

I hope my response comes off as indifferent, but I'm sure both Annie and Cass know better.

Annie smiles warmly at me and I think she is trying, in her own kind way, to encourage me to do whatever I need to do. Her eyes get misty and I feel like a schmuck for not telling her about Sara.

"Nicky, I think it would be a good idea if you and Sara had a chance to catch up with one another. It's okay. I understand and I really want you to have the time to be able to sort out whatever you need to sort out. I love you and I will always want what's best for you," Annie tells me.

See, I told you Annie is the best and I certainly do not deserve her love, but I'm very glad I have it.

Cass shoots me one of her penetrating looks, but I know she won't violate me by probing my mind. I imagine she will ask me later and I will tell her the whole story. For now, I get her message loud and clear. I can hear her voice in my head saying, *we will talk about this later, and you'd better not hurt Annie.* Even though Cass is my best friend now, I know her loyalties are to Vic and, by extension, Annie. This trumps her loyalty to me. Although Annie has come a long way, she is still relatively fragile and I can't blame Cass for being overprotective.

I notice the exotic looking woman standing off to the side.

Sara introduces her as her elusive friend, Ting. I've forgotten that I met her earlier at the funeral but it was such an emotional time that I don't remember meeting her years before.

I step forward to greet her. "So you're the one who set up the cabin all those years ago. Thanks to you I'm a sushi snob."

"Sara always did have good taste in women, but you were different. I didn't know if it was a good or bad thing, but it was important to her, so I helped. Hmm, a vampire, you weren't a vampire back then?" Ting raises her eyebrow.

"No, no, I didn't get turned until many years after Sara left. I guess there are a lot of secrets floating around. This is quite the eye opening visit."

"Indeed." Ting chuckles as she glances over at the rest of our little group of visitors.

As if Sara and the rest of our group remember the whole reason for our visit, Sara turns to Vic. "God, I'm sorry, Vicky. I'm supposed to be showing you around and helping you understand our world. Please come with me and I'll show you to where all of you will be staying while you visit the compound. I understand that you don't want to live here permanently, but you will always be welcome to come and visit anytime you wish. The call to the pack will only grow stronger as you get closer to the year mark. If you will allow me, I can help you through your first shift."

So now, all the pieces shift into place for me, as I realize that Sara is the one Vic told us about. Apparently, Vic and Sara had some kind of wild night of sex, where Sara bit Vic and, bam, nine months later Vic tells us she's turning into a shape-shifter.

Vic confirms my suspicions, when I overhear her whispering to Cass that Sara's the one.

I don't feel particularly comfortable with Sara taking on the role as host. After all, she is the one responsible for turning Vic into a shape-shifter, a fact I'm not eager to embrace.

I see Vic quietly surveying everything and I notice that my interaction with Sara is not lost on her keen observation skills. I understand her wariness. Annie is her best friend and I know she's smart enough to pick up on our history. I can also imagine that Vic might not necessarily be too comfortable with Sara—especially with Cass by her side.

Vic narrows her eyes at Sara. "What will that entail? Can Cass join us for this lesson?"

I know how Cass can get sometimes, but I think she is trying not to be too possessive or overly jealous of Sara. I've seen that look on her face before and I can tell she is happy that Vic wants her to be involved.

I'm trying to erase from my memory the knowledge of Vic and Sara doing the horizontal mambo and Vic turning into a shape-shifter from of a night of passion with Sara. I don't have any right to be jealous. I'm with Annie now, but my emotions have been in freefall from the minute Sara came back into the picture. I can't help feeling jealous now that I know it's *my* Sara that was Vic's one-night stand.

"Yes, of course Cass can join us. It might help to have her love and support. However, if you become too distracted by her presence we can adjust things at that time."

Now, if I'm really uncomfortable with the possibility that Vic and Sara might be spending some alone time together, I can imagine how Cass is feeling.

I look at Vic and I can tell she wants to talk things over with Cass.

"Would it be okay if we retired to our cabins and got a little rest—maybe freshen up a bit?" Vic asks.

"Of course. We can all meet for dinner later. Come this way." Sara leads us to our cabins.

Once Annie and I settle into our cabin, I'm transported back to my time with Sara in the cabin in the woods—my first time. The time I will never forget. I shake my head as if this will shake the memory loose and send it flying into a big black hole never to return. Annie touches my arm and gently turns me around to face her.

She presses her lips to mine. "Nicky, I love you. That will never change, but...."

"No, please, Annie, I don't like statements that include the word *but*."

"Nicky, just listen to me, no interruptions, okay?"

"Okay."

"I'm not blind. I know you have a history with Sara—a deep history. I also know she still loves you and you still love her."

I open my mouth to argue.

Annie places her finger gently on my lips. "Please, let me finish."

I nod. God, I love this woman.

"I know you have a history and that someone as amazing as you had to be loved by another at some point in your life. We all have a history. Our past is what shapes us into who we are—the good and the bad. I love who you are and I'm convinced Sara is a big part of that. You two have unfinished business and if we have any hope at all of making things work between us you need to explore that. I promise, I will be here no matter what. I love you enough to want you to be truly happy regardless of what your decision will be. Sara seems to be a good person and in one really

123

important way, she is more compatible to you—as a shape-shifter she will have a very long life. We've avoided discussions about the future, but you know they are inevitable at some point. I want you to figure this out with Sara, and if you come back to me, I'll welcome you with open arms. If you don't, I'll cherish what we had. I will never forget how you brought me out into the world and allowed me to live again."

"Annie, you're right about a few things. I won't lie to you and tell you Sara meant nothing to me. She meant everything to me and we do have unfinished business, but it's not what you think. I never got to say goodbye to her and I do still love her, but I swear she is my past and you are my future."

"Spend the time with her, Nicky. Figure it out. That's all I ask."

I pull Annie into my arms and kiss her with such passion that we both sway. I don't want to lose this wonderful woman. I'm confused and my life is spinning out of control, but I know that deep inside Annie's the best thing that ever happened to me. I guide her to the bed and our lovemaking is gentle and sweet—like Annie.

†

A couple hours later, I hear a soft knock on our door. I pull on my jeans and throw a sweatshirt over the naked upper half of my body. I open the door a crack and then widen it, as I notice Annie putting on her own sweatshirt.

Ting is grinning at me. She looks over toward Annie and her smile widens.

I love that Annie has a way of bringing out the best in everyone.

"I hope you both are hungry. There is a feast in the common room and I came to show you how to get there."

In my estimation, Ting is being a little more than a good host.

"Thank you, Ting, that is very kind of you." Annie smiles warmly at Ting.

"It's my pleasure." Ting bows her head.

I don't like the way she is smiling at Annie and I'm even more concerned at the way I think Annie is responding. Annie is always polite, but usually I see her shying away from others. She is not shying away from Ting. I notice right away how Ting has a gentle way about her and an exotic beauty that is hard to miss. I have no right to be jealous, but I am.

†

They aren't kidding when they tell us there is a feast. The common room is an enormous open area heated by a massive fireplace. There are long, natural log tables with matching benches. The room is set up to feed an army and the food covers every square inch of several twelve-foot tables while other tables are clear of everything but fresh flowers. I've never seen such a vast variety of dishes.

"May I get you a plate of food or a beverage, Annie?"

It seems to me that Ting is directing her attention specifically to Annie. Okay, now I'm getting irritated and I'm convinced that Ting is enamored with Annie.

"Okay, first, Annie is perfectly capable of getting her own plate, and second, if anyone is to get Annie a plate of food that would be me—her girlfriend." I emphasize the last word.

"You're jealous. That's so cute." Annie chuckles.

I seethe. "Am not." I revert to my petulant child persona.

"Ting, that is very kind of you but, as Nicky so eloquently put it, I'm perfectly capable of getting my own plate."

I don't like what I consider flirtatious banter with Ting one bit. I glare at Ting as if to say hands off—she's mine. Shit, what am I turning into—some kind of back woods mountain girl?

I notice Sara hanging out on the periphery watching this whole exchange. She casually strolls up to our small group. "May I get either of you anything to drink?"

I glare again at Ting as if to say, *see, at least Sara is directing her offer to both of us.*

125

"Thanks, Sara. I see there's water available and I don't need anything different," I respond.

Alcohol doesn't really affect vampires, but I'm not taking any chances. I want to be one hundred percent aware of everything. It's an irrational thought process, but this whole experience has me off kilter.

Sara looks at Annie. "Annie?"

"Thanks, Sara, water is good for me, too."

Sara sits at another table, but I notice her stealing glances in my direction. I think I'm being subtle as I catch myself looking in her direction several times during our meal. On a few occasions, our eyes meet and I imagine that I see such longing in her eyes that it startles me.

I still don't have the answers to my questions. The big question being—why didn't she tell me about herself? Why did she feel she had to leave?

I feel Cass's stare.

It's my humble opinion that Ting is somewhat bold when she sits with our table. Although she has a shy demeanor, I notice how she is not hiding her fascination and attraction to Annie.

I notice that Vic seems to be taking everything in and I wonder what she makes of this whole scene.

I want to break whatever fantasy I imagine is going on in Ting's head. "So, Ting, how old are you?" I blurt out.

The question doesn't seem to faze her. "I am six hundred and three years old. Because of my age, I am considered one of the elders. I don't feel like an elder, but the younger shape-shifters seem to look to me for advice and guidance. I am not sure I am deserving of their respect," she answers.

I'm sure I'm not the only one who notices that Ting is both humble and beautiful. *Shit.*

"Wow, you look pretty good for someone who is more than six hundred years old." I emphasize her age in a vain attempt to highlight our differences. After all, I'm still only thirty-four.

"I am blessed with good genes." She smiles.

Damned if her smile is not dazzling.

126

I'm sure Vic is curious, since she joins the conversation. "How did you come to be a shape-shifter?"

"I am a natural born shifter. Both my mother and father were shape-shifters. Sometimes it only takes one parent, but you are guaranteed to become a shape-shifter when both parents are shifters."

"Are your parents still alive?" Vic asks.

"No, I am afraid they were hunted when I was very young. I never knew them." Ting shakes her head.

Shit, she's an orphan. My sweet Annie is such a compassionate person that I fear this latest piece of information will make any attraction she feels toward Ting even more compelling.

"I'm so sorry," Vic replies.

I don't doubt for a minute that she is sincere.

The rest of the group nods.

"Don't be. I was raised by the loving pack. You cannot miss what you never had in your life. I never lacked love or affection. This is a very nurturing environment to grow up in."

"Are there differences between natural born shifters and people—or rather shifters like me who are made?" Vic asks.

"Yes and no. Natural born shifters grow quite naturally— much like human children until they hit puberty. The urge to mate and shift grows strong after puberty. It is difficult, but we are forbidden to mate, have sex, or shift until we at least reach the age of twenty-one. There is good reason for this because once a shape-shifter has sex or shifts, the aging process slows down considerably. The more shifts or sex, the slower the aging process. Can you imagine staying in puberty for fifty or one hundred years?" Ting shakes her shoulders.

The gesture looks to me like she is trying to shake off an unwelcome guest.

"I waited until I was twenty-two. My first love was a beautiful human and you could very well be her ancestor, Annie. You have the same eyes. She died a long time ago in my arms. We had many beautiful years together." Ting glances over to Sara then back to me. "I told Sara not all react as her father did but she did not listen."

I want her to know that vampires can also live their lives with a human. "Yeah, Cass's first lover was a human and she died in her arms after forty years together."

"Yes, I have heard that beautiful story. You are the reincarnation of her lover. Is this correct, Vicky?"

"Yes, we think so. So are you saying that the more sex I have, the slower the aging process," Vic asks.

"Yes, we believe that is the way it works."

Perfect. I've got her now so I want to reveal her as a player. "So, you must be getting it pretty regularly to look as young as you do."

Cass glares at me.

I'm being rude. I don't care. I get the impression she believes Annie is her reincarnated first love and I don't like that one bit.

"Yes, our sex drive is strong and I wish to remain young for when my reincarnated first lover returns." She looks at Annie.

Shit. My comment backfires on me and I can't help what I blurt out next. "Well, you can just stop looking at Annie like she's your lover reincarnated."

"I apologize. I know that you and Annie are a couple. I am sorry if I have offended either one of you." Ting stands up, bows to us and gracefully exits the room.

I can tell that Cass is pissed at me now, because she has *the look*.

"Nicky, would you stop being such a petulant child. Ting was being very helpful with information that Vic needs to know and understand and now she is going to have to seek Sara out to get her questions answered. Are you happy now?"

"No, I'm not happy now." I sulk. "I wish I'd never come here. Being blissfully ignorant has some advantages."

I think Sara catches the last part of the interaction between Ting and me and comes over to sit at our table. "It seems like Ting has other matters to attend to. I'm sure you have other questions that I would be happy to answer for you."

"How often is it successful when your serum enters a human through a bite, or scratch, or however it gets there?" Vic asks.

"Are you asking how often we are able to create, for lack of better terminology, a shape-shifter?"

I want to know the answer to this question, as well. If it's a lot easier than making a vampire. I wonder why Sara didn't bite me.

Sara glances at me.

"The odds can be as high as ninety percent, especially when the shifter is mature. Ting's first lover was in the ten percent and so was my father." Sara looks down.

I don't think she can meet my eyes. I'm positive she knows what I'm dying to find out.

"Why did you bite me? We were not going to be long term lovers," Vic asks the question that I myself am wondering.

"I know. I have asked myself that question again and again, but I don't have a good answer. I could say I got carried away, but it has never happened before. I have always been able to control myself. I'm deeply sorry."

"Don't be. It solved our problem." Vic looks at Cass with love. "The universe works in mysterious ways and I believe everything that is meant to be occurs for a reason. There are no errors in the universe. You don't have to feel bad for giving me this gift. Sara, look at me."

Sara looks up at Vic.

She seems so sad that my heart is breaking for her.

"I look at this as a gift. You have given me a gift and I will be forever grateful to you," Vic says.

"Sara, I am also in your debt. I do not know how I will ever be able to repay you," Cass adds.

Sara gives Cass and Vic a genuine smile, the first smile I think I've seen since we entered the compound.

Why? Why? Why? That question keeps racing through my brain. I know I'm not leaving this compound without the answers.

Chapter Sixteen

As we're leaving the dining hall, common room, or whatever this massive facility is called, Sara touches my arm. "Nicky, we need to talk. I need to talk to you."

I'm ready to bite back a snarky comment like, *yeah, well, I wanted to talk thirteen years ago, but you never gave me that option,* but instead I nod. Annie and I have already talked and I know I have her blessing to seek closure.

Annie kisses me on the cheek. "I love you," she whispers.

I don't say anything back. Why don't I tell her I love her, too? I just let her take the left fork in the path that leads to the lake, as Sara and I take the one on the right. I glance over my shoulder and see Ting step beside Annie. I see Annie laugh and I'm about to abandon my talk with Sara, but she touches me on the arm. My need for closure is too great, as I look into the eyes that feel like home to me.

We walk along the path in silence. I'm convinced neither of us is quite ready to break the silence. I'm in the eye of the storm and it's peaceful there but the winds on either side of the eye threaten to destroy me.

I don't relish interrupting the calm, but someone has to make the first move. "Shit, Sara, why did you have to come crashing back into my life just when everything is starting to work out for me. Annie is a wonderful woman—"

"You came into *my* world. I didn't crash back into yours."

130

"Sara, that was not a real question, it was rhetorical."

"Oh."

"Stop looking at me like that."

"Like what?"

"Like you looked at me the last night we made love."

"I never stopped loving you, Nicky—never."

"Stop, don't tell me that. I love Annie now. You don't get to come strolling back into my life confusing me into falling back into your arms."

"I know, I know. I lost that privilege a long time ago."

"No shit."

"Can I ask you something?"

"You just did." I look away for a moment and then return her gaze. "Sorry, being a bitch again. Sure, go ahead, ask away." I throw my arms in the air.

"Annie is a human, right? Yet she knows about you. I thought that was forbidden. Have you talked about how you will deal with your relationship in ten years, or twenty years when she starts to grow old and resents your youth? I'm not advocating that you leave her or anything, I'm just wondering."

"Although it is forbidden to reveal ourselves, circumstances forced our hand. We were given special dispensation to tell Annie and Vic, but honestly it would not have mattered. I love her and I wanted her to know everything." I switch gears on her. "Why didn't you tell me? We could have figured something out."

"You mean like my mother and father?" She raises her brow. "You saw that disaster unfold when my father died. How can you ask that?"

"Was it more of a disaster for your mom or for your dad?"

"On my father's dying bed he begged me not to put you through what he went through. He told me if I really loved you, I had to let you go."

I'm pissed now. "Well, he didn't have that right to decide things for me. How do you know what I would have wanted? You never even gave me the chance to decide. I'm not your fucking father. Besides, you told us that ninety percent of the time it works. You can't get much better odds than that. Why didn't you bite me?"

There it is hanging in the air. It's finally out there—the question she knows I've wanted to ask ever since she enlightened us.

"Don't you think I thought of that? Don't you think I wanted to have a future for us?" She starts to cry.

Remember, I have seen Sara cry maybe three or four times. She melts my black heart with her tears and I start crying right along with her.

"Did you know I cried myself to sleep for months after you left? I wanted to die, Sara. I just wanted to die. Lisa tried to get me to go out for a year—a whole fucking year. I wouldn't go. I was sure you were coming back. I looked for you. Did Mary tell you that?"

"Yes, she told me and yes, I know what you went through. Trust me, it was no picnic for me either. Ting told me I was being stupid and I should let you decide."

"So why didn't you?"

"Let me ask you something. What will Vic do about her family? Will she fake her death and destroy them like you were forced to do?"

I feel the direct hit. "I don't know, she hasn't decided yet. Besides, the shifters didn't forbid her from telling them. What does that have to do with why you didn't bite me?" I'm back on the offensive.

"Humans don't always react very well to the news that you've become some kind of animal. That's how they see us, you know."

"I would never have viewed you as some kind of animal. I loved you."

"What about your family?"

"What about my family?"

"Look, Nicky, I know you. You don't follow the rules, yet you faked your own death so your family would not find out—damned good fake, too. You fooled me."

"Yeah I know. I saw you."

"That was you in the black hoodie?" Sara nods to herself.

I realize that her suspicions are confirmed.

"I knew there was something familiar about you. I should have guessed."

"So, what's your point?"

"My father told me about his family's reaction to mom. They looked at him like he was some kind of deviant. They told him to never come around again, and if they ever caught my mom in her wolf form, they would hunt her down and kill her for bewitching my father. They threatened to capture her and then put my father in an institution for sexual deviants. I couldn't take that chance with you. I didn't want you to have to choose between your family and me. I loved you too much for history to repeat itself. Can you honestly say you don't miss your family? Besides, you had your chance to tell me at your funeral but you didn't. I could ask you the same question."

"Of course I miss my family. I miss Lisa, too. You could have at least given me the option," I argue.

"You could have done the same. You must understand at some level. I did what I thought was best. I was trying not to be selfish."

"Well, it was selfish. You made the decision for us. That's not a partnership, that's a dictatorship."

"Aren't you the pot calling the kettle black—Miss fake-your-own-funeral? I don't recall you getting any input from me."

"Well, I could hardly get input from a ghost. You left remember?"

"Again, you had a chance at your funeral, yet you never took it. Besides, my father's plea was so heart wrenching, it was hard not to listen to him. Mom wasn't helpful either. She said that after she wasn't able to change him, he became bitter when his health started declining. Their final years were difficult. We were both a constant reminder of his mortality and our near immortality. It was too much for him to bear in the end. He died a very bitter old man."

"He was wrong you know. You have to know that my family would not have turned you or me away. They loved you. Well, Mom didn't love you so much after you left. She's kind of like a mama bear and you hurt her little cub. I'm surprised she even let you stay at the funeral."

"Yeah, at first it was really frosty. I could tell how angry your mom was at me. Lisa was mighty pissed at me, too."

"I know, I heard. It was hard on Lisa. She tried to be strong for me after you left, but I remember hearing her cry at night and I would see how red her eyes were the next morning."

"She must have seen how distraught I was at your funeral, because the ice melted a little and she hugged me. I guess she tried to remember the good times. I think she forgave me that day." Sara frowns.

"I know that look, there's something else you're not telling me. Okay, spill it, Sara."

"You don't know about Lisa and Gabby, do you?"

"What about Lisa and Gabby?"

"Gabby left her. Lisa won't tell me why. I get the feeling something more is going on, but Lisa is like Fort Knox. She's not talking. I haven't been the greatest friend. I keep tabs, but I don't visit. I don't know how to explain how I look the same after so many years."

"Shit, that bitch. I knew she was no good for Lisa. If it wasn't for our code, I would hunt her down and drain her."

"You would not."

"Okay, maybe not, but my thralling skills sometimes come in handy. I could make her do some really embarrassing things in public and teach her a few lessons."

"God, I've missed you, Nicky. I honestly thought I was making the right decision. I'm so sorry."

I look at Sara and I realize I do still love her and I miss her too, but too many years have gone by and I love Annie. I also realize I'm a big hypocrite. Sara is right. I understand now that our assessments of our immortality or near immortality are the same. I accept her rationale. Our time together has long passed. I know deep inside that we had our opportunity and for whatever reason the universe is telling us it was not meant to be.

I take a step closer to Sara. "I've missed you too."

Sara reaches up and brushes a tear from my cheek. She pulls me into an embrace.

I don't offer any resistance. It feels so natural for Sara to hold me. I inhale her scent. She smells like spring and fresh wildflowers. She smells like Mountain Laurel—a kind of sweet smell. It is so reminiscent of the old days that all of a sudden, I'm transported back fifteen years and I'm nineteen again. Before I became a newling and lost my innocence. For just a moment, we are back at school. It's just like the old Dan Fogelberg song, *Auld Lang Syne*. I breathe in her scent again, and I realize she doesn't smell like Annie who is my new home—my true north. I pull back.

Sara looks me in the eyes. "I will always love you, Nicky, don't ever forget that."

"I'll always love you, too. You were my first love. You never forget your first love."

We pull apart just a little and Sara places a kiss on my lips.

It's not a kiss with a promise of a future. I recognize it as a goodbye kiss. The kiss settles me because it provides me with the closure I desperately need. I understand we are entering a new chapter in our lives and I think Sara understands that too.

We smile at one another and then I hear it—the crinkle of leaves. I turn to see Annie running back in the other direction.

Ting is following her and calling out. "Annie, wait."

Shit, shit, shit. I have to find Annie. I know she thinks I've chosen Sara, but that's not what has happened. Things are now crystal clear for me—Annie is my future. Sara is my past.

Sara is looking at me.

I know there is a look of horror on my face.

Sara pushes away from me. "Go, hurry, she'll understand. You can explain it to her. It's so plain on your face that Annie is the one."

I don't know where she has gone, but I start running down the path and run into a growling, black wolf.

135

Sara approaches the wolf. "Ting, stop it. You don't understand. Annie and you saw something and you are jumping to the wrong conclusion. Don't do this."

I'm rooted to my spot on the path. I don't understand. I look at Sara. "What's going on?"

"Ting is challenging you. She is taking a stance. She wants to fight for the right to court Annie."

"No fucking way. I'm not going to fight her. I don't want to kill her."

"Don't be so sure that you will be able to kill her. Let me handle this. Please, Nicky, do not act rash and do not provoke her."

"I'm not provoking her, but I sure as hell am not going to let her *court* Annie, unless that is what Annie wants. Annie is not some possession we get to fight over as a prize at the conclusion"

"I agree, but the old ways are deeply ingrained in our culture. Let me talk to Ting. She is reasonable. She is just letting her emotions get in the way of a clear thought process." Sara steps in front of me.

I'm relieved as she effectively puts a barrier between the black wolf and me.

"Ting, can you please shift back so that we can talk?"

I'm fascinated as the black wolf transforms into the woman, Ting. I can't look away. It's a beautiful transformation. Ting is naked as she walks up to us. A vision of a proud warrior flashes before my eyes. This is how I see Ting.

Ting's voice has a calm but eerie tone. "You have ten seconds, Sara. I cannot say I am disappointed. I always sensed your deep love of Nicky."

"Ting, I do love Nicky. I will always love Nicky and she will always love me, but our time to be together has passed. We were saying goodbye. We were putting closure on our former relationship. This is something I never allowed for either of us with my abrupt departure. Perhaps if I had not acted so rash things would be different, but Nicky has chosen Annie—not me."

Ting shifts her penetrating gaze in my direction. "What have you to say about all of this?"

"I needed closure. I needed to understand why Sara left. She's right, I will always love her, but Annie is my future—not Sara. If we made different choices thirteen years ago, things might be different, but there are no mistakes in the universe. I believe that. I'm meant to be with Annie and I think Sara is meant to be with someone else. Please let me go to Annie and explain this to her."

"If you ever hurt Annie again, I will be there to explore what this universe may have in store for us. I will not interfere unless you make a poor choice in the future."

I nod at Ting before hurrying down the path.

Cass meets me in front of the cabin and steps in front of the door.

I don't need to deal with this obstacle right now. "Oh, for fuck's sake, will you get out of my way? I need to talk to Annie."

"Vic is with her. You will let them talk. I warned you not to play with her feelings. I believed that your intentions were honorable and that you truly cared for her."

"God, Cass, how can you possibly believe that I could hurt Annie? It's all a big misunderstanding. She saw something and misinterpreted what she saw and heard."

"I am not sure confessing your love for another woman and kissing her on the lips has much interpretation other than the obvious."

"Fuck you, Cass, and your self-righteous bullshit. We were saying goodbye and not that it's any of your goddamned business, but I will always love Sara. That doesn't mean my future is with her. You know that I adore Annie. She's my future and we need to have a serious discussion on what that will look like."

Cass's eyes narrow. "Annie is a remarkable woman and she deserves to be happy. I believe you are the one to make her happy, but I think you need to let Vic calm her emotions first. She might have given you some speech about you needing to get closure and wanting you to be happy, but Annie is still very fragile and right now her heart is broken."

"I know. Don't you think I know that? That is why I have to help her understand. I know I can make her understand. Please, Cass, let me talk to her."

"I will ask."

Cass enters the cabin.

I'm petrified. I realize what I have to lose. I can't bear to lose her. I know with certainty she is my future and I know how to ensure it. I'll ask Sara for a favor, a big favor. I know I probably have no right to ask, but I'm pretty sure she won't turn me down.

Cass, shaking her head, comes out of the cabin. "She says she can't talk to you right now. She is convinced you need to spend more time with Sara to be sure of what you really want. She loves you and just wants you to be happy. She wants you to stay here at the complex for at least another month. She says you need to spend time with Sara, and if after that month you still want to talk she will be ready."

"Fuck. Okay, I'll give her a month, but I'm not gonna agree to remain here the whole month. I have something I have to take care of. I have another friend in trouble and I don't give a shit about the code or any fucking consequences. I'm going to go see her in California. I'm tired of all these secrets and the fucking code. I may even go see my parents. So, you better be prepared to talk to the High Council, because your charge is about to go rogue. If I'm gonna lose Annie, I don't have any reason to care much about anything."

Cass steps in front of me and draws me into a hug. "Have faith, Nicky. Everything will work out. I could ask you to please not be rash, but I am sure it will not do any good. You do what you need to do and I will help them understand. I promise Vic and I will take care of Annie."

"Will you please help Vic understand? I don't want her thinking I hurt Annie."

"I will. I promise."

Chapter Seventeen

I shuffle along the path with my head down and tears streaming down my face. Sara and Ting approach with caution. I'm not interested in making any small talk or answering their questions. I need to find out more about Lisa and I believe Sara has all the answers.

I don't relish staying in the compound. If Sara is going to accompany me to California to help our friend, I need for her to provide me with alternate accommodations for the evening.

It's clear to me that Sara doesn't know what to say.

Ting looks at me and jumps right in. "I see you were not able to repair your relationship."

Right or wrong, I can tell that Ting looks hopeful. A wave of anger crashes over me at what I believe is her insensitive observation. "Oh, you'd like that, wouldn't you? No, that is not the conclusion to draw at this time. She has asked for a month. I didn't get a chance to talk to her, but whatever Annie needs, I will honor her wishes. Before you go running to her cabin to offer your support and sympathy, she has all the support she needs right now with Vic and Cass by her side—so back the fuck off."

Sara puts her hand out when Ting growls. "Ting, stop. Nicky, I'm so sorry. I didn't mean to cause you problems."

"I need your help, Sara. Before all the shit hit the fan, you were telling me about Lisa. I need to find out what's going on with her. I'm going there, and if I have to read her mind, I will. She was my life raft after you left, so it's the least I can do to support her now. Besides, it looks like I have a month of idle time and a distraction will help."

"I thought the vampire code restricts you from revealing yourself. I think that coming back from the dead is a pretty big reveal."

"You think I give a fuck what sanctions the High Council will impose on me? I may have lost the one good thing that matters in my life right now. There isn't anything else they can do to me that means a damned thing. Cass said she will back me up no matter what."

"All right, I have your back, too. Whatever you need, Nicky, just ask. Loyalty and friendship must mean something in your world. It means a lot in ours."

"I have a very convenient means of travel now that can transport me wherever I wish. I just need an address. If you're coming with me, you need to make whatever arrangements you can and I'll meet you there at whatever time you can arrange. I would suspect that this won't be possible to arrange until tomorrow, so I might as well stay at the compound tonight. I'll need alternate sleeping arrangements. I'm sorry, Sara, but it cannot be in your cabin."

"Of course not. I understand. I'll make the arrangements and perhaps something good will come out of this mess." Sara turns to Ting. "Ting, I know that right now you and Nicky may not see eye to eye on everything, but I could use your help."

Ting nods.

"Can you see what cabins are available for Nicky while I make travel arrangements for myself?"

"Come with me. I will take you to another cabin and will arrange to have your things transferred." Ting starts down the path.

My jaw becomes rigid as I follow her. "I'd really appreciate it if you didn't arrange to personally have my stuff transferred to the new cabin. Can you please at least give us a chance to mend things without your interference? I promise, if we don't work it out, I'll step aside. No matter what, I want Annie to be happy. If that means you will be the one to make her happy, I won't stop you."

"I give you my word. I will not interfere. You must have some redeeming qualities for Sara to love you so deeply."

"Thank you. I think."

†

Ting shows me to an empty cabin on the outskirts of the compound. The cabin is a perfect match for what I deserve. I've finally done it. I guess I deserve banishment to the Siberia of the compound. I can barely stand myself, so I can imagine what others must think of me now.

I'm surprised Cass is still talking to me. Good thing Vic isn't quite accomplished as a shape-shifter yet, or I can imagine her trying to rip my head off right now.

I have one chance to get things right and the least I can do is help an old friend. Consequences be damned. It can't get much worse, can it?

I'm sitting on the bed with my head in my hands when I hear a soft knock on my door.

Sara enters, sits next to me, and puts her arm around my shoulders.

It feels good to have her comfort me but I hate myself even more for allowing it. I'm afraid someone will see us and I'll be screwed even more than I already am. It's strange though, I have this sudden epiphany that it really is only comfort. I don't want to make love to Sara. I just want her friendship and I'm genuinely glad she's back in my life. I want Annie to read my mind. I want Cass to violate the rules and probe my brain. At least then, someone will know the truth.

Sara doesn't say a word to me. She just lets me cry on her shoulder until I'm emotionally exhausted.

She kisses my forehead. "Get some sleep, Nicky. We have a big day tomorrow. You need to be prepared for Lisa's reaction and her questions."

Sara crosses the cabin and quietly exits.

I'm left by myself with only my depressing thoughts to keep me company. I don't even have the energy to change. I sprawl out on the bed and, even though I'm exhausted, it takes me several hours to fall asleep. I can't stop my destructive thoughts from swirling around angrily in my head.

All I can think about is Annie. My beautiful Annie—she's the one. How can I possibly be so stupid to have been confused for even one second? I don't need a month, an hour, or another second, but that's my punishment for doubting our love for even a millisecond of time. Was it doubt though, really? I try to think back over my emotions and I'm not so sure. Can the need for closure create doubt? It did feel like home when Sara embraced me, but I didn't want to sleep with her. Shouldn't that count for something? Oh, well, too late now. The damage is done.

I'm too tired to hunt down a deserving drainee. I believe that somehow, Sara knows this and she doesn't knock on the door the next morning. Perhaps she knows I will not be able to come out into the sunshine. The darkness matches my mood.

Sara sends me a text message to let me know her flight arrangements. I don't know how she got my phone number but I imagine Cass has given it to her. I hope it wasn't Annie. The arrangements seem to fit, because Sara isn't able to get a flight out until the afternoon. She will not arrive at Lisa's place until evening and the timing is perfect for me.

I'm tempted to try to talk to Annie again, but I owe her the time she has requested. It's what she wants and giving her that control is important. I know this. No matter how much my heart is breaking, I just want to make her understand that I won't go against her wishes.

The minutes tick by so slowly that I wonder how I'll ever survive the day. I'm being overly dramatic, but it feels like I'm in a prison of my own making. I suspect this is what prisoners have to contend with every day. The sheer boredom and inactivity must drive them completely bonkers. I pick up my journal and begin writing again—my story is far from over.

†

Finally, it's seven thirty in the evening and I get a text from Sara.

Pulling up to Lisa's. 310 Sycamore in LA. C U soon
On my way now, I text back.

One thing I really like about being a vamp is the easy travel. I fog myself to the location Sara gives me and find myself in front of a modest brownstone. It's not flashy but it's Los Angeles, so Lisa must be doing okay for herself.

Sara exits from her rental car and joins me. "So, how do you think we should approach her? It's going to be a shock. She thinks you're dead."

"I know. I think maybe you should knock first and I'll kinda hang back in the shadows. Maybe you can try to prepare her before I show myself."

"All right, that sounds like a good plan."

Sara knocks on her door.

Lisa doesn't answer right away, so Sara knocks again and this time Lisa opens the door.

From the way she looks at Sara, I get the impression she is surprised to see her. I was hoping Sara would have contacted her to prepare her for this visit, but it doesn't seem like Sara felt this was necessary.

Lisa was always a beautiful girl, but now she has grown to be a very beautiful woman. She looks pale now though and rather sickly. It appears to me that she might be getting over the flu or something.

Lisa is standing in the doorway. "Red, my God, what are you doing here. I haven't seen you in ages. You promised you would keep in touch after…" She doesn't finish her sentence.

I wonder if she realizes it might be a mistake to bring up that old memory.

"I'm sorry, we came unannounced. I hope we aren't interrupting anything," Sara explains.

143

"We?"

"Yeah, sorry, I have a surprise for you and I don't know how to make this any easier. I'll explain everything, or rather we'll explain everything, but it might be a bit of a shock, so...."

I step out of the shadows and Lisa promptly passes out. Sara catches her before she hits the floor.

"Shit, I expected her to be shocked, but I didn't think she'd fucking pass out on us." I sigh and look up to the sky as if the answers are up there for me.

"I don't think the shock is the only factor here. I can smell it." Sara has a worried look on her face.

"Are you out of your fucking mind, she's not drunk."

"No, not drunk. We need to let her tell us."

"What the hell are you talking about?"

"We can talk about it later. Let me get her to the couch first."

Sara carries Lisa to the couch and gently puts her down. She kneels next to the couch and tenderly brushes a wisp of hair aside.

Lisa's eyes slowly flutter open. She turns her head in my direction. "You're dead. I was at your funeral. Red, I think I'm having a reaction to the medicine."

"No, hon, you're not having a reaction." Sara's voice is so gentle and sweet. "Nicky is alive. We have a lot to tell you and you need to tell us some things too. Don't you? There are reasons why we both did what we had to do. There are rules and we're about to break a bunch of them."

"Rules? What are you, CIA or something? Oh, God, you saw something you shouldn't have and now you are in some kind of witness protection program. You had to disappear and Nicky had to fake her own death." She looks back and forth between us. "No, wait. Nicky, you were destroyed when Red left, unless you missed your calling as an actress there is no way you could have faked your depression. I was there."

"Lisa, we're not CIA, or in witness protection. Our story is far more bizarre. We had to chance your reaction, because we knew you were in trouble. I think I know part of the story," Sara explains.

144

I'm so glad Sara is here with me, because she is always the patient, calm, and comforting one.

I see what looks like a pained expression on Lisa's face and she turns to Sara. "You promised you would stay in touch but you lied. What the fuck difference does it make now?"

"I kept tabs. I knew when Gabby left you but I didn't know why."

I sense that Sara is trying to smooth things over.

I've rarely seen Lisa this angry, but when she turns her gaze in my direction, I definitely get the distinct impression that she is mightily pissed. *Shit*. Not only do I think she is pissed, but I'm pretty sure it's more than that—she looks wounded. I've betrayed her.

"Why? Why did you fake your own death? Why didn't you call more often? I missed you and I missed Red. You weren't the only one who lost something when she left."

I take a step closer and then I notice how fragile she seems. "God, no offense, Lisa, but you look like shit right now. Can I get you something to eat or drink?"

"I don't see you in what, nine years—I think you're dead and all you can say is I look like shit. I wish I could say you look like shit too, but you two look the same as you did in college. I mean, what the fuck?"

She begins to laugh now.

This is the old Lisa—the one I remember from college.

"Look, what we have to reveal may seem impossible, but both of us are prepared for whatever consequences arise." Sara takes Lisa's hand. "I didn't know Nicky was alive until yesterday. We ran into one another in a very unlikely place and I told Nicky you were in trouble and needed our help. Will you listen and try to be open to what we have to tell you?"

Lisa nods.

"Do you remember how old my father looked when he died?"

Lisa nods again.

"I'll bet you thought my mom just married a man three times her age. That isn't the case at all. My mom is much older than my

145

father was when he died. My mom and I are shape-shifters and we have unusually long lives. My mom was not able to provide my father with the serum to prolong his life or convert him to a shape-shifter. She tried but it wasn't successful. My father convinced me that if I really cared about Nicky I would let her go and not have her experience the agony he experienced when he chose my mom over his family."

Lisa's mouth is hanging open, looking as though she thinks Sara has completely lost her marbles.

I decide to interject a bit of my story.

"So, um, I didn't know Sara was a shape-shifter until yesterday. I had my own unusual event. Right after you left for California I went to a gay bar and suffered a fatal stab wound at the hands of some psycho dude. I would have died that night, except Sabrina gave me a gift—a really rare gift. Before you get all freaked out, just remember that all that Hollywood crap about vampires and werewolves is just that—crap. I'm still me, just an enhanced and virtually indestructible me. Vampires are actually righteous beings. I've never killed anyone who didn't deserve it."

"Have you two lost your fucking minds?"

I look at Sara and she shrugs. "I guess a demonstration is in order. Since it would require some douchebag to demonstrate and that might kinda freak Lisa out, I think you'd better do the demonstration. Besides, I've never seen you shift to a wolf. I only saw Ting shift from a wolf to a woman. If it hadn't been that little bitch, Ting, I would have thought it was kinda hot."

Sara sheds her clothes and the transformation is mesmerizing. The shift to wolf is so beautiful. I can barely take my eyes off the beautiful reddish brown fur. I reach out to touch her.

Lisa sits up and starts backing away. Her face is ghost white again.

I think she's about to black out.

Sara shifts back. "I'm here. Are you okay?"

Lisa is shaking her head.

I get the impression she is doing this to somehow remove what she must believe is a dream or a hallucination.

146

Sara puts her arms around Lisa. "Lisa, you're not dreaming, nor are you having a reaction to the chemo treatment. Nicky and I are right here and we'll be here as long as you need us. Well, I'll be here for as long as you need me. Nicky has to do something very important in a month."

I look at Sara as I realize what she's just said. "Lisa, what's going on? Why are you getting chemo?"

"I don't know how to react. I'm sorry. I thought the biggest shock in my life came when I found out I'm probably going to die before the age of thirty-five. I have breast cancer."

The way she says this sounds so nonchalant, that I wonder how long she's known to be so blasé with the announcement.

"I look like shit today because I got a big dose of chemo and it's kinda hard on my body. Some days are better than others and there's still a chance I'll make it," Lisa explains.

I'm sad about this news, but I'm pissed that Gabby is not here with Lisa. "Where the fuck is Gabby? I'm gonna kill that fucking bitch for bailing on you."

"It's not her fault, Nicky. She doesn't know. I bailed on her first. When I found out, I changed the rules. I started distancing myself from her and then told her I had lied and now didn't want to have children anymore. I insinuated that I might be seeing someone else on the side and that our marriage was too boring for me. I pushed her away."

"You have to tell her. She'd want to know. I'd want to know if I was your wife," I say.

"It's too late now. She moved on. It's better this way."

"Oh for fuck's sake, it's not better this way. You were married to her for what nine years?"

Lisa shakes her head. "Gabby and I both settled. We couldn't have the one we really wanted, so we convinced ourselves we were in love with one another. You know if you can't be with the one you love, love the one you're with. You know how lesbians are so predictable. We followed the lesbian rule book—date, fuck, move in together, and then get married.

147

"Shit, I've made a career out of falling for unobtainable people—starting with my very own first girl on girl action. She ran so fast I thought I saw road runner tracks in the cement outside my family home. Gabby's ex came back onto the scene and then I got sick. I do love her. I just wasn't in love with her, so she deserves to be with the one she wants. I engineered it so she wouldn't have any guilt for getting her happy ending. Enough said. Just drop it, Nicky."

"Fine, I'll drop it, but you aren't going to get away with pushing Sara or me away." I smile reassuringly at her.

Lisa gets an impish grin on her face.

Despite her pale complexion, I once again see a little of the old Lisa. "So, you're a hot sexy vamp and Red here is a hot sexy werewolf. Do you have, like, sex powers now?"

She grins, and just like that, I'm transported to our college days and none of the years or distance matter anymore.

"Sorry to disappoint, but no sex powers," Sara responds.

Sara always takes the practical path. Me, I want to tease a bit and embellish our changed situation.

"So, Nicky, if you're a vampire, can I see your fangs?" Lisa asks.

"No, no way."

"Aw, come on, Red here showed me her beautiful wolf. I wanna see those sexy fangs."

"I don't think so. Look, Lisa, I really don't want to scare the shit out of you, but I can demonstrate a less menacing parlor trick."

I fog out of the room to just outside of the brownstone and knock on her door.

Sara answers, because I believe she's convinced that Lisa is drained from her recent treatment.

Lisa has a big smile on her face as I walk back into the living room. "Wow. That was fucking amazing. What else can you do?"

"I can read minds and I can thrall people to convince them to do whatever I want. Not that I need to do that with women, you know, but I can if I want. Well, we're not really supposed to thrall anyone for personal gain. It's one of the rules. We're not supposed to read minds either, unless we're tracking down some low life."

"What? Vampires have some kind of code of conduct?"

"Yes, they do, and of course I've already violated it a few times." I'm not really bragging, just stating facts.

"What about werewolves. Do you guys have a code, too?"

"We're shape-shifters who happen to shift into wolves—not werewolves—and yes, we have a code," Sara adds.

"Are you as bad as Nicky at breaking the rules?"

"No, not as bad as Nicky, but I guess I owe our little reunion to bending the rules a bit. I had no idea Nicky was the famed Little Wild One."

"Why am I not surprised Nicky has a nickname? So, are you two back together then?"

Sara looks at me and I notice her eyes get a little misty. I shift uncomfortably.

"No, Nicky is with someone else now."

"Well, I hope I'm still with her." I jump in to add to the story. "No big surprise, I fucked up yesterday and I'm on a one month forced separation."

"Nicky and I were saying our goodbyes as lovers and Annie, her partner, misinterpreted our actions. It's hard to rebuild a past based on so many wrong turns. I'd like to think we can become good friends. If I'm honest, it probably isn't my first choice, but Annie seems to be such a wonderful woman and I won't get in the middle of Nicky's happiness. Annie is her choice and I accept that our time came and went," Sara says.

Lisa gets a strange look on her face. I'm tempted to read her mind, but I don't.

"Okay, so what's the plan now?" I ask. "I hope you have a couple of guest bedrooms like in your past house, because it's probably not a good idea for Sara and me to bunk together."

I think I detect a look of discomfort in Lisa.

"Uh, I don't. I only have one guest bedroom."

"I'm used to sleeping pretty much anywhere. Nicky, you take the guest bedroom," Sara says.

149

"No, I can take the couch. Nicky, you can take the guest bedroom and Sara can bunk in my room," Lisa says.

I recognize Lisa's attempt to be the gracious host. I'm eager to offer my own solution. "I can always just fog in and out. It kinda saps my energy if I do it too often, but I can manage."

"If everyone is going to insist on being some kind of martyr, why don't I just bunk with Lisa and then I can be there in the middle of the night in case she needs anything," Sara offers.

"Hey, that's a great idea," I add.

Now I'm really wondering what is going on as I notice Lisa's expression. I decide since I'm already breaking the rules, why not totally smash them. I probe her mind because I want to know what she's thinking.

Shit. What do I do now? How am I going to be so close to Red and share the same bed with her? I'm a terrible friend pining after my best friend's lover. Well, ex-lover, but this is all so wrong. I thought all these years of not seeing Red would finally break my unhealthy obsession. I'm a total shit. I hate myself right now for even having the slightest hope that maybe she'll start to see me in a different light. Of course, she won't, you idiot. Remember dying. Cancer. I'm so fucked.

Shit, shit, shit. I just violated my best friend's mind and I can't believe I never saw this. God, it all makes sense now, the late night crying, the red rimmed eyes, her solitude for so many years until Gabby. I should be pissed. I should be jealous, but I'm not. Lisa never once made a play for Sara. She always respected our relationship. She was always supportive and encouraging from the very first day we met. The guilt of loving Sara all these years must have been excruciatingly painful for her. I admire her restraint and I vow to see if maybe Sara and Lisa can be happy together. I know Sara loves Lisa, but can she think of her in a completely new way?

I want to steer this in the right direction. "Sara, that's a great idea. You need to bunk with Lisa. Don't be such a stubborn shit, Lisa. Don't let your pride rule. Please let us help you. Let Sara be there for you in the middle of the night, at least until we see how you do after this round of chemo."

I smile to myself. Maybe the universe has a better idea about how things should unfold. Maybe everything that happens *is* for a reason.

I don't think Lisa knows how to respond. I'll bet she's thinking that if she protests too much, we might get suspicious about her motives. I've backed her into a corner and I smile at my match-making abilities. I know it's against the rules, but I consider thralling Sara, just so she at least considers the possibility of a relationship with Lisa.

I'm really warming to the idea of these two very important people in my life coming together. Yeah, I can handle that. I can handle that a lot better than seeing Sara with someone else. I'll wait to see how things unfold naturally, but I don't throw out the idea of giving things a little push in the right direction. I may be a total bitch sometimes, but I'd like to think that when it comes to the people I love, I can act a little less selfishly.

"All right, thank you, Red. I hope I don't keep you awake. I sometimes get sick in the middle of the night."

"I'll be right there by your side, always." Sara's voice softens.

I imagine she's letting her know how much she cares, at least that is my hope for what is happening.

Chapter Eighteen

I'm already plotting and planning as Sara and Lisa head off to bed. The distraction of being there to support Lisa and seeing if there might be something more to their relationship to build on is a godsend to me. It keeps my focus away from missing Annie and wondering if I'll ever see her again.

I haven't hunted in a few days, so if I hope to be in the sun tomorrow, I know I have to get out there and find a deserving drainee. I miss Cass. She would know who to stalk. I don't remember Los Angeles that well from my previous visit, but I vaguely recall some particularly seedy places that I can go to find what I need.

I decide to text Cass, it can't hurt. Maybe she can give me some pointers. Maybe she can tell me if Annie is okay. I grab my phone and send a quick text.

Hey Cass. Arrived at Lisa's. She has cancer. Going to stay here for now. Any good places to hunt in LA? Annie ok?

Address? she texts back.

310 Sycamore. Why?

Cass does not text me back. Instead, she fogs into the living room and turns her penetrating gaze in my direction.

"I am sorry to learn of your friend's illness. I will not reveal much about Annie, but she is doing okay. I am sorry to disturb you, but I am afraid we are summoned by the High Council again.

I was expecting this, but I was not expecting it to happen so soon. Unfortunately, we must leave at once. They are not pleased."

"Fuck. Okay, I understand. Can I at least let them know I need to be gone for a bit?" I point in the direction of Lisa's bedroom.

"Yes, of course."

I knock lightly on Lisa's bedroom door.

Sara opens the door. She looks surprised to see Cass and arches her right eyebrow. She quietly closes the bedroom door behind her as she joins me in the hallway.

"I'm sorry, Sara. I've been summoned to the High Council. It's time I paid the piper. I'll be back after I straighten things out. Can you let Lisa know what's going on, but don't let her think it's a big deal or anything. I don't want her to worry. She has enough on her plate right now."

"Will you be okay? They don't execute you or anything, you know—for violating the rules."

"No." I laugh a little, but it's a nervous laugh. "I already asked that when I got in trouble before."

"Okay, take care. I've only heard good things about Cass. I'm sure she'll be able to help support you with this."

"Yeah, she is a big help. Don't worry."

"Nicky, time to go," Cass calls from the living room.

"Yeah, yeah, coming. Don't get your little panties in a wad. Sheesh. I don't think one more minute is going to make much of a difference in sucksville."

†

It's déjà vu as I look into the steely gazes of the seven vampires of the High Council. From the looks they are giving me, I'm pretty sure they aren't too happy with me. I get the distinct impression unhappy is an understatement—I think they look royally pissed. I wonder if they are considering a new sanction and execution is no longer out of the question. Helena always seems to be the one to represent the council. In addition to the touch of

153

anger I hear in her voice, I think I also hear a note of disappointment

"We had an agreement, Nicole, that you would not reveal yourself to anyone except your lover. You broke that agreement. It has not even been one month and we learn of not only your broken agreement but also your intention to break it again with your family. We understand that you are a newling and can be quite impulsive with your actions, but we take our agreements very seriously. How can we possibly respond in any other way than to sanction you as we have outlined previously. Can you give us one good reason why we should not proceed to thrall you and take away any remembrance of your vampire abilities or your love for your humans?"

On anyone else, the frown on Helena's face would somehow mar her beauty, but it doesn't. It only makes me squirm in discomfort. From my viewpoint, she stands in a long line with everyone else I've disappointed lately. That does not stop me from challenging her.

"Will I be impertinent if I ask all of you a question?"

Helena sighs, then waves her hand. "Very well, ask your question."

I take that as my cue to proceed. "Did any of you have family or close friends at the time the gift was offered to you?"

One of the more serious looking vampires smiles at me—at least she looks pretty damned serious to me.

"Very good question, Nicole, you are a cunning one. To answer your question, no, I did not. There was a great plague in my village and most everyone was either dying or dead at the time the gift was offered to me. I think I understand your argument. How can I possibly understand the difficulty of agreeing to such a sacrifice if I have never had to face this choice?"

I think I may have found an ally and I'm excited to find what I consider a small crack in the seven-person brick wall. "Exactly. The last time I was here, Cass told me that when agreeing to the gift, I was agreeing to the responsibility required and the consequences that follow. I know I wasn't forced to accept the gift, but do any of you believe that I could possibly understand those responsibilities and consequences in the split second decision I made to accept the gift."

"We do understand, Nicole, and this is the reason we have been lenient." Helena nods and smiles.

At least I imagine her smile is friendlier now, so I push on. "I have another question. Why do the shape-shifters give their pack the choice? Yet we don't? They have the same issues, but they allow them to reveal themselves to family and very close friends without breaking their code. I remember what you told me the last time you summoned me when I broke the code. *We have evolved our code over the years. Each new consideration leads to another evolution.* Don't you think it's time for another evolution? Why can't we adopt the shape-shifter code on this topic?"

"That is a very interesting argument. I would very much like to speak to one of the shape-shifters and learn more of their experiences," Helena answers.

At this point, I start getting excited. I think maybe, just maybe, I might squirm out of this mess. Cass is smiling next to me. I think she is proud of me because I haven't reverted to babbling or saying really inappropriate shit. I'm making decent arguments.

"I have a close, shape-shifter friend. I'm sure I can get Sara to talk to you."

I can't believe I'm offering up Sara without even talking to her, but I'm convinced she will help. I'm anxious to get back to Lisa, because I'm worried about her health and trying to figure out how to keep her alive.

"Sara is your ex-lover. Correct?" Helena asks.

Shit. Where do they get their information? It's like she has eyes in the back of her head or something. She's worse than my mother who always seemed to know when my sister Tess and I were doing something wrong.

"Um, yes, that's right," I say out loud.

"Yes, we would welcome the opportunity. I would also like to speak to an elder. I would like to hear of the experiences from one who is older and has a broader history and perspective. I would like to understand how their code has evolved. We will take this into consideration before rendering a decision. However, there is still the issue of breaking your commitment to the High Council. Integrity and loyalty are two traits we must insist upon."

Shit. I almost squirmed out of this, but I have to admit this is something I don't really have a great argument for.

I give it my best shot. "I know and I accept that I fu...uh...made a huge mistake with that. I should never have agreed to that. I was forced to weigh my loyalty to my best friend, who has always been there for me and needed my help, with my new vampire family. How could I expect to choose one over the other? It's kind of like the choice given to Sophie. You know, the movie *Sophie's Choice,* where she had to decide which one of her children would die. I mean what kind of fucked up choice is that? Oh, sorry. I mean that was an impossible choice. So anyway, I heard she was in trouble and she's the one that kept me from falling into the abyss. I owed her."

I know I'm rambling now, but I continue to explain things. "You know times have changed a lot. It's not the dark ages anymore. They don't chop off your head for heresy. I honestly don't think that by telling Lisa or my family, I'm gonna start a war on vampires. Could you maybe consider altering the rule a bit and instead allow us to make a case for revealing ourselves to a choice few. So, if I'm not being too impertinent, I'd like to ask permission to tell my family—you know, in case you decide to take my suggestion and change the rule or something."

"If you can arrange for Sara and an elder to come and speak to the High Council, we can consider this further before rendering our decision."

Helena ignores—okay, maybe ignore is too strong—but I don't hear a response to my request to reveal myself to my family.

"I am impressed with your ability to argue your case. It appears as though Cassandara is not needed after all. We will convene when you have had the opportunity to arrange a meeting."

Whew. I'm amazed at their response. I wonder if I haven't pissed off Ting too much. Maybe Sara can get her to talk to the High Council. I believe Sara still cares for me, even if those feelings are complicated right now. I'm confident she will talk to them.

I'm still worried about Lisa and even though I know I'm not completely out of hot water, I feel an obligation to my dear friend.

"Um, Helena, do you think it would be possible to have this meeting in California? Do you have a house in Los Angeles or somewhere near? I could arrange the meeting quicker with Sara if you come to Los Angeles, because that's where she will be hanging out for a while. Shifters don't really have the ability to fog in and out like we do. They have to rely on more traditional transportation. However, there is another option."

I hurry to explain further while I still have their attention.

"Ting, who is an elder, lives here in the Pacific Northwest and if Sara could arrange it, she might be willing to come to the Athena House, or you could go to their compound if we could arrange an invite. It might be a nice way to have the entire High Council meet the elders. Maybe there could be a new alliance? Just a thought."

The seven High Council members exchange looks with one another and I stop myself from probing their minds. It's hard for me to resist doing this, but I do. I'm in enough trouble—I certainly don't need to add to my misery. Helena smiles at me again and I get the feeling she likes my idea.

"We would be honored to meet with the elders if you are able to arrange a meeting."

I look over to Cass because I know she will have to help me with this. I don't think the elders are too enamored with me right now, but I believe they are intrigued with both Cass and Vic. I'm hoping the positive feelings will help me wiggle out of my current predicament. Cass nods her head. I trust that she knows me well enough now to anticipate what I'm asking without me asking her.

"How will we contact you to let you know?" I ask.

"Cass knows how to contact us." Helena waves her hand as if to say okay we're done, or get the hell out now because I tire of your antics. I'm not really sure which—I'm just guessing, but I certainly don't need a second gesture.

☦

I fog back to Lisa's house in a jiffy to give her an update and beg for Sara's help. I don't even bother to let Cass know where I'm going, but she appears not even one second later in Lisa's living room.

"Perhaps you should update Sara first before we approach any of the elders. Sara may be able to help grease the skids."

"Aw, Cass, I'm so proud of you. That's a great American saying. Did Vic teach you that one?"

"I do not believe this is the time to be discussing American slang, Nicole. You need to take this seriously. Please talk to Sara right away so that we can make the necessary arrangements. The High Council has been far too patient and I do not wish to test this any further than necessary."

"All right, no problemo. I'll talk with Sara right now."

I knock lightly on Lisa's bedroom door and Sara answers. I immediately notice her particularly grim expression.

"Hello, Nicky, I'm glad you're back. The treatment is making Lisa really sick and I'm not sure what to do to help. It breaks my heart to see her like this."

"I think you being here is the most important thing. I hate to add to the already huge pile of shit, but I'm in a bit of a bind right now. I promised the High Council I wouldn't reveal myself to anyone else but Annie and I broke that promise. I sorta suggested that the vampire code was out of date and they should take a page out of the shape-shifter code book, because you all are much more progressive with your views. Now, they want to talk to you and to the elders. Ideally, they would love to meet with all the elders at the compound, but that would require an invitation. I think they might be willing to come to Los Angeles to meet with you so you don't have to travel back to the compound, but then the elders would have to come here. Travel is much easier for us. Did I fuck up again and promise something that I shouldn't have?"

"Well, I can't really speak for the elders, but I'm happy to help. Somebody needs to stay here with Lisa."

"Oh, I can do that. They're probably really sick of hearing my lame excuses anyway."

"I think the elders would enjoy hosting the High Council. They're really curious about vampires and were excited to explore a revitalized alliance. I'll bet I can get Ting to talk to the other two elders. Let me see what I can arrange."

Cass joins us in the hallway. "Do you need any assistance with this? Vic may be concerned with Annie right now, but I am sure she would be happy to help in any way she can. She still cares about Nicky and she believes what I have shared regarding the status of your relationship with Nicky. Her first loyalty is to Annie, but that does not mean she will not support Nicky."

"Thanks. If I need your help, I'll ask," Sara says.

I don't feel like she says this rudely—I just think she is already in her efficiency mode.

Sara continues. "Let me talk to Ting first. How much trouble are you in, Nicky? What will happen to you if they're not satisfied with offering our differing perspective?"

"Don't worry about it. This is not your problem," I answer.

"You wouldn't be in this predicament if I hadn't told you about Lisa. Please, tell me the truth."

I suppose Cass believes I'll make a joke or water things down, so I suspect this is why she jumps in and answers for me. She may be a tight ass sometimes, but I believe she still cares about what happens to me. I'm lucky to have so many in my corner.

"To answer your question, Sara, Nicky is in a lot of trouble right now. The High Council is currently considering thralling Nicky to the point that she will not remember she is a vampire and will not remember she loves Annie. They will strip her of any special gifts—including the ability to see the sun again. There is often great pain associated with this sanction—both physical and mental."

I don't quite understand this yet, but I find out soon enough. I always have to learn the hard way.

Sara turns to me and her voice is so soft and gentle, it feels like a caress. "That harsh decision from the High Council will destroy your spirit. I'll do everything in my power to keep it from happening. If I were more selfish, I would let it happen and then perhaps I might have a second chance to change our destiny. I would be able to re-do our past."

She looks into my eyes and I see such love in her expression that, for a moment, it breaks my resolve. Annie is my future.

Sara looks away for a brief moment and then catches my eye again. "I cannot do this to you, I love you too much to interfere with what I know is the right path for you."

I love her so much for this. In this instance, I let go of all my past hurt and anger and completely forgive her for leaving me. I understand and really believe now that Sara's decisions always consider everyone but herself. I want her to be happy. I want her to find love again. I'm obsessed with this need to ensure her happiness. I don't have any words for her right now, so I just quietly speak. "Thank you."

First, I need to resolve my troubles, and then I can concentrate on being a good friend to Sara.

†

Sara retrieves her cell phone from her bag and steps into another room.

I assume she is calling Ting.

Cass watches her leave with a curious look on her face. "She is quite a woman. At first, I'll admit, I was a little jealous. I did not know her intentions with Vicky. It must be hard to let her go. I understand now how you must have loved her very much and how you will probably always love her. Are you sure that Annie is the one? Are you sure of your choice? I do not wish to see Annie destroyed, but I want you to be sure."

"Yes. Sara is a wonderful woman and I will always love her, but I'm one hundred percent positive of my choice. Annie is the one for me. She will always be the one for me."

Sara is smiling as she walks out of the guest bedroom.

"Ting agreed to talk to the other elders. She seems confident they will want to extend an invitation to the High Council. She is very curious and welcomes the meeting. She believes the other elders will wish to meet the High Council." She frowns. "Let me go check on Lisa. I'm worried about her." She walks back into the master bedroom.

I'm paying attention to Sara's actions and I can tell how much she cares about Lisa, but I wonder if it will turn into something else. I have a fleeting thought that maybe Sara's serum can cure Lisa and give her a chance. I want to suggest this to Sara, because I want to ask her to give Annie her serum.

I know this is a lot to ask of her. I can just see the headlines now. *Ex-lover gives gift to new lover to enable happily ever after for an ex she still loves.* Yep, I'm an asshole. I don't know who else to ask.

I'm sure as hell not going to ask that drooling shit bag, Ting. I know I'm not being fair, because she is agreeing to meet with the High Council, which will save my ass, but I still don't like what I view as her excessive attention to Annie.

I wonder if I can ask Vic, but I don't know if her serum is strong enough or if you have to have a natural born or elder bite someone to give them the life healing serum. These are all questions I need to ask, but how do I ask them without coming across as a selfish prig. I'm pretty sure there is no way around it because, in fact, I am a selfish prig.

I wonder if Lisa or Annie will accept the gift of extended life as a shape-shifter. I know Annie doesn't have any close family, but she does have Vic's family's love and support. I'm pretty sure Vic is getting ready to tell her family about all the changes in herself, so one more daughter being a shape-shifter is probably no big deal. Lisa's mom is already gone, so she only has her father to contend with and I feel confident he would want her to live even if it means she has to become a shape-shifter.

I'm interrupted from my internal musings by Sara's ring tone, *Born to be Wild*. I chuckle because I would never categorize Sara as wild, but now that I know she is a shape-shifter, I guess it fits. She must still have her wry sense of humor.

Sara has her cell phone plastered against her ear. "Yeah, okay...Yeah, I think that would be best... All right. I will make flight arrangements as soon as I can. Nicky can stay with Lisa. Sure, no problem."

She punches the button on her phone to end the call and looks up at me. "I assume you heard. They want me to fly back so that we can all meet with the High Council together. I'm sure I can get a flight out tonight or early tomorrow morning and we can set up the meeting for tomorrow, probably early afternoon. How does one o'clock sound?"

The phone call from Ting seems quick. I didn't think Sara would make the arrangements so quickly. I wonder if they have been waiting for an opportunity to meet with the High Council and my fuck-up has provided them the perfect situation to capitalize on.

"That sounds perfect." I turn to Cass. "Can you let the High Council know?"

"Yes, I will act as a liaison and provide proper introductions. If I sense there is an opportunity to add to the discussion on your behalf, I will do so. Although this is serious, the High Council is fair minded. I believe they will listen to another perspective and this may go in your favor."

"Thanks, Cass. I don't deserve to have you in my corner, but I'm glad that you are."

"Nicky, you often sell yourself short. You do not believe you are worthy enough, but you are. We all have our imperfections. This does not make us unworthy of love or happiness. I almost lost Vic to my—how do you put it—oh yes, my propensity to be a *tight ass*. Your impulsiveness is who you are, it is something that may get you in trouble, but it is not something you need to change. Temper perhaps—but not change. Annie would not love you if you were more like me and less like you."

"I agree. Nicky, you are a wonderful woman." Sara smiles in my direction. "You have to stop believing you are not deserving of the love and support we all want to provide. Well, not Ting, but she has her own agenda."

I let a tear trickle down my cheek and pull them both into a group hug. They are both somewhat stiff to the hug for what I assume are very different reasons, but then they relax and we're all hugging and crying together.

Sara breaks from the hug. "I'd better make my flight arrangements."

I'm eager to be alone with Lisa. I want to get her to admit to her feelings for Sara and to feel her out on my plan. Maybe, just maybe, everything will work out. I'm hopeful for the first time since this whole mess started.

Chapter Nineteen

Sara gets a flight out for later that night. She throws necessary items into her travel bag, then goes back into the bedroom to give Lisa an update on the latest developments.

As she walks out the front door, she looks back at me. "Please take care of her, Nicky. She's not as strong as she wants us to believe. I don't think the chemo is working. I can smell the cancer all over her body and it's spread to other areas."

Apparently, shifters have an enhanced sense of smell and are more accurate at detecting cancer than any fancy piece of imaging equipment. Not that I have anything to worry about now, but I think I would much rather have a beautiful shifter sniffing me than go for a CAT scan or mammo.

I know that she has to leave, so I don't tell her about my idea for Lisa. Instead, I just look her directly in the eye. "Don't worry, Sara, you know how much I love Lisa. I'll take good care of her. I promise."

Cass, who was standing there, fogs out. I presume it's to meet up with Vic and Annie who are probably still at the compound.

I wonder if Annie knows about the latest developments. I want her to meet Lisa, but I want the plan to be in effect first. I hope it's not too late for Lisa. It seemed to take a while for the serum to work on Vic. I don't completely understand how it all works, so the sooner I can set the plan in motion, the better.

I knock lightly on Lisa's bedroom door before I enter. "Hey, can I come in?"

Lisa looks like shit, but her eyes are open.

She motions me in. "Same old Nicky. You sure have a way of attracting trouble." She chuckles. I know she is teasing me.

I sit on the edge of her bed.

I decide it's time to clear away all the bullshit and get everything out in the open. "Lisa, I'm sorry, but I know. I know you're in love with Sara. I read your mind. I know I shouldn't have done that, but I'm glad I did. I'm not mad or anything. I'm happy about it. I want you and Sara to get together."

Lisa looks shocked by what I've just said. She opens her mouth, but nothing comes out.

Of course, I revert to my *go to* state of action and start blabbering like a fool. "Look, I know things are kinda fucked up now, but I have a plan. See, I realize that you being in love with Sara is a good thing. I think now that we have closure and you know all our secrets, Sara has a clear path to see you in a different light. I know she loves you. She's just never had the opportunity to see you in a different way. I mean, what's not to love. You are gorgeous, funny, warm, and loving. If I wasn't so in love with Annie, I might try to jump your bones. No, wait, this is coming out all wrong. I mean you are wonderful. You would be so easy to fall in love with. I think you should tell her how you feel. It might get her to consider things differently. I see the way she looks at you with love and concern. She just needs to hear how you feel and I'll bet that will start the ball rolling. So what do you think? Am I right?"

Lisa starts laughing and then she starts coughing.

I pull her into my arms and hold her until her coughing fit stops.

She has a smile on her face as she looks at me. "God, Nicky, I've really missed you." Her smile fades. "Here's the truth. Yeah, I've been in love with Sara for a long time. I never wanted to get in the middle of your relationship. It's way too late now. The chemo's not really working. I'm dying, Nicky. I don't think I have more than six months. It's a nice fairy tale to think that after all these years I might be able to share my feelings for Sara and have her fall madly in love with me, but that's just not possible anymore."

I'm not about to give up. "Yes it is, Lisa."

She starts to respond.

I hold my hand up. "Wait, just listen to me. Shape-shifters are not just long lived, they have this serum that can be transferred to a human. The serum speeds up the healing process and there is a small side effect where you would feel the call to shift, but it's a small price to pay. Maybe the serum can cure your cancer, then you and Sara can live a long happy life together and make lots of little baby shifters."

"What does Sara think about this?" Lisa looks as though she might be considering this new information.

"Um, I don't know. I haven't had the time to talk with her about it yet. Besides, I'm kinda in some serious shit right now and she's had to concentrate on helping save my ass. I know that's not really fair to you because you really need her now—probably more than me."

"I don't think a day to two is going to matter much to me, but I do believe it will make a lot of difference to your predicament. She told me a little of what is going on and you're in trouble because of me, so stop beating yourself up."

"How would you feel about becoming a shape-shifter if that is a possible outcome?"

"Wow, I've never really considered the possibility of living past the age of thirty five. I guess I settled into the reality that I'm dying. If I'm completely honest with myself, I would say I don't want to die and I'm willing to try anything."

"Awesome. So here's the plan. Everything has been kinda wonky lately, so I'm sure Sara isn't even thinking straight right now. Maybe she hasn't considered the possibility that her serum could be the answer. I can talk to her about that, but you have to tell her how you really feel about her."

"I can't believe I'm talking to *you* of all people about this. I've kept this a secret for so long, that I don't know how to tell her now. If the serum works, she might think I'm saying this because I'm so grateful to her for saving my life. I don't know, Nicky. We have a really good friendship. I don't want to fuck that up. She walked out of my life before and I don't know if I can chance losing her as a friend again. She just came back and I should be grateful for that and not be greedy for more."

"You deserve to be happy too. Sara needs love in her life and if I can't give it to her, I want it to be you. I know she's basically been doing the same thing I did for ten plus years. She had a one night stand with Cass's lover and I suspect that's her life right now—a series of brief affairs. Trust me, I lived that, it is no way to exist. It doesn't feed your soul like loving someone does. I know that now."

I know that I'm rambling, but I still have to tell her a little about Annie. "I can't wait for you to meet Annie—that is if she's still talking to me after our one month separation. You're gonna love her—I hope not in the same way you love Sara, because I may be okay with Sara, but you better not fucking fall in love with Annie, too. I'll admit to being a tad possessive with Annie."

"No worries. I've met some really wonderful women and none of them touches me like Sara. I've always loved her and I think I always will." Lisa shakes her head. "God, what a relief it is to finally admit that to you. It was killing me to think that every day I saw Sara and continued to feel that way about her, I was betraying our friendship."

"I understand. It's all going to work out. I promise. If all else fails, I'm gonna be here to hold your hand. I'll do whatever it takes to try to save you even if it means turning you into a vampire. It's not such a bad life. There are definitely a lot of perks to being a vamp. It's late and I promised Sara I would take good care of you and you need to sleep. I'll be right here if you need me. Okay?"

"Okay. I think the worst of the side effects are over and I don't think I'll get sick again. I'm really tired now. Thanks, Nicky. You're the best. I really mean that."

I push back a strand of Lisa's limp blonde hair as her breath gets shallow and she starts to fall asleep. She looks so fragile. I hope we're not too late to save her and I vow to talk to Sara as soon as she gets back. I climb into bed with Lisa and put my arms around her in an effort to protect her and keep the cancer from eating away at more of her body. I fall asleep with my arms wrapped around her. This scene has played itself out before, only Lisa was the one who wrapped her arms around me and held me as I cried myself to sleep after Sara left. Everything seems to come full circle. Besides Cass and Vic, Lisa is the best friend I ever had. I guess now Sara will also become a good friend. At least I hope that is what will happen.

†

I slowly become aware of my surroundings as the sun filters into the room. Shit, I forgot about the sun. I have to close the blinds before the sun filters completely into the room.

Lisa stirs.

She is too sick to take care of this for me and I don't want to cause her any more pain. I carefully remove my arms and slip out of bed. As I cross the room to attend to the blinds, I feel a pain so excruciating it renders me completely helpless. I double over in pain as the sunshine blankets my body. *Stupid, stupid, stupid.* How can I forget about this? I bite my tongue to avoid crying out in pain. I guess it's all moot now, because I'm probably not going to survive this.

I don't know what happens when we're exposed to the sun and we haven't drained a human. I wonder do we die or do we just suffer in pain until the sun sets again? I don't know if I can honestly survive this level of pain for that many hours. I haven't ever bothered to ask what happens. It's all a mystery to me.

I close my eyes in an effort to block out the sunshine and stop this searing pain. It doesn't work. As I'm writhing in pain on the bedroom floor, the room is suddenly dark again. I think this is it— I'm dead now.

I feel a soft hand on my shoulder and I jump so high my head hits the ceiling. "What the fuck?"

I'm back down on the floor after my close encounter with the ceiling.

Cass is looking down at me. "Sabrina felt your pain and telegraphed it to me. She did not know where to find you, but she believed I would know. I needed to be at the compound today for the meeting, so I went out on a hunt last night. I've closed the blinds. You have to be careful, Nicky. The sunshine can create excruciating pain if you have not hunted the night before."

"No shit, Sherlock. I forgot to do that with everything else going on. Would I have died?"

"No, but you certainly would have wished for death. This is why the High Council's most extreme sanction is so devastating. Even with a permanent thrall to avoid the sun, there is always a chance for exposure as an unaware vampire lives out their life without blood."

"Thank you, Cass. You seem to be always pulling my ass out of the fire."

Lisa moves in the bed, yawns, and opens her eyes. She manages to pull herself to a sitting position and looks at Cass who is standing in her bedroom.

"Uh, good morning." She glances down at me on the floor. "What's going on? Nicky, you don't look so good." She looks back at Cass. "Sorry for my ghastly appearance. I don't think we've met. I'm Lisa."

Lisa tries to get up.

I don't want her to try to be a good host so I stop her. "No, don't get up. I'll get the coffee and make us some breakfast, because I know that's where you were heading. I just had a minor mishap. I forgot about the sun coming in through the window this morning. Cass came to the rescue and shut the blind for me." I turn to Cass. "Would you mind checking out the kitchen and closing the blinds in there?"

"Oh, I'm so sorry, I don't have blinds in the kitchen. I'm feeling okay this morning. I think I can handle coffee and eggs," Lisa says.

God bless Cass who steps in. "Hello, Lisa. It is an honor to finally meet you. I am a friend of Nicky's. My name is Cassandara, or you may call me Cass. Nicky has spoken fondly of you. We don't require food, but I believe I can find my way around a kitchen. What would you like to eat this morning? Or would you prefer I go out and bring something back?"

I'm so happy Cass found Vic, because she is such a good egg and she deserves all the happiness that Vic brings her

"I don't understand." Lisa blinks her eyes. "Are you a vampire too?"

Cass nods her head.

"How can you be in the sunshine, but Nicky can't?" Lisa asks.

"Vampires can only be in the sunshine if we drain a host."

I rush to explain the rest, because I think the explanation will come better from me. "We have a strict code, one I have never violated. They only allow us to drain deserving hosts. I may be a fuck up and violate some of the vampire code, but I've never violated this part of the code. We're like your modern day vigilantes. If you watch the show, *Dexter*, we're sorta like that, only we don't chop people up and dispose of the bodies. Every human who we drain, deserves it. Trust me on that one. We've probably saved countless lives by taking care of the worst of society."

"So, what happened to you this morning?"

"A little bit of pain." I shrug. "No big deal."

Cass glares at me.

Lisa looks back at me. "Why do I get the impression you've just glossed over a few things?"

"Nicky can be very foolish and she sometimes does not realize the consequences of her actions or her lack of attention to details."

"Boy, you sure have her pegged correctly. She has mentioned you. You must be a good friend and I'm glad she has someone in her life to keep her out of trouble." Lisa looks wistful. "I haven't been able to be that for her in quite some time."

"Yes, well, even if I did not wish to have this role in her life, I am afraid I have no choice now."

Cass is referring to the previous sanction from the High Council. They dictated that Cass has to continue to mentor me—keep me under wraps and out of trouble. I try not to think of her as my jailor and don't really mind the sanction. Cass grows on you.

"Aw, Cass, you know you love me. I've been a good influence on you. You're not as big a tight ass as you were. I still have my work cut out for me, but you are making some progress. Good thing we were sanctioned to live together with Annie and Vic, or I might not be able to help you as much as necessary."

Lisa and Cass both laugh.

"Lisa, what can I make or get you for breakfast?" Cass offers.

"As long as you're offering, I'd die for a breakfast burrito from the little Mexican stand down the road. It's about three blocks away."

Lisa looks a little better this morning and I'm grateful for that. She misses my cringe at her words, *I'd die for a breakfast burrito*. It reminds me of her impending mortality unless we can turn things around.

Cass smiles at Lisa.

I've already told her about Lisa's cancer, so I suspect she can tell how ill she is. I love her for wanting to help.

"I think I can find it. Nicky, would you like one, as well?"

"Yeah, that sounds great. I'm afraid I'm gonna have to stay in the bedroom where it's dark until sunset tonight. I hope that will be okay."

"Of course," Lisa says. "I should probably hang out here anyway. Although I'm feeling much better today, I'm still not ready to run a marathon."

Cass disappears in the blink of an eye and returns about ten minutes later with three enormous breakfast burritos.

171

Lisa's eyes glimmer with excitement and it's as if she's no longer sick.

Cass hands Lisa a large orange juice.

I get a vanilla latte with extra cinnamon.

Lisa arches her eyebrows. "I guess I'm not getting any coffee this morning."

Cass looks down at her feet and mumbles. "I've read somewhere that juice is better for you after treatment."

Lisa smiles at Cass.

I think she is clearly touched by this simple gesture.

✝

Lisa and I entertain Cass with our escapades during college.

She is not surprised to learn about how our antics are legendary.

Lisa is laughing hard as she tells her about her short-lived sorority chapter.

"See, Nicky didn't much like my sorority sisters, Missy and Amanda. So, one night she sneaks into the sorority house and writes in indelible marker on the official Tri Delta shirt—that we're supposed to wear at official hosting functions—*I'm not a lesbian, but my girlfriend is.* I think it's hysterical, so I'm laughing so hard I'm about to pee my pants. My sorority sisters didn't think it was very funny. Even though they knew it was Nicky, they couldn't prove it. The story got around to the frat houses and they dubbed Missy, Mysticpussy and Amanda, A*man*dontdo. When they heard the names they had been given, they demanded that I move out of the dorm room and stop hanging out with two well-known lesbians. I told them to fuck off."

I chime in with my own version of the story. "Did I ever tell you that Missy caught me in Starbucks one day and started ranting and raving at me? So I announced loud enough for everyone to hear, *Aw, baby, don't be that way. Everyone gets pubes caught in their teeth when they eat pussy. If you want me to shave next time, I will.* That shut her up and for the next four years whenever I saw

172

her or Amanda they sprinted in the other direction. I think they missed their calling. They should have gone out for track, but they probably thought there were too many dykes on the team."

Cass looks at her watch. We've been having such a good time going down memory lane that time has just flown by.

"I'm sorry, I have to leave shortly. The meeting with the High Council is in a few minutes. I cannot be late. This meeting is important to Nicky's future."

"Thanks, Cass. Will I have to be present after they talk with the elders? I won't be able to leave until Sara gets back. Can you please explain that to them?"

"I will try but I really must go now." Cass looks down at her watch again then disappears in a fog.

Lisa turns her piercing gaze back to me. "Okay, Nicky, spill. How much trouble are you in?"

I go into a long diatribe about my current situation.

"I was pissed and I kinda got a little overzealous with this guy who kidnapped Vic, Cass's lover. I don't really have time to give you all the gory details, but here's the reader's digest version of what happened. There were these four guys who started this sick club called the *Wallflower Club* and they would go around picking out women to rape and sometimes murder. Unfortunately, Annie was one of their victims.

"When Cass first met me, I was doing a little *clean-up* work with one of those four sick bastards. Shortly after, we started tracking down the other three club members, but we had to be careful not to drain them all too quickly. It was already a little dicey that two of the four young healthy men died under suspicious circumstances. We wanted to spread out the deaths.

"Anyway, one club member got nervous. He was convinced that Vic was somehow responsible for the other's deaths. In his pea brain, he thought that since Vic was present at the assault and her efforts to get the case prosecuted failed, this was somehow related, so he kidnapped her. He had no idea that, quite coincidently, we were already tracking these fuckers down.

"So anyhow, Vic saw everything and we had to reveal ourselves to Vic and Annie. We would have done it anyway. I wasn't about to keep that secret from Annie. Anyway, I kinda promised I wouldn't reveal myself to anyone else, but when Sara told me you were in trouble, I ignored my promise. Now we're trying to argue that the code is outdated."

"Okay, so you've told me why you're in trouble, but you still haven't told me how much trouble and what the consequences are."

"They don't execute you or anything barbaric like that."

"You're still not telling me anything. I think I have a right to know since I'm the cause."

"You are not the cause. I wanted an excuse to tell my family anyway—this just helped pave the way."

"Come on. What's going to happen to you?"

"Hopefully, nothing. It's a stupid fucking rule."

"They must have made it for a good reason. I think you should try to see things from their perspective. It might help."

"I know, but they should try to see things from my viewpoint too."

"It sounds like they are. It appears as though you are the one not trying to understand."

"Hey, whose side are on you on anyway?"

"Yours, Nicky, always yours. Now, tell me what might happen to you."

"The worst they can do is take away my special gifts and make me forget I'm a vampire. I could care less about that, but I do care about not remembering Annie. I don't even care about not seeing the sun again. It's Annie I can't live without."

"Oh, I'm so sorry, Nicky. I really have to meet this Annie. You must really love her."

"I do, I really do. I'm not sorry for what I did. I would do it again. I'm glad I came with Sara, but it would suck if I lost Annie and went back to my former life."

"Sara still loves you. Maybe it would work out between you two."

"No, I don't think so. She would always know that I chose Annie. Really, Lisa, our time has passed. I don't know how I know this, but I just think you two have a real future. She hasn't seen what's been right in front of her eyes all along, but she will."

"It may be too late for all of us."

"Nope, I refuse to believe that. I want that happy ending like in Annie's books."

"Annie's books? Is Annie a writer?"

"Oh. my God, that's right, you don't know. Annie is famous. She writes all those hot lesbian vampire books—you know, the ones they made that blockbuster movie about. Ironic, huh?"

"God, I love those books. They used to get me so hot. I wish I still had the energy to get hot. Chemo really sucks the life out of you."

"Why don't you take a nap? It looks like we tired you out. It will probably be a while before I know anything anyway. It might help to have a distraction. Got any smutty novels I can read while you nap?"

"Sure. Gabby bought a ton. They're all on my Kindle. It's on the side table there."

Lisa settles in for her nap. It doesn't take her long to fall asleep.

I'm happy for the distraction reading will provide as I wait to learn my fate.

†

An hour and a half passes and there is still no word. I'm getting nervous now. How can the meeting possibly take that long? I start imagining every little possible catastrophe. Cass can't bring herself to tell me that the most severe sanction is their answer and I'll never see Annie again. I think this serves me right for being such a fuck up. I have absolutely no remorse for my behavior. Lisa's right, I make no attempt to try to understand their viewpoint. I suck.

Just as this thought process starts spiraling out of control, Cass's gentle touch on my shoulder startles me. I don't realize she's back.

She smiles down at me.

I take that as a good sign. I don't want to wake Lisa up because she needs her rest, so I motion for her to meet me in the living room.

I sit on the couch and look at Cass expectantly. "Well, what happened? Are you going to tell me, or are you waiting for the tooth fairy to give you permission?"

"No need to be snarky. I know you are nervous, but it is better than expected. The shape-shifters are very gracious hosts. The elders and the High Council had a very nice discussion about one another's perspective on the code. We were able to sway the High Council to consider a more temperate position. Sara gave a very impassioned plea on your behalf and helped them understand the depth of your relationship and loyalty to Lisa. I added a few of my own observations, which I believe helped. You remain on probation. I am required to continue to mentor you as outlined in the previous sanction. You are forbidden to reveal yourself to your family until you are prepared to present your case to the High Council. They have indicated they will consider your request, but you must give them the respect of their years of wisdom and ask *prior* to acting."

I grab Cass and pull her into a grateful hug. She is stiff at first but then hugs me back. I think Vic is having a good influence on her.

"Oh, my God, Cass, that is the best fucking news I've heard all day."

"Nicole, you know how I feel about profanity. I have relaxed my stance when you are angry or frustrated, but must you also use profanity when you are happy?"

"Sorry. Old habits...."

"Sara is in the process of arranging for a flight back and will probably arrive sometime this evening."

"How's Annie? Have you seen her? Is she doing okay? Has she asked about me?"

"She is doing fine. She knows all about the meetings with the High Council. Give her a little more time. She is still not sure about what will make you happy. She is glad to hear you will be helping Lisa. It reminds her of who you are, Nicky. She still loves you. Of that, I am sure. You must have faith."

"I do, Cass, I do. I will never give up, unless I think she'll be happier without me."

"She will not and someday she will realize that you will not be happier without her. How is your friend?"

"I'm sure you must realize she is dying. Sara says she smells the cancer all over her and she doesn't think she has much time. She confessed that she's in love with Sara, but she's dying and the chemo is not working. I told her she needs to tell Sara how she feels. I'm gonna ask Sara to give her some serum, because maybe it will alter the effect of the cancer on her body."

"I do not think you should get your hopes up. I suspect if that were an option, Sara would have already tried it."

"She didn't bite me all those years ago."

"True, but you were not dying."

"It doesn't hurt to ask."

"Yes, that is true. I just do not wish for you to count on this making everything all right. Will you be okay if I get back to Vic? I feel like an inadequate partner. I have not been able to spend much time with her since everything started happening yesterday. It has been quite a journey these past couple of days."

"Of course. Go back to Vic and if it's okay, will you please tell Annie I love her and I miss her."

"She knows."

Cass disappears.

I'm so relieved that my sigh is probably audible to Lisa sleeping peacefully in the next room. I settle back into the bedroom with the Kindle, but this time I can concentrate on the love story in the book I'm starting to read. I completely forget about asking Cass for leads in Los Angeles, but I don't worry too much. I'm sure I'll find the seedy parts of town again and something will come my way.

Lisa wakes from her nap.

I get her something to eat.

Her brief rally is gone. Her skin looks more pallid than it did earlier in the day. I can tell she's struggling and I feel helpless to make her feel better. The soup I bring her promptly comes back up.

"I'm so sorry. I wish you didn't have to see me like this," she says.

"It's okay. Don't worry, hon, everything will work out."

I don't want to find a drainee until Sara gets back. I want to tell her about my plan first.

†

Sara quietly enters the brownstone. It's midnight.

Lisa is finally asleep again.

"How is she?" Sara asks.

"She's had a rough day. After an initial rally this morning when Cass was here, she's taken a turn for the worse. She's been sick and in pain all day."

Sara's look is grief stricken.

I hate how distraught she appears by my update. It seems to be the perfect time to offer my idea. "Look, Sara, I know you don't want Lisa to be in pain."

"Of course I don't."

I ignore the irritation in her tone because I know she is just worried about Lisa. "Have you thought about biting her and giving her some of your serum? It works ninety percent of the time, maybe it can work with Lisa."

Sara has a pained expression on her face. "Oh, God, Nicky, if only it were that simple. Don't you think we would save so many people with cancer if it were that easy? Once a person becomes terminal our serum doesn't work. It only works on healthy humans. Even on a healthy human, the serum doesn't work for several months—Vic didn't feel the effect of the serum for eight months."

"Oh." I look at her and smile. It's time to tell her. "I know I shouldn't have done it, but I kinda read her mind and well, she loves you, you know?"

"Yes, and I love her too."

"No, I mean she's in love with you. She has been for a long time. I'm telling you this now, because I don't think she will when she learns your serum won't help. She told me the chemo isn't working and she's gonna die."

Sara sits down heavily on the couch and begins to sob. "Oh, Nicky, what are we going to do?"

Her reaction tells me all I need to know. I'm convinced she's in love with Lisa and just doesn't know it yet. I ask her, "Do you think you might be in love with her, too?"

"I don't know. I never really thought of her in that way. It's a lot to take in right now. I know with every fiber of my being that I don't want her to die. I don't want to lose her or to ever lose touch again. She was the only other person I kept tabs on."

"I've been reading the old vampire documents that outline our history. I've been wanting to ensure a way to turn Annie, because I don't think I can bear losing her like Cass lost Vic—well, Verina—because I'm pretty sure Vic is a reincarnation of Verina, Cass's first lover. I suppose I could wait five hundred years like Cass did, but you know patience is not my strong suit. Anyway, most of the time, there is a strong connection between the human and the vampire. It hasn't always been a lover's connection. I was a fluke. Sabrina managed to give me her blood at just the right time, but that was just pure dumb luck. I think I can turn Lisa, but that means I have to be by her side just as she's passing. What do you think? Do you think she'll go for it?"

"I think it's our only option at this point." Sara gets a hopeful look in her eyes. "The chemo isn't working and it's tearing her body apart. Regardless, I think she should stop the chemo. We can take turns caring for her."

"I'm in—no matter what happens between Annie and me. If we get back together, do you think it will be odd if Annie comes here to help? I'm pretty sure she would want to do that."

"No, I'd like to get to know Annie. I think it will be weird at first, but I think it could work out."

"Me, too. Will you open yourself to the possibility of Lisa as your lover?"

"We'll see. I can't force something, but I'll admit that, although I've never considered it before, I do care a great deal for her. Who knows what the future will bring? I've always known that Lisa is a wonderful woman. I need to check on her now."

I follow Sara into Lisa's bedroom.

Lisa stirs and smiles at Sara. "You're back."

"Yeah, and everything is great. No more trips needed. Nicky got lucky again," Sara tells Lisa.

"Oh, I'm so glad."

"You're stuck with both of us now. We'll be right here for as long as you need us."

"Thanks. I love you guys. I'm pretty tired right now, but starting tomorrow I would like to pass the time by you filling me in completely on both of your lives. I want details of the missing years."

I grin at Lisa. "You got it. I think we'd all like to know about those missing years."

Lisa's eyes flutter as she settles in and falls back to sleep.

Chapter Twenty

Lisa has stopped getting chemotherapy treatments.

It looks like she's having a good day, because I don't see her grimace in pain.

We decide to spend some time in the sun. Fortunately, I'd hunted the night before and am prepared to join them.

Lisa glances over at Sara.

Sara nods.

I don't fully understand the look that passes between them.

Lisa breaks the silence. "Tell me about Annie. I want to know everything. I want to know how you met."

I glance at Sara and wonder if my story will be painful for her to hear.

She smiles back at me.

I get the feeling Lisa and Sara have already discussed this and Sara is ready to hear our story.

At first, it feels awkward talking about Annie. Sara seems genuinely interested, so I tell them all about her. It becomes a bit therapeutic for me as I remember the past seven months and my life with Annie.

"All right, I'd love to tell you about Annie...."

My memories are one of the few things sustaining me now and I relay most of them to Lisa and Sara.

†

I remember the first time I see Annie. She captures my heart that very first night.

I manage to drag Cass out for a night of fun. She tells me, *I'd really rather not, Nicole, but I do not have a choice, do I?*

I remind her of the orders from the High Council and that she can't leave me to troll the bars alone.

I hear the music before I even step foot into The Orchid. The music has a sweet, haunting sound that literally pulls me inside. I glance at the stage because I want to know the singer whose voice is responsible for that angelic sound.

I'm not prepared to encounter the sky blue pools that meet my gaze and seem to penetrate my soul. I feel an instant peace and calm. This is unlike any other feeling I've ever experienced. This beautiful angel literally takes my breath away.

Cass looks at me. "Please refrain from thralling that poor girl on stage. I sense she is very fragile and I do not wish you to shatter her."

I've learned that Cass has a sixth sense about people. I also have a special sensitivity to emotionally damaged humans and I feel how special she is. I'm not about to pass up an opportunity to meet this beautiful woman.

Fortunately for me, Cass is staring at Vic and makes a beeline for her table, which is right in front of the stage.

I follow her without taking my eyes off Annie, who is singing onstage.

Cass introduces herself to Vic and offers to buy her a glass of wine.

I notice her stiff introduction and give her a few pointers on the way to the bar.

As I'm getting my beer, Cass is running back to the table with the wine for Vic. My eyes travel to the stage and I catch Annie looking in my direction.

She blushes and looks down.

I love how shy she seems. It's especially endearing to me. I instinctively know I need to tread lightly and go very slowly if I want to get to know her.

Cass is such a goober. After she comes back to the table with the wine, she introduces herself again and uses both of her hands as she gently strokes and caresses Vic's palm. She places a soft kiss on the underside of Vic's hand and gives Vic some bullshit line about it being a European handshake and it works.

This is genius thinking. I figure *what the hell*, I might as well try this with Annie. I think I'm being all smooth, but I find myself wanting to treat her with love and respect. I go slow and ask her permission. I can tell she is struggling with what I think is an innocuous touch. I remember thinking at the time that I wonder what makes her so fragile and suspect that she's endured some kind of trauma. I desperately wanted to be the one to take away all her pain.

I gently take her hand in mine and with just the barest of touches press my lips to her palm. My touch is like a butterfly landing on her hand. I have a visceral reaction to this connection. It feels like home. Every other person in the room, including Cass, fades into the background. In my mind, we are the only ones that occupy this space.

†

Our first date is an evening at the theatre. I'm not prepared for how epic Annie looks when we pick her and Vic up the next evening.

I'm feeling a little out of place with the silk button-down turquoise shirt and tailored black pants Cass makes me wear.

Annie enters the room in her snug, low rise jeans and slowly approaches our group.

I notice how timid she still is, but she looks directly at me. I instantly melt inside her beautiful blue eyes.

I can't help myself when I start rambling trying to expel my nervous energy. "Annie, you look amazing. I mean really spectacular. Not that you didn't look good last night. I couldn't take my eyes off you. I told Cass it was okay to wear jeans. Look what she made me wear—a stupid monkey suit. I'm wearing my Levi's next time—that's for sure. But really, shut the front door, you look epic in those jeans."

Three sets of eyes just stare wide eyed at me, as I make a total ass of myself before letting them know I'm done rambling. "Okay, shutting up now."

"I think your outfit is perfect, Nicky. I'm glad she made you wear it. I...I...don't really have any nice clothes, so I had to wear jeans. I should have gone shopping. I'm sorry." Annie whispers her response.

I jump in because I don't want this wonderful person to feel inferior in any way. "No, no way, this really isn't mine. I had to borrow these clothes. What you are wearing is perfect. We are the ones who will be overdressed tonight. Trust me on this. We will be in the minority, not you." I glare at Cass.

Vic jumps in. "Well, I don't care if I'm in the minority, I will take any excuse I can get to put on my sexy red dress, and Cass, you look wonderful. The dress suits you. Annie, your outfit suits you, as well. No second guessing. We all look amazing. Let's have a toast and get this evening off to a good start."

✝

Our third date is almost cancelled when one of Vic's friends stops by unannounced.

When we arrive, Annie is cloistered away in one of the bedrooms.

"I messed up this morning. I'm so sorry. Annie heard my friend and me talking about something and it's upset her. I tried to calm her down, but things are...well,...they're...uh...difficult for her now. She's barely holding it together," Vic tells us.

I'm desperate to have Annie join us, so I offer to talk to her. I think Vic sees something in me that night and allows me to talk to Annie.

I find my way upstairs and take a deep breath before I knock lightly on Annie's door. "Annie, it's Nicky. I know you probably aren't in the mood to talk with anyone right now, but if you let me in..." I pause. "You call the shots—whatever you need. I just need to make sure you're okay. You don't have to say a word. I'm going to open the door now and if you want me to go, just shake your head no and I'll leave. I promise."

I'm extra careful as I open the bedroom door. What I see breaks my heart.

Annie is sitting on the bed with a tissue in her hand. It's obvious to me she's been crying.

She doesn't look up, but she doesn't shake her head no either.

I quickly push forward. "Anytime you want me to leave, all you have to do is shake your head. I'm going to take a step inside the room now. Okay?"

Annie's nod is so subtle, I almost miss it.

"Everything is going to be fine. You're doing great. Do you trust me?" She nods her head again. "That's great, Annie. I'm going to come in the room farther now. Still okay?"

Annie nods yes again.

"Would it be okay if I sat next to you on the bed if I leave some room between us?"

I notice that Annie's breathing begins to increase as she starts to hyperventilate.

I back off a little because I think she needs a little more time and space. "How about if I wait ten seconds before sitting on the bed? Would that be better?"

She looks up briefly at me and nods again. I hope she sees the concern in my eyes.

I'd like to think she does, because she continues to allow me to come farther into her bedroom. "Okay, I'm almost to the bed now, but I think I'll wait just a little longer to give you a chance to get comfortable."

I have keen hearing and I hear Annie's heart start to pound. I feel her fear. "I know this is scary stuff, Annie, but we can do this. You have all the power here."

I take a chance and ease myself gently onto her bed, barely causing a ripple. I'm not in a rush. For the first time in my life, I'm patient as I wait on the bed. I'm determined to let Annie do the driving and control everything. I sit with her in companionable silence for at least five minutes.

Finally, Annie speaks to me. I can barely hear her and I have supernatural hearing as a vampire.

"Why are you here?" Annie asks. "You can have anyone. Why bother with a broken toy. I know you date a lot of women."

I'm a total shit and I do fuck around a lot, but I want this to be different so I make my plea to her. "No, Annie, I don't date a lot of women. I have brief relationships. I don't want to do that anymore," I say emphatically. "You're not broken. I'm the broken one here. Trust me, brief meaningless relationships leave a person empty. I don't want to feel empty. Please help me with this emptiness I feel."

I can't believe it as I start to cry. I'm not playing on her emotions or trying to score with her. I feel real emotion and it slips out. This is enough to break the impasse.

Annie reaches over and takes my hand.

I've never felt more joy than in that simple gesture. I think I fall in love with her at that exact moment.

"I don't know why I trust you, but I do. One step forward, two steps back—but today—maybe just for today—it will be two steps forward, one step back." She hurries on. "I want to go sailing today. I want to take that second step forward now."

My heart swells just like the Grinch and I swear it becomes ten times its original size. "Oh, Annie, I can't even put into words how frickin' awesome that is. We had better head downstairs. I'll bet Cass and Vic been shitting big fat bricks the whole time we've been up here. Oops, sorry. I know I really need to clean up my language. Cass is always correcting me. I promised her I wouldn't cuss on our dates. Please don't tell her. She'll start again with the, *language Nicky, language, don't you know any other words than those of a common gutter rat.* Then I just shrug and piss her off again. She, like, never cusses. Have you ever heard of anyone who can't even say *shit*? I mean shit isn't really a bad word. There are lots of other words far worse—you know like fuck, or ass-wipe, or dick-wad. Oh, uh, shutting up now."

We have a wonderful day on the water and I amaze myself with how patient I am with her. I know that I love her, because I don't even try to kiss her for another month and a half.

†

I'll never forget that first time I kissed Annie. It happens when we go away for the long Labor Day weekend.

We enter this beautiful suite with a Jacuzzi tub and everything.

At first, it's awkward and I'm not quite sure what to say. "Uh, do you like the right or left side of the bed?"

"I...I...don't know. I usually sleep kind of in the center," Annie stutters.

She is so adorable when she's really nervous.

"How about you take the side closest to the window. It's a gorgeous view. That should be nice to wake up to," I offer.

"Not as lovely as seeing you first thing in the morning."

I'm flabbergasted as she makes this bold proclamation.

Annie slaps her hand to her mouth after saying this to me. I'm charmed and chuckle to ease her discomfort.

The next words just flow out of my mouth. "Oh, trust me, I'm only offering because I don't think there is a view in the world that will be more beautiful than seeing you lying beside me in the morning. I could easily learn to live with that every day of my life."

"That is so sweet. Thank you, Nicky. Thank you for giving me the option today. It means a lot."

When we first arrive at the resort, I make sure to give Annie the option to bunk with Vic instead of me because I don't want her to feel pressured. I'm really glad that she chooses to share the suite with me and I'm especially happy that I was smart enough to give her the option.

187

I want to know when it will be okay to kiss her, so I jump right in. "Can I ask you something personal?"

"Well, it can't get more personal than sharing a bed, so, yes."

"Will you tell me when you're ready for me to kiss you? I mean, I'll ask before I do it, but I kinda need a sign when it's okay to ask."

"I'm ready."

Oh, my God, I think I've landed in heaven. I sigh. I cannot imagine feeling more content.

"Annie, can I hold your hands?"

Annie nods.

"I'm gonna pull you close. Is that okay?"

"Yes."

"Can I touch your face now?"

"Yes."

"May I kiss you now?"

"Yes."

Annie begins to tremble. I don't think she's afraid. I'm pretty sure she is trembling in anticipation. I lean in and barely brush my lips against her mouth. It's the sweetest kiss I've ever experienced and I just know it's filled with the anticipation of future kisses.

"I think I would like it if you kissed me again—maybe a little longer."

I hesitate for a second. Annie comes closer. I gently take her bottom lip into my mouth and allow my tongue to caress her lips.

Annie's mouth opens to allow my entrance.

I don't realize how new this is to Annie.

She pulls away from the kiss.

I misread her signals. "I'm sorry. Oh, Annie, I'm so sorry. I didn't ask for permission to go that far with the kiss."

"No, it's okay, really okay. It's just I've never kissed anyone before. I don't understand what's happening. The sensation—it's really like how I describe in my books. I feel it all over. I feel it...um...you know...in other places."

"Oh, thank God. I'd be worried if you hadn't felt it in other places. It's a good thing, Annie. I promise—it's a good thing."

"I know. I write about it all the time. I just never thought it would happen to me. I'm surprised is all."

"A good surprise?"

"Oh, yes, a good surprise."

"Can I ask you another question?"

"Sure."

"Do you think I will be able to kiss you now without asking permission each time?"

"Yeah, I'd like that. Surprises aren't always easy for me, but I think I'd like those kinds of surprises."

I feel more confident as I gather Annie in my arms and deliver a passionate embrace. The two of us sway.

I feel Annie's legs give way, but I hold her close against my chest. "I've got you and if you'll have me, I'm never letting you go."

†

Annie and I don't make love for two months after we meet. It's oddly reminiscent of my first time with Sara. I tell her repeatedly that I can wait and I mean it. I'm willing to wait for her to be ready for however long it takes, because that is how much I love her.

After a spectacular day on the water, I barely get inside our suite when I embrace Annie. "You gave me permission to kiss you whenever, but I don't think I clarified where I have permission to kiss you. May I kiss your neck?"

Annie nods.

I begin kissing her neck and work my way to her mouth. Our kiss begins slowly, and as the intensity increases, I think both of us moan at the same time.

I put a small amount of distance between us, because I'm afraid of going too fast. "I'd better stop now, while I still have some semblance of control left."

I take Annie's hand and lead her to the sofa. I take a chance and ask Annie about the newspaper article that upset her earlier in the day. I've already done some research and I know it relates to the trauma Annie endured.

"I know it's probably none of my business and I probably shouldn't ask because it seemed to really upset you, but...."

"You want to know about the article in the newspaper?"

"Uh, yeah. I only ask because whatever it is, I want to do whatever I can to erase the bad memories and keep seeing your beautiful smile. I think I already know, but it might help to talk about it."

"Oh, believe me, I have—every week for the past three years with my therapist and every once in a while with Vic. Mostly I talk with Vic, because she feels so guilty for being the one to take me to the party and I don't want her to feel that way. It's old news. I just sorta got rattled when I saw the paper today. I'm okay now."

"Annie, I want you to know I will always be here for you. Whatever you believe, I want you to know that you are stronger than you think. You survived."

"Barely. Vic has been my only friend for so long. Then you came along."

"Well, I hope I'm more than a friend."

"You are. Can I ask you something personal?"

"Sure."

"Why do you need to clear your head?"

Since I have to find victims to drain, I've been slipping from our bed in the middle of the night. I've told Annie I have insomnia and sometimes have to take a walk to clear my head.

"In some ways you and I are not so different. When I say I understand, I mean it."

"You mean you were...I...I...can't even say the words. Isn't that pathetic?" Annie stutters.

I cannot even imagine how Annie has been able to recover from the trauma of being gang raped. Yeah, my beautiful Annie is a rape survivor like me, but she had to deal with four of those animals.

"No, it's not. The words are ugly to say. I understand. I have a confession to make. I did some research on you and Vicky. I found out about the case and when I saw the paper today, I put two and two together. I got angry and wanted to rip their limbs off. The other two, you know, because two are already dead. Cass calmed me down."

"Oh, Nicky. Thank you, but Vicky has already tried to be my crusader, and honestly, I never wanted to go after them. I just wanted to forget it ever happened. I know I'm a coward, but I just couldn't gather the strength to testify."

"I don't blame you at all. Karma has a way of taking care of everything."

I twirl my hair as I relish the knowledge that karma didn't take care of them—the vampires did. We got all of Annie's attackers. Sometimes being a vampire truly has its advantages. The world is a much better place now that those bastards are not roaming the earth.

"You know, I don't really understand it, but oddly, I do feel better. It's like I can talk about it with you because you understand and I'm not getting any flashbacks. You feel really safe."

"Annie, I love you. Oh, shit, I just said that out loud, didn't I? Sorry. Sometimes my mouth gets ahead of me and I blurt shit out. I'm impulsive and all that, but it doesn't mean I'm lying or anything. I'm not just saying that to get in your pants either. I can wait. Honestly, I can. I mean even though it has been a long time, I can still wait. Oh my God, I'm rambling again. Okay, shutting up."

Annie smiles. She takes my hand and leads me into the bedroom. "You might be able to wait, but I'm not sure I can anymore. Oh, and by the way, I love you, too."

"Oh." I'm rendered speechless.

I beam as I walk into the bedroom with Annie. "Can I undress you now?"

"Yes," Annie agrees.

I take my time with Annie. I'm savoring the experience much like a gourmet meal. I intend to roll every delectable bite around in my mouth and savor the taste. I remember every delicious moment.

Believe it or not, I'm shy at first. I'm wound so tight that one touch sends me spinning. I understand the saying, out of body experience. I feel like my body is floating.

I slowly work my mouth down Annie's torso, and her breathing becomes more irregular. I gingerly spread her legs. "Annie, can I please taste you?"

"Oh, my God, yes, Nicky. Please hurry."

I part her lips and run my tongue, feather light, up and down her clit. I can sense that the hint of things to come sends her into a tailspin. She arches her back and I wonder if she is doing that to seek more contact, but I won't be rushed. I take her engorged bud in my mouth and gently suck. Annie erupts like a volcano and calls out my name. I work my way back up, canvassing her body in little kisses and then take her gently into my arms.

I feel Annie stiffen and I'm so worried that I've rushed things. "Shh. It's okay. I'm sorry. It was too soon. Please tell me you don't regret making love."

I can barely hear Annie respond.

"I...I...I've never done this before. I don't know what to do next. I don't know how to please you."

"Oh, is that all you're worried about? Listen, I'm easy. Um, I don't mean it like I'm a slut easy," I say.

Annie giggles.

"I just mean that pretty much anywhere you want to touch me is okay. My whole body is one big erogenous zone. Here give me your hand. I'll guide you."

I take Annie's hand and guide her between my legs. I'm so wet and ready for her. I direct her to make small circles around my most sensitive areas. It takes less than a minute. Although I've been perfectly content to wait, my release is definitely overdue.

I can tell by Annie's reaction that she is awed by her ability to elicit this beautiful response from me. Annie begins to caress me and it seems like her touch is more daring now.

"Not that your touch isn't incredible, but I need to tell you it's one and done with me. I can really enjoy the afterglow, but you shouldn't feel bad if I can't climax again."

"Good to know. Can we just lie here together and touch one another?" she asks.

"Absolutely, I think I may also have to test out my theory that you are not the one and done type."

"Research is good," Annie remarks.

I burst out in laughter. My research continues well into the night and my theory proves to be correct. I'm also surprised to learn that I'm not a one and done type as Annie's talented tongue and hands explore my body all night long.

I don't tell Sara and Lisa every detail about Annie and my relationship with her, but I told them enough to let them know how much she means to me. I didn't tell them how we made love all night long. I also didn't explain how no other experience ever came close for me.

I never forgot my first time, because the memory of this moment with Annie was branded into my brain. Even if I live to be ten thousand years old, I will never forget my first time with Annie.

The rest of my memories, I let swirl around in my head and I place them on an imaginary shelf, as I gaze longingly at them every night that we were apart.

I will do anything to get Annie back. She is my world.

Chapter Twenty-one

Sara and I settle into our caregiver roles.

Late in the evenings, I get to know the seedier parts of Los Angeles. California might be all sun, surf, and sand to everyone else, but the sun doesn't shine on the rats that frequent the back alleys. The grease and grime caked all over the brick walls of the bars we frequent shines like black tar. I don't even want to get anywhere near those walls—it's as disgusting as the dish room back in college.

Cass comes to visit every few days and although she doesn't talk much about Annie, I get the feeling that things are okay— status quo for now—no real changes.

Lisa's pain continues to get worse, so Sara hires a home care nurse. We are desperate to keep her comfortable. Sara seems to have a harder time seeing Lisa in pain than I do. I imagine this is because Sara might be coming to terms with her feelings for Lisa. I recognize the signs and believe she has finally realized she's in love with Lisa.

When I tell Lisa that Sara's serum is not the answer, she takes the news with what I have come to know as her typical stoicism. She doesn't tell Sara how she feels about her. I don't want to fight with her, especially if my plan doesn't work.

I decide it's time to approach her with plan B—turning her into a vampire.

I send Sara out to get Lisa's favorite food, in case she can get a few bites down. Although she's no longer getting chemo treatments, she still has no appetite. I get her some awesome weed and it seems to help. I don't care about legalities. Marijuana is still the best drug I know to increase appetite and relieve cancer pain.

I knock lightly before I enter her bedroom. "Lisa, can I talk to you for a few moments?"

"Only if you don't try to get me to tell Sara how I feel."

"No, I promise this is about something else."

"Okay."

I can hear the hesitancy in her voice.

"Look, I know it was disappointing to learn that Sara's serum won't help with your disease, but what if I was able to give you a gift—the gift of immortality by turning you. Would you want this gift?"

"I don't know. Will I look like a scarecrow for all eternity?"

I chuckle. She doesn't look like a scarecrow, but she doesn't quite look like herself. Despite her sickness, Lisa is still beautiful.

"No, Lisa, you will be beautiful. I know a lot of vamps who were dying of a plague or some other horrible sickness at the time of death and they are all total hotties."

"Will I have to drain people?"

"Yes, if you want to hang out in the sun. At first I was kinda horrified by that, but trust me, you get over it pretty quickly when you see how much good you can do by taking those bastards out."

"What is it like taking someone's blood? Is it hard to get used to?"

"No, not really. We don't require a lot of blood to stay young and it elicits a kind of sexual response in hosts. The first time I took a little blood from this girl—she moaned. I'm pretty sure it was a good moan. It wasn't unpleasant at all."

"It's still not a guarantee is it?"

"No, but you don't really have anything to lose. I've been reading up on our history and even though it doesn't work very often—in fact the odds are pretty shitty—I really believe it will work for you. I can't do it without your permission though."

Lisa closes her eyes and I wonder if she's fallen asleep.

"You have my permission. If it's the only chance I have, I want to take it. I'll accept the consequences of my choice. I know what they are because of the path you've taken," she answers me quietly. "If it works, Sara can know, right?"

"Yes, the High Council does allow us to reveal ourselves to shifters. We have a strong alliance now."

"They owe that alliance to you, Nicky."

"No, they owe that alliance to Sara. She bit Vic and since Cass and Vic are soul mates, the rest is history."

"So what you're saying is that a vampire and a shape-shifter can make a good couple."

"Yes, they can. Apparently sharing blood and serum strengthens the bond and gives longer life to the shifters."

"Do Vic and Cass share blood and serum?"

"I think so, but I don't know. I never asked because I thought it might be too personal. If you want me to ask, I will."

"No, that's okay. One of the benefits of dying is I get to ask impertinent questions."

"I'm going to make this work, Lisa. I promise you I will."

"I believe you, but if not, maybe the afterlife is not such a bad place. Maybe I'll see my mom again. I'd like that."

I don't even want to think about the possibility of it not working. Lisa is way too young to die. I won't let it happen.

†

The month seems to drag by so slowly that every day is agony for me. It feels like college all over again.

I don't let Sara or Lisa know, but I'm back to crying myself to sleep every night that Sara is with Lisa. When a vampire cries herself to sleep, it doesn't show as much the next day but I don't think I'm fooling them.

I miss Annie so much it feels like the sun's rays are bombarding my body. I hurt to the depths of my core. I know I'm not hiding it from Cass—I'm certain she knows. I don't know how much she shares with Vic, or with Annie, because the Cass I've come to know always holds her cards very close to the vest.

Finally, the day comes and I wake up in a cold sweat. What if I can't convince her of my love? What will I do?

I haven't asked Sara if she will bite Annie, because I know it's premature. I have to get Annie back first and then I can ask for this favor. Favor, ha. A favor is such a nonchalant way to describe what I intend to ask of Sara. It's probably not fair to ask this of her, but I don't care.

I'm ready for the day. I find a particularly nasty serial rapist and ensure he will rape no more. I'm ready to spend time in the sun now.

I'm writing in my journal when Cass appears in the living room. "It has been one month. Annie is ready to talk to you. Are you ready for this?"

"God, I hope so, Cass. Do you have any advice for me? This is the most important day of my life. What can I do to convince Annie?"

"Do you really want my advice?"

"Yes, please. Tell me what I can do."

"You can buy her a ring and ask her to marry you."

God, I'm such an idiot. Why don't I ever think of things like that? The answer is so simple. She needs a tangible symbol of my commitment to her. I have some money set aside but nothing like Cass. My paltry resources embarrass me.

"Fuck. I don't have enough to get her the ring she really deserves. Cass, I promise, I'll pay you back, but can I borrow some money from you?"

"Of course you can, Nicky, but it's not the size of the ring that will matter to her. You could present her with a simple silver band. It's the meaning behind the gesture that will matter."

"I want both the meaning and the actual jewelry to match. Will you help me pick it out?"

"Of course."

"Okay. Let me tell Sara what's happening and then we can go."

I knock lightly on Lisa's bedroom door before I go in.

Sara has her arms wrapped around Lisa in a protective, loving embrace. Her eyes lift to meet mine.

I saw the nurse come earlier with a dose of morphine in her hand, so I suspect that is why Lisa does not stir.

I whisper to Sara. "It's time, Sara. Annie will talk with me today. I'm going out right now to get her a ring. I'm going to ask her to marry me."

Sara nods and starts crying. "I'm not sure how much longer it will be. Keep your phone handy. I may need you to come back in an instant. I'm sorry. I know the timing is bad and this conversation with Annie is important to you."

"No, I understand. The minute you text me no matter what is happening, I'll come back. I know we won't get a second chance to get the timing right."

"Thank you, Nicky. I'll be eternally grateful to you if you can give Lisa this gift."

I want to run right over and hug her, but I don't want to disturb the tranquility of the moment. I just nod. "I know it will work."

†

I drag Cass to every expensive jewelry store in Los Angeles, but I can't seem to find the perfect ring. Annie's hands are so delicate. The one and two carat monstrosities in their elaborate settings do not seem to fit.

Cass tags along with me and doesn't say a word even after I've taken her to twenty different stores. Finally, I think she reaches the end of her patience and leads me to a family owned boutique where I see the perfect ring. The diamond is small in comparison—probably not more than a half a carat, but even I can see it is flawless with the highest quality clarity that is available in a diamond. Unlike all the other rings, this diamond is deeply set into the gold with shimmering blue opals on each side.

The opals remind me of the color of Annie's eyes and I know this is the one. "I'll take it."

"Don't you want to know how much it is?" the storekeeper asks.

"Nope. This is the one. Whatever I can't afford, my friend will loan me." I point to Cass.

"Whomever this is for is a lucky woman." The owner smiles fondly at me.

"Oh no, I'm the lucky one—that is if she accepts."

The owner puts the ring in a brilliant blue box and tells me the ring is six thousand dollars. I'm happy that I can afford this with no assistance from Cass.

†

It's funny the things you think about when you're making important decisions. I take a little side trip and think about my life and how I've been looking at the need for financial resources. During the past ten years, I didn't worry much about money. I took a little here and there from my drainees. I didn't feel any guilt about this. Sometimes I kept the money, most of the time I found some homeless youths and distributed the cash as evenly as I could. I had a special place in my heart for the homeless gay teens. I didn't want them to resort to prostitution or drugs.

They called me the blonde angel—blonde devil is more like it. They didn't really know me. They only knew that I was their ticket to the next hot meal and sometimes if they were really lucky— a place to stay. I didn't need the money. There were vampire safe houses everywhere. Transportation was never a problem and food was a luxury not a necessity. Food for these young men and women was not a luxury.

During the past several months, since I've met Annie, I'd decided to keep more of the money, because I didn't want her paying for everything. This was the only reason I had any money saved.

I think maybe it was time I get a real job, but finding consistent drainees is not always easy. I know that most of the world operates during the daytime hours. But this problem can wait. First, I need to get the girl to say yes. I'll worry about how to support her later.

I'm feeling optimistic for the first time in a month. Somehow, I just know everything will work out—it has to.

I ask Cass where Annie is staying. I don't want to assume anything. She tells me Annie's been sequestered in her studio apartment, writing non-stop.

I feel guilty because Annie writes as a form of therapy and I know I'm the cause for this new backslide. I've sent her into isolation again.

Annie writes brilliant novels. I'm so proud of her talent. I don't want to be the cause of her pain, yet I'm pretty sure that I am.

Cass looks over at me and smiles. "It's time, Nicky. You have the perfect ring. Annie is waiting. Don't keep her waiting too long."

Her smile gives me a boost of confidence.

I take a deep breath and I fog into Annie's studio apartment. She is staring out the window. I don't think she is looking at anything. She appears to be deep in thought. She looks so beautiful that she takes my breath away—again—just like the first time I ever laid eyes on her. For a second, I literally cannot breathe and I think that maybe I'm having the second panic attack in my life.

She must sense my presence.

When she turns to look at me, she smiles.

Her brilliance is overwhelming. I have no doubt I want to spend all of eternity with her.

I smile back and I do the first thing that comes to mind. I drop to one knee and pull out the blue box. I'm about to beg her to marry me when my phone buzzes.

Annie must hear the phone buzz because I see her look down at the offending noise.

I pull my phone out of my jeans. "Oh, God, Annie, the timing sucks I know, but I have to answer this. Lisa is so close and if I'm not there when she passes—well, we won't get another chance."

"Go. I promise I'll be here waiting."

Annie looks at me with such love and compassion that even though it seems impossible, I fall deeper in love with her.

I glance at my phone. The text message is short and to the point.

It's time.

I look back at Annie. "I'm so sorry."

†

I disappear and fog back to Lisa's.

Sara is still holding her. The tears are trickling down her cheek in a constant stream—just like a spring melt in the mountains.

I take my place next to the bed and take Lisa's hand.

Lisa's eyes flutter open for a second and I think she recognizes me. She starts to talk.

I stroke her hand. "It's okay. Don't talk. I can read your mind."

I'm glad you're here. Can you tell her I love her?

"She knows. She loves you, too. I can tell."

Sara is now sobbing as she tries to talk to Lisa. "Oh God, Lisa, please don't leave me, I do love you."

I'm not afraid. Please don't blame yourself if this doesn't work. Take care of Red.

I will my fangs to come out so I can slice open my wrist at the exact moment I need to. I can feel Lisa's heartbeat slow down. It is no longer a steady beat. It is erratic and unpredictable. I wonder how I will possibly be able to get the timing right. I don't feel her heartbeat any longer now, so I slice my wrist and begin to offer the blood to Lisa. The silence in the room is deafening.

I'm startled when Sara interrupts me. "Wait. Not yet," she says.

It sounds like she's yelling because of the silence in the room, but she barely whispers this command. I don't know what makes me wait, but I trust her judgment.

No more than thirty seconds pass.

"Now, Nicky, do it now."

I place my wrist against Lisa's mouth and I command her to drink. At first, I don't think it's working, because I don't see any movement, but then Lisa's eyes open.

Lisa is a beautiful woman, but the transformation is astounding. The haunted look in her eyes disappears. Her body fills out a little more after her radical weight loss. Her skin begins to glow as she loses the pale sickly sheen that has been present since we reconnected.

Sara is crushing Lisa against her body. "Nicky, Nicky, look. It worked. Oh, thank God, it worked. Oh, God, Lisa, I love you…. I mean, I'm in love with you."

Sara's proclamation is not really a surprise to me.

"Thank fucking God for that, any chance we can skip to the good stuff now?" Lisa grins at Sara. "I haven't had sex in like, a year."

Lisa is so cheeky. I've always loved how she'll just blurt out these borderline inappropriate comments. Like me, she has no filter sometimes. It breaks the tension though and we all burst into laughter.

I'm so pleased with my matchmaking abilities that I think that maybe that's what I should do for a living.

"I think that's my cue to leave now. Besides, I kinda got interrupted earlier at a very inopportune moment. Before you both go right to the gutter, you didn't interrupt our lovemaking. I started to ask Annie to marry me when I got Sara's text and I have to admit to being kinda scared about her answer. I didn't get a chance to talk to her yet. I'll be back later—much later—to take you out and introduce you to the life. I can also ask Sabrina and Juno to help. Juno was a big help to me when I first became a newling."

"Go," both of them yell in unison.

I don't need them to tell me twice.

†

I fog back to the apartment. Annie is sitting on couch. She has the blue box in her hand.

My hands are sweaty now. I feel like an adolescent on her first date.

Her smile settles my nerves. "Is Lisa okay?"

"Yes. It worked. I have so much to tell you. I kept a journal of sorts this past month. I want you to know everything. I want you to know every little thought—every feeling I've had. I know I'm not a great writer like you, but I wrote my story. I want you to read it. It's an honest depiction of everything since my first day of college. At times, it's not very flattering to me, but everything is there. This is the only way I know how to explain what happened and get you to understand that I have no doubts. Before I was interrupted, I think you probably guessed that I was about to ask you to marry me. You don't have to answer me just yet, but if you can give me an answer after you read my journal, I would be eternally grateful."

I pull the journal out of my backpack and hand it to her.

She takes the book and opens it to the first page.

I start pacing her living room.

She chuckles a few times and then looks up at me. "Nicky, if you're going to continue to pace, I won't be able to read this without distraction. It will end up taking me longer to read."

"Sorry."

"No need to be sorry, but can you give me a little space?"

"Oh, sure, sure. Can I go into your bedroom and wait?"

"Yes, that is a splendid idea."

I go into the bedroom and throw myself on the bed. I begin to bite my nails—I know, such a human thing to do. I bring Annie's pillow to my face and inhale her scent. God, I miss her so much. I don't know what to do with myself while I wait.

The glow from her laptop is like a beacon to me. I hope she won't get angry if I read her latest story. The glow seems to taunt me and I can't help my curiosity. I pull the laptop onto my lap and settle back on the bed. I read the first page and I know it's our story. She's writing our story. It's filled with love, laughter, friendship, and yes, agony. Her book transports me into the story even though I've lived it—the story is through her eyes, not mine.

I imagine she may be feeling the same thing as she reads my diary, except the story is more about me. Of course it is, because I'm a self-centered bitch. Annie is selfless and I don't deserve her. I almost leave as the sudden realization hits me that she's far too good for me.

At that exact moment, she opens the door. Tears are cascading slowly down her face and she says one word that changes my life forever.

"Yes."

I think that maybe I'm hearing things. Maybe I'm hallucinating the answer I want to hear.

She speaks again. "Yes, Nicky, I will marry you. I love you more than I ever thought possible. Just for the record—you are not a bitch, asshole, or any other such derogatory name. If you don't stop beating yourself up for being imperfect, I may have to reconsider my answer."

Her words are so soft I almost don't hear what she says. Fortunately for me, acute vampire hearing often comes in handy.

I set the laptop on the nightstand and I'm off the bed and into her arms in seconds. I'm kissing her and caressing her as if she might disappear on me. The joy I feel at this moment is unlike any other joy I've ever felt in my life.

I take the blue box out of her hand, open it and pull the ring out so that I can place it on her finger. I look up at her to make sure it's okay and she smiles brightly at me. I place the ring on her finger and the fit is perfect. She is perfect.

I start babbling right away. "Cass and Vic can stand up for us. Lisa and Sara have to come, too. The two of them are together now. I'll bet it's pretty steamy in Lisa's bed right now. They seem to be a perfect match. I think I may have had something to do with that. Maybe I can pursue a career as a matchmaker. I have another idea that I wanted to ask you about, but you probably already read about it in my journal. I haven't asked Sara yet, but I think she'll do it for me. I don't know how you feel about it, but I'd like for you to at least consider it. I don't think fifty years is enough time. What do you think?"

"I think you need to take me to bed. I think we can talk about the rest later, but the idea has merit."

I don't need a second invitation. I slowly remove her shirt and kiss her shoulders. Annie shivers as I lead her to the bed. I try to control the excitement that is building quickly. Our arousal is swelling like a Tsunami as we both fall on the bed. I want to slow this down. I don't want this to be a quick fuck. I want to make love to her all afternoon. I want her to feel the love in every touch—in every kiss.

I don't know who moans first, but it sends my arousal into the stratosphere. "God, Annie, I've missed you so much. You feel like heaven. If I don't get to touch you soon, I know I'm going to explode."

Annie slips out of her pants.

I toss the rest of my clothes over the side of the bed. I brush my hand down her back and caress her perfect ass.

She kisses my neck.

I flip her on her back and slowly make my way down her stomach. Her nipples become rock hard as my hand lingers over them. Annie arches into my touch. I find her center warm, wet, and inviting, as I slip my tongue inside.

I hear a rush of her breath as she responds to my tongue. "Oh, my God, Nicky, what you do to me."

I hear her heartbeat increase and I continue my exploration. She's so close now, but I don't want her to come just yet. I want to delay and extend her pleasure to the point where she is screaming out my name. I back off just a little.

She whimpers. "Nicky, please."

"Shh. We'll get there. We have all day."

She sighs,

I feel her melt back into my touch. My tongue begins to make small circles around her clitoris and her arousal climbs again. I know she wants me to go inside, so I push two fingers in, as I continue to give special attention to her clit. I'm gently sucking as I stroke in and out. Her peak is the most beautiful thing. I feel every contraction against my fingers. She does cry out my name as her contractions continue for what seems like minutes, but is probably only seconds.

Annie collapses back on the bed and grins at me. "I'd forgotten how good you are."

"I never forgot this and I dreamed of you every night. It was all I had to keep me sane for a month."

"I'm sorry, Nicky, but I had to be sure. I had to make you take the month so that you could be sure. I know it was hard, but I'm still glad I did it. It gave you time with Lisa. I can't wait to meet her."

"Well, the feeling is mutual. She can't wait to meet you either. You are gonna love one another."

"I think I still have enough energy to ravish your body now."

"Um, no need. I kinda went over when you did. It was just so hot to see you like that, I couldn't control my reaction," I confess.

"We still have the rest of the day."

Annie and I make love the rest of the day and I'm the happiest woman on earth.

I want to talk to Annie about Sara biting her and her openness to joining the shape-shifter pack, but I fall asleep several hours later. I wake up and it's early evening. If I want to be out in the sun tomorrow, I know I need to hunt tonight, but I don't want to leave Annie just yet. Annie stirs and her beautiful blue eyes open.

She smiles at me. "Hello, love. Should I make us something to eat?"

"I can pop out and get us whatever you want." I'm excited to share our news with everyone. "Can I text everyone now?"

"Oh, yes, that's a great idea. You text Sara and Lisa and I'll text Cass and Vic. How about some sushi? Now that I know how much you like it," she teases.

Her grin is infectious, and everything is right with the world. I grab my phone.

She said yes. She can't wait to meet Lisa. Need to talk to you. Have a big favor to ask.

Congratulations☺ How about we meet at the compound? Would like to introduce Lisa to the pack.

Good idea. I can get Vic and Cass to join us.

I turn to Annie who is in the process of finishing her own text. "Sara and Lisa want to meet us at the compound. I know there are some unpleasant memories of your last visit there but perhaps we can start fresh."

"Vic suggested the same thing. She and Cass are so happy for us."

I look up and Cass is standing at the foot of the bed.

Annie and I both pull the covers up to our necks. "What the fuck, Cass? Ever heard of knocking?"

"Sorry. I was just so excited by the news that I wanted to congratulate you both in person."

Cass looks sheepish to me, so I let her off the hook. "Oh, it's okay. You did help me pick the ring out and gave me damned good advice."

"Vic and I have our own announcement. Would you be open to a double wedding?"

"Shit, Cass, you dog. You never said a word. You could have at least told me your plans."

"Well, I wanted to wait to see what happened with Annie— you know in case...."

"Got it. Did Vic talk to you about meeting up at the compound? I need to talk to Sara about something."

Cass starts to frown.

I can tell she is not happy. "Oh, stop with the disapproving looks. Annie already knows what I want to discuss with Sara. It's a good thing, I think?" I look at Annie for confirmation.

She nods.

I know she likes my idea.

"No, she didn't get a chance to tell me about the meeting at the compound, because I threw on my clothes and popped out as soon as I heard the news of your engagement," Cass tells us.

"Since a shape-shifter's serum bite works ninety percent of the time, I thought those odds are in our favor. I want Sara to bite Annie. I know it's asking a lot of her, but now that she and Lisa have found one another and I gave Lisa her life back, I think Sara will want to do this for us. I would have asked Vic, but I don't think she has the ability to ensure the same amount of success."

Cass doesn't say anything at first. She seems to be deep in thought. "Sara is a natural born, but only one of her parents is a shape-shifter. Have you thought about asking Ting? Her serum is pure. I'll bet that will virtually ensure success," Cass suggests.

I know I'm being unreasonable and jealous, but I can't help it. "No, no way. I don't want her touching Annie. Besides, it didn't work for her first lover. Maybe she shoots blanks."

"You are so cute when you're jealous." Annie laughs.

"I'm not jealous," I say, pouting. "I just don't like her. Besides it worked with Vic, so I don't see why it won't work for Annie."

"Don't let your pride get in the way of your future happiness. From what we learned, the success rate is higher when the serum has never been transferred to another and the serum is from a pure shifter," Cass argues.

"Fine, I'll talk with Sara and get her opinion on this." I look at Annie. "Ultimately, the decision is up to Annie."

Annie kisses me on the lips. "I love you, even when you go all cave girl on me."

My dopey smile returns and I let go of the covers and pull Annie into an embrace. I realize we are still naked and hurry to pull the covers back up.

"Okay, Cass, now that everything is settled, can you get the hell out of Annie's bedroom?"

"Of course." Cass stiffens and is now as rigid as a board. "We will meet you at the compound at five o'clock tomorrow. That should provide Lisa and Sara plenty of time to make travel arrangements since Lisa hasn't been shown how to travel yet as a vampire. Vic will make the arrangements. Do not be late. Do you need assistance with your hunt tonight?"

"Uh, yeah, that would be great. Come back around midnight. I'll be ready," I tell her.

"I think we should take Lisa with us tonight."

"I did tell Lisa that I would be back later to introduce her to the life. I was gonna ask Sabrina and Juno, but I didn't really talk about going on a hunt. Don't you think that will be too soon?"

"We can ask, but the sooner she learns the rules, the better. Our mistake with you was letting you roam on your own too long."

"All right, I will text her to let her know to expect us tonight."

Chapter Twenty-two

Annie, Vic, Cass, and I arrive at the compound early the next day. I feel kinda bad about taking Lisa out hunting the night before, but she tells me she wants to be in the sun and a few hours away from Sara won't kill her. I assume she heads back to Sara right after our hunt. Since Annie and Vic can't really fog anywhere, we take Cass's car. It's a smokin' hot Mercedes that I helped her pick out.

"I feel like I practically live here. It's like they're my second family or something. God, I feel kinda bad about spending so much time here and not telling my own family," Vic tells us one evening.

I think she's waiting for the High Council to give their permission for Cass to reveal herself. She probably wants their secrets revealed all at once. I know the meeting between the High Council and the elders helps.

I like Vic's family and I want them to know about me and hopefully about Annie too if everything works out the way I hope it will.

I realize I don't know anything about Annie's family and I don't want to make the same mistakes I made with Sara. I get the sense that there is a painful story there and I want Annie to feel comfortable sharing it with me. I've never seen or heard her call or write her family in the whole time we've been together and I don't know why. We have plenty of time to learn more about one another.

Ting greets us.

I have to admit she is being gracious. She shows no sign of irritation or anger at seeing Annie by my side.

She glances at the ring on Annie's finger. "I hear congratulations are in order. I am happy to hear things have worked out for you."

"Thank you, Ting," Annie responds for both of us.

I respect the way Ting is handling her loss.

She shows us to the same cabins assigned to us on our previous visit and I'm hopeful this will not resurface bad memories for Annie. I don't see any outward signs that Annie is uncomfortable. I love this about her as she seems to move on so easily. I've never seen her dwell on the past like I do. I'll bet all her therapy after the rape helps with this.

Ting tells us about the evening celebration. "There is another feast this evening. Sara and Lisa are due to arrive around four thirty. This should give them plenty of time to settle in before the feast at six. Shall I retrieve you just before six, or do you remember the way?"

I want to bite back that *we don't need you to* retrieve *us*.

Cass interjects before I can make a snarky comment. "Thank you, Ting, you have been gracious as always. I believe we can find our way without your assistance."

There is nothing snarky about Cass's statement. Once again, I'm being a total bitch.

"You're fine," Annie says and kisses me on the cheek.

I wonder if she somehow picked up mind-reading capabilities or perhaps she just notices my sour expression.

†

Annie and I are settling into our cabin and relaxing after the long drive from Seattle. The banging on the door is loud. I stand

211

up and give Annie a look like, *what the fuck*. I open the door to a beaming Lisa.

"Stop hibernating in the cabin. Haven't you two had enough make-up sex?" Lisa brazenly enters the cabin and grabs a startled Annie, pulling her into a hug. "I'm so happy to meet you finally. You were all Nicky talked about for the entire month she stayed with me. It was bloody sickening. If I wasn't already on my deathbed, I would have told her to get her bony ass moving to make sure she groveled until you took her lame ass back."

I think, *God, I love this woman.*

Annie starts laughing.

Even though Annie normally shies away from physical contact from strangers—for some reason, she doesn't immediately pull away from Lisa.

Sara follows the tornado, Lisa, into the room. "Hello, Annie, it's good to see you again. I presume you know who this little spitfire is. Let me formally introduce you to my future wife, Lisa."

I squeal as I grab both Sara and Lisa and crush them into a hug. "I knew it. I just knew it was gonna work out. Vic and Cass also just got engaged. I think we ought to have a triple blow out bash. Cass has more money than God, so she can foot the bill for all of us."

"Um, I'm not poor you know," Sara pipes up.

"Well, I am, so I'm more than happy to accept her abundance of resources," I declare.

"I'm so glad to finally meet you, Lisa. I read Nicky's diary and it's clear how much you mean to her. As for financial resources, I'm not poor either," Annie asserts.

I glance over to Annie. "Really? I thought I was going to have to look for a job or something. Why do you live in a studio apartment then?"

"It is a safe place for me and I didn't want to venture too far. I just never got around to moving. Since we were all talking about moving in together after the High Council sanctioned you and Cass, I just never saw the need to move. I got a lot of money for the screenplay and my books have sold well. Vic is smart about investments and I guess mine have done exceptionally well."

"Well, hot dog, I got myself a rich beauty queen, but I swear I'm not a gold-digger, because I didn't know before I asked you to marry me. I truly am the luckiest vampire on earth," I add with enthusiasm.

"It sounds like Nicky and I hit the jackpot. I'm not poor, but I'm not rich either. I had to spend a lot of my resources when I got cancer and then I couldn't work. I still insist on contributing to this big bash we're all gonna have," Lisa suggests.

"Honestly, I don't think any of us much cares who pays for it only that it happens."

I look at Sara. "Shifting gears for a second, I need to talk to you, Sara. I have a huge favor to ask and I need you to be completely honest with me."

"Nicky, anything, anything you need. You saved Lisa and I can never repay you for that. I can't think of anything I wouldn't do for you at this point," Sara tells me.

"Wait until you hear my idea before you respond."

"All right."

"It seems like shifters and vamps make good pairings, and since it is so difficult for us to make newlings, one option Annie and I are exploring is for someone to turn Annie into a shifter. She's not sick, so our chances are good, right? I don't think I can do what Cass did and wait for Annie to return after we only have fifty or so years together." I glance back at Annie for the confidence to continue.

She nods at me.

"I want you to bite Annie and give her your serum," I blurt out.

"I will do this for you and Annie, but I want you to know all the facts first," Sara says.

"Okay, tell us."

"First of all, since I have already transferred some of my serum to Vic, the possibility of success is severely diminished."

"How much of an impact?"

213

"I'm sorry, Nicky, maybe, at best, a thirty percent chance of success."

I slump down on the bed. The air whooshes out of my balloon of happiness. "I see," I mutter.

"Wait, Nicky, don't lose hope. It's a good idea. We can ask someone else," Sara offers.

"Not Ting," I declare emphatically.

"Why not Ting? I know she would do this for Annie. She is a powerful elder and her strength has increased over the years. I'm confident her chance for success would be ninety percent or better," Sara argues.

"If her chance for success is so great, how come it didn't work for her first lover, who she claims might be somehow connected to Annie?" I cross my arms.

"Ting was very young when she first fell in love, so I'm not surprised it didn't work. Let me talk to Ting. Please. Nicky, don't let your stubborn pride get in the way."

"You bit Vic during sex. It doesn't have to include sex, does it?" This is my greatest irrational fear.

"No, of course not, but they will need to have a connection."

"Define connection."

"I'm sorry, Nicky, but if they are not intimate they will need to spend time with one another. They will need to become friends."

I don't like this, I don't like this one bit, but I love Annie and I trust Annie. I look into her eyes and I see nothing but love.

"All right, it's up to Annie."

"Nicky, I love you and only you. I will never love another, so if this is what is required, you'll have to trust me. Besides, I have a feeling that Ting will become a good friend to both of us. You need to give her a chance," Annie tells me.

"I do trust you. I'm just not sure I trust Ting, but I'm not marrying her, am I?" I catch Sara's eye. "Okay, talk to Ting and let us know what she decides."

"This is going to be so epic." Lisa claps her hands. "From what I understand, there is some kind of legend that a new alliance between vampire and shape-shifter occurs with the return of a great love. Now that we have a triple love, just think how powerful that will be. Good things happen in threes."

"Bad things happen in threes, too," I mumble beneath my breath.

"I heard that, Miss negative." Lisa smacks my arm. "Remember, I have extra sensitive vampire hearing now. Don't let that green streak of jealousy overcome your good sense. I can't wait to meet this Ting person. She must be smokin' hot for you to be jealous."

"Hey, future wife sitting right here. I hope you're not overly anxious to meet Ting, or I might start to get jealous," Sara adds.

"You have nothing to worry about." Lisa's expression softens. "I've loved you for, like, forever. My arm almost fell off after carrying the torch for so many years."

Sara kisses Lisa tenderly.

I can't help my smartass remark. "Aw, isn't that the sweetest thing. The sugar high is making me sick. Let's go get some real food to counteract the effect. Isn't there a feast waiting?"

Chapter Twenty-three

Sara corners Ting at the feast and I see her nodding at Sara. I'm so tempted to try to listen to the conversation and I'm even more tempted to read her thoughts, but I don't. I may be a fuck up sometimes, but I draw the line at some things. I won't invade someone's privacy for my own personal benefit or curiosity. Whoop-de-do for me. I do have some scruples.

Sara walks over to Annie and me and pulls us aside.

"Ting has agreed to your plan. She believes Annie will make a wonderful addition to the pack and, before you go all cave girl on me, she understands that your relationship is sacred and she will not violate it. She admires you, Nicky, and would like to start over. She wants to develop a friendship with you, as well as with Annie."

I don't quite know what to do about this new piece of information. I take back every rotten thing I've ever thought or said about Ting as I look at Annie. She looks so hopeful that I pull up my big girl panties and vow to clear the slate and sincerely make an effort to befriend Ting.

"I'd like that," I say and I mean it too. I would really like to start over with Ting.

"That's great, Nicky. Ting is special. I know you will grow to love her as much as I do. She has been a good friend to me," Sara tells me.

I look over at Ting and send her a genuine smile. I can be amiable sometimes.

She strolls over to our group. She looks directly at me and extends her hand. "Truce?" Ting is very charming.

I extend my hand back to her. "I'm sorry, Ting. I have been a total ass to you and yet you still agree to help us out. I think maybe we should shoot for more than a truce. I want to get to know you as a friend. I can be a total bitch, but I can also be very loyal. You are deserving of a faithful friend. I'll never be able to repay your kindness."

Ting grins. "Don't be so sure of that."

I think that maybe Ting is teasing, but I hear a note of truth in her voice and I wonder what strings might be attached to the favor. I know this is a sacrifice for her because if she gives Annie her serum and it takes, she will have less chance of giving her serum to another. I can't figure her angle in all of this, but I'm so grateful I don't care.

Ting turns her gaze upon our newest member and extends her graceful arm. "Hello, I am Ting, you must be Lisa." She turns to Sara. "Sara, you really do have exquisite taste in women."
Ting smiles back at Lisa. "I am very pleased to meet you."

This is the first time I've ever seen Lisa flustered.

Sara smacks Ting on the arm. "Stop flirting with my future wife."

"I am doing no such thing. I merely made an observation."

Lisa seems to get back on solid ground and recovers from Ting's initial comment. She extends her hand to Ting. "Shit, Sara, no wonder you never brought Ting to meet us. If I met her first, I might have never held that torch for you."

"Ha, ha. Ting is a shameless flirt. It's best not to take her too serious. I on the other hand have substance." Sara pulls Lisa into a passionate kiss. "Besides, I am a far better kisser than she is."

"In your dreams, Sara, in your dreams," Ting fires back.

"I don't know about Sara's dreams, but she has been in my dreams ever since college—my wet dreams that is," Lisa quips.

"God, Lisa, have I ever missed your one-liners." I love this woman. "No matter what outrageous thing I say, you always seem to top it. Welcome back."

†

We all gather at one of the tables.

Vic and Cass see us and walk over to the table.

I'm a little nervous seeing Vic again. I wonder if she blames me for Annie's heartache this past month, but my concern is short-lived as she pulls me into a hug.

"Nicky, how are you? I've missed your diarrhea of the mouth." She smacks Cass playfully and looks at Annie. "These two barely say shit when you're not around to provide comic relief."

I see Vic look toward Lisa as she notices that there is a new member of our little tribe of lesbians. "Oh, sorry, I'm so rude." She sticks out her hand and offers it to Lisa. "Hi, I'm Vic, Cass's partner, future wife, whatever. Cass told me she's met you and has nothing but nice things to say about you. I'm so glad Nicky was able to...." Vic's voice falls off.

I think she must realize her faux pas.

Lisa waves her hand at Vic. "Hey, no worries. I'm glad Nicky turned me, too. Cancer is a bitch. I'm glad to finally meet you. You make a very beautiful couple."

"Thank you. Yes, Cass is stunning." Vic is beaming as she looks at Cass.

All through dinner, our group is laughing and joking. Ting has a wicked sense of humor and despite our rough start, I find myself appreciating her wit and charm. It's getting less awkward to be around her.

I suggest to Annie that she might want to take a walk with Ting while I spend some time with Lisa. She takes me up on the offer and I watch Annie and Ting walk away.

Sara excuses herself. "I have some business to attend to."

Vic and Cass walk away from the group and begin to stroll through the grounds.

I'm left alone with Lisa. I want to make sure that she is doing okay with her new abilities. "So, how are you doing? Was last night too much for you?"

"No, it wasn't. You were always more soft hearted than I was. I really wanted to be out in the sunshine today. So if the price of getting to spend the day in the sunshine is draining some douchebag—so be it. I'm glad you chose a particularly nasty person for me. It made it easier."

"You're going to make a much better vampire than me. So, did Sara tell you about our plan?" I ask.

"Yeah, she gave me the broad strokes."

"What do you think? Did she tell you how long she thinks it will take before Ting can try to give Annie the serum?"

"No, not really. Why?"

"Oh, I don't know. Everything seems to be falling into place for me and I'm just wondering when the hammer's gonna drop. I guess I'm just anxious. You never know what life will serve up next and I want to make sure that Annie's chances are secure before anything weird happens."

"You mean like get cancer, right?"

"Sorry." I cringe.

"Don't be sorry. I understand, I really do, but you need to make sure the odds are the best possible odds you can engineer. I don't think a month or two is that long to wait."

"Really? I just went through a month of hell. Trust me, a month is a really long time."

"I know it feels that way, Nicky, but a month is a drop of water in an ocean. Don't fuck this one up because of your impatience."

"Thanks, Lisa. You always did know how to cut straight through the bullshit. I needed this little pep talk from you. I don't suppose that me sending Ting and Annie off on a walk is going to quite solidify the connection they will need to make our chances of success certain."

219

"No, hon, afraid not. I can tell you from experience that anything worth having is worth waiting for. I had to wait fifteen long years for Sara and believe me it was worth every hour of every day."

"Of course you're right. I'll defer to Ting and Sara. They will know when the time is right."

Chapter Twenty-four

Annie and I end up staying at the compound for another two months. Sara and Lisa spend part of their time at the compound and part of their time in California. Vic and Cass visit quite often. Whenever the six of us come together, we spend time making plans for the wedding of the century. The shifters in the compound are so excited about the upcoming nuptials, they can't help but provide useful suggestions. Some of the suggestions are good—some, not so much.

Ting and Annie spend time together, and as I get to know Ting, I respect her even more. I'm not jealous anymore. Ting and I hang out sometimes and I'm grateful for our growing friendship. I get the feeling that she understands that I'm anxious about the upcoming attempt to transition Annie to a shifter. We've both told her how important this is to us.

One evening as Ting and I are taking a walk in the compound, she broaches the subject

"Nicky, you have been exceptionally patient. I did not think you had it in you. I am impressed. This is not what I would expect from the Little Wild One." She grins.

"Yeah, I know. Impulsive, impertinent child is a common descriptor. Lisa has a way of cutting through all the bullshit and helping me separate what is important with what is not important. I trust you to tell me when the time is right."

"The time is right. I feel not only a connection to Annie, but I feel a connection to you, as well," Ting pronounces.

My stomach flips. I wasn't expecting her to tell me this tonight. "Oh, God, now I'm really nervous. Our entire future is at stake."

"I know. I wish I could guarantee success, but I can only tell you that I feel everything will work out. I have a question for you."

"Shoot."

"Are you and Annie planning on having children?"

"Wow, where did that come from?"

"I have my reasons for asking."

"Um, well. I love kids, but I don't think vampires can have children. If we do, Annie will have to carry them. I know she likes kids and I'm pretty sure she's good with them too. We haven't really talked about it, but I don't think it's too farfetched to consider."

"There are male shifters who would offer their sperm if you decide to have children."

"I guess I would want my children to be as strong as possible—so that's a good idea."

"How would you feel if, years from now, someone like me fell in love with one of your children?"

The question startles me and at first I think, *ew*, but then I remember that shifters don't come of age until their first sexual experience. Ting could very well fall in love with someone hundreds of years younger and it wouldn't seem strange at all to anyone else. Love is love.

She is watching me, as the range of emotions cross my face.

"You know, Ting, I'm really glad you waited two months to share this with me. You know my legendary temper and I might have reacted very differently two months ago. This is why you agreed to the plan," I state.

"Yes. I consulted the Universe and came to realize that Annie is meant to be with you, but her physical likeness is so much like my first lover. I cannot ignore the possibility that she has come into my life for a reason. I believe that reason may be one generation away and I want your blessing if it is meant to be."

"Okay, but only if you promise not to deflower her until the age of twenty one. Wait, better make that twenty-three. Don't make me pull out the shotgun—loaded with silver bullets."

Ting laughs.

I scowl at her. "That wasn't a joke. I don't want my daughter taken advantage of or transitioning to adulthood before she's ready. I'm dead serious about that, however, I'd love having a six hundred year old shifter as a daughter-in-law. It might change our whole relationship dynamic. I'd relish being the powerful mother-in-law."

At this, we both burst out laughing. It's so ridiculous to envision me as Ting's mother-in-law.

✝

Ting and I enter our cabin.

Annie looks up and stops tapping on her laptop. She is still writing the story she started about us.

I think we're about to give her a whole new chapter.

She sees our broad smiles.

"You both look like the cat that ate the canary. What's up?" she asks.

"It's time. Nicky and I needed to discuss a related topic before the transformation," Ting replies.

I'm nervous again, because I don't know how this will work.

Annie shifts awkwardly in her seat.

I jump in and fire off several rapid questions. "So how does this work? Will it hurt when you bite Annie? Do you have to bite her, or can you give her your serum in another way that is less intrusive? Can I stay and be with her?"

"Okay, let me take one question at a time. I will need to bite Annie because that seems to be the most effective way. I suspect the bite will hurt for a short time, but you must not wash the bite area. We could try to isolate my serum and inject Annie, but this is not a method that has been tried before, so the success rate is unknown. Yes, Nicky, you may stay if you wish. It will be easier and less painful if I shift to my wolf. Will that frighten you, Annie?" Ting asks.

"No, I've seen you shift before and you're a beautiful wolf. It won't frighten me," Annie answers.

"Very well. I think it is best if we don't dally too much. After I shift, I would recommend that you make contact with my wolf. You may stroke my fur. This is not sexual, Nicky," she adds quickly. "It just cements the bond. I will be as gentle as I can be, but the skin must be broken. I apologize in advance for any discomfort I may cause."

I stand behind Annie and stroke her neck and shoulders. I'm letting her know I'll be right there with her.

Annie nods to Ting.

Ting carefully removes all her clothes.

She is spectacular in her nakedness, but I don't view this as anything sexual. I'm also not concerned that Annie might see her in that way. She is our friend. The shift is just as beautiful as I remember.

Annie reaches out to the wolf and strokes her soft fur.

Ting's wolf nuzzles her hand and gives it a quick lick.

I'm not sure if I'm supposed to touch her or not, but I figure she's my friend too, so I stroke her fur, as well. I guess this is the right thing to do, because she nuzzles my hand and then softly licks my palm.

Annie gets down on her knees and puts her arms around Ting. It looks like she's giving her an affectionate hug. Annie must sense that this makes it easier for Ting to bite her neck.

I kneel beside Annie and touch her arm, never breaking contact. I imagine Ting is as gentle as she can be, as she nips her neck and breaks the skin. There is only a small amount of blood. Ting doesn't go anywhere near her jugular vein. It's over in seconds

The next time I blink, Ting is naked again, reaching for her clothes. After Ting puts her clothes back on, she examines the bite. She nods her head.

I look at her expectantly. I think she senses that I need to hear the words.

"It is a good bite. You must keep it open. Do not wash it. Do not touch it. Just let the serum absorb into your system. Unfortunately, we will not know anything for several months. Annie, you must tell someone if you begin to have dreams about wolves. Our pack will probably feel you, but if you start to have dreams or odd sensations, you must tell someone at once."

I glance up at Ting. I have tears in my eyes as I whisper my gratitude. "Thank you, Ting. Thank you."

"Yes, thank you, Ting. You are a true friend. We will never forget what you have done for us," Annie adds.

"Nicky, will you tell Annie of our conversation?" Ting asks.

"Yes, I will tell her tonight."

Annie looks at me and raises her right eyebrow.

I give Annie a reassuring smile. "I'll tell you later. It's nothing to worry about."

Ting exits our cabin.

Annie strokes my arm. "So, what were you two cooking up besides tonight being *the night*?"

"Annie, what are your thoughts on children?" I ask.

"We've never talked about kids."

"No, we haven't. Kind of a big topic to avoid talking about, huh?"

"Vampires can't have children, right?" she asks.

"No, we can't." I shake my head sadly.

"So I guess I'll be the one to carry our children."

I squeal in delight. "Oh, Annie, I love you. How did you know I would love to have a bunch of little Annies running around?"

"I know more about you than you think and so does Sara and Lisa. It will just be one more child for everyone to raise."

"Ha, ha, very funny. I suppose I'm the child everyone thinks they're raising."

"So what does this have to do with the conversation you and Ting were having?"

"Well, Ting thinks that maybe one of our little wolf pups might be her destiny. Um, like she might fall in love with one of our children and she wanted our blessing."

I see on her face that Annie is going through the same range of emotions. The smile on her face lets me know she's come to the same conclusion.

"I suppose we could do worse in the daughter-in-law category," she declares.

Epilogue

So sue me because I made you wait to get your happy ending.

Annie starts getting dreams about wolves about six months later. I suspect she is tired of me asking her about her dreams every morning. I'm a total pain in the ass for six months.

One morning, she's grinning at me as I open my eyes. "I got one."

I'm not awake yet. I grumble back at her, "Got one what." Then I realize what she's telling me. I sit straight up in bed. "A dream, Annie? Did you have a dream about wolves?"

"Yes."

I try not to get too excited because it could just be a dream about wolves without meaning anything. "Call Ting right now."

"Nicky, it's only six am. I don't want to wake her up."

I'm not listening to reason. I grab my phone and before Annie can stop me. I hit the speed dial to Ting. The words come tumbling out. "Annie had a dream. Do you feel her yet?"

She tells me that she did feel something and was wondering.

"Awesome. Oh, Ting, I can't tell you how happy I am right now." I'm nodding and grinning like a fool. "Yeah… yeah… I'll tell her."

Annie looks at me.

I relay everything Ting is telling me to Annie. "Ting says that you need to pay attention to your body and notice if you have increased strength. She also says you might want to call Vic. She's been through all of this and kinda knows what to expect. Ting says as a natural born she's only heard stories second and third hand. She doesn't know what to expect but Vic does."

†

Vic and Sara often go out for late night runs. They've become good friends and Sara teaches Vic how to shift and the first shift goes amazingly well. I wonder if Ting or Sara will be the one to teach Annie.

The High Council starts loosening their rules and allows Cass and me to reveal ourselves to Vic's parents at the same time she tells them about the changes in her life. They are surprisingly nonchalant about the whole thing.

I learn a little more about Annie's parents and it takes all the self restraint I can muster not to hunt them down and confront them for what shitty parents they were. In my mind they both border on being deserving drainees, but Cass reminds me that not every horrible person meets the code. Annie has made peace with her childhood and considers Vic's family her real family. Unfortunately, we don't get to pick our own family and blood is not thicker than water.

I still haven't gathered enough courage to tell my own parents, but it's getting close. I want to make sure everything goes as planned with Annie.

We all decide to wait until we're sure that Annie is a shape-shifter before we set a date for our triple wedding. I want to be able to invite my family. The rest of my chosen vampire and shifter family support me in this.

†

Eight more months fly by and I'm standing in front of a mirror looking at my reflection. I scowl at the white dress that

Cass, Lisa, and Sara convince me to wear to my wedding. I convince everyone that a white tuxedo is better suited to me.

Annie gives me *the look*. "Nicky, I'm sure you would look hot in a tux, but you'll look even better in a dress."

That does it. I go out shopping with Cass, the tight ass, and Sara and Lisa, the twin smart asses. I finally find a simple white dress at Banana Republic. It's casual enough to fit my criteria, but fancy enough to meet their prissy standards. All of us are in white dresses, but I'm the only one tugging my dress and wanting to kick off my shoes to go barefoot.

I don't tell anyone that I secretly loved the pedicure they drag me to the day before but I suspect Annie knows when she snickers at me.

I give the dress one more tug for good measure.

Someone is knocking on the door. I think that maybe it's Cass or Lisa, but Ting peeks her head inside.

She whistles at me. "Damn, Nicky, you are looking fine today." She chuckles. "You look great, but boy, do you look uncomfortable."

"I know, I know. All the damned women in my life ganged up on me and you're looking at the result. I look stupid, don't I?"

"No, no, you look great. Look, this is not about you. Don't you think you can suffer through wearing a dress for a few hours if it will make Annie happy? By the way, that reminds me I have a bunch of messages for you. Your mom said, *quit tugging on your dress, you'll stretch it out*. Your sister, Tess, told me to tell you that Annie's just as nervous as you are, but no worries, she's handling it. Do not worry—she will make sure Annie shows up. Sabrina said Lisa is being a royal pain in the ass, and at this point, she would have preferred you asking her to stand up for you instead of Lisa. Your dad just told me to give you a kiss on the cheek for him. I wish I had recorded the conversation between Vic and her sisters and Cass's reaction. They had us all in hysterics— except Cass, of course. You're kinda right, she can be a little stiff sometimes. I think that maybe she is just nervous. It was nice of Vic's sister to stand up with her since you couldn't. Sara just said thanks for everything. Lisa said she's glad she got her wish because she will most definitely be dancing at your wedding. Whew, I think I covered everything. Oh, wait, I have one more message. Juno said she cannot wait to see you in a dress, and then she doubled over in a fit of laughter."

"Yeah, well, I'm glad for the photographer, because this is the first and last time anyone will see me in a dress," I grumble.

"Wait until you see Annie. She is stunning."

"How come you get to see her and I don't?"

"Bad luck. Now come on, it's show time. Helena and Faustina are here too. The room is positively vibrating with so many powerful vamps and shifters. This is the soiree of the century—millennium, even."

"Hey, Ting."

"Yeah."

"Thanks for being my best mate. All the others are in the ceremony but even if they weren't, you'd still be my first choice because of what you did for Annie and me. We'll never forget it."

"Aw, shucks, Nicky. I believe you just gave me a compliment."

"Oh, shut the fuck up."

We walk into the room full of people, and as Annie comes from the opposite direction, Ting is dead on. She is absolutely stunning in her white, flowing dress.

Ting, Sara, Vic, and Annie all go on regular runs in their wolf form. Annie is more confident now and her confidence is so damned sexy.

She told me last night that she's pregnant. Jacy, one of the elders, is happy to be our sperm donor and the first insemination takes hold.

I figure Annie won't mind if I tell Ting, so I whisper in her ear, "Annie's pregnant—you're the first one we've told. You gotta act surprised when we make the announcement later on."

Ting beams at me and pulls me into a crushing hug. "Oh, Nicky, I am so happy for you both. You are going to have beautiful children. I can't wait."

"Me neither. I'm so excited. You have to help me. You know what a fuck up I can be."

"Shh. You're the only one who thinks that. I always knew that things would work out. For once in your life, will you listen to those who love you when we tell you what a wonderful person you are? Annie is lucky to have you, and yes, you are lucky to have Annie. We are all lucky to have one another."

"Truer words have never been said," I exclaim.

The room is filled with my friends and family and all is right in the Universe. So many of us have come together recently and the love and joy that flows among our supernatural and natural family is awe inspiring.

Lately I've noticed that Sabrina and Juno are becoming especially close. They are helping me indoctrinate Lisa into the code. I wonder if I should try to nudge them together a little more. I've done such a great job with Sara and Lisa, that I think, *what the hell*. I'm born to be a matchmaker.

Annie looks at me and mouths two beautiful phrases to me. *I love you. You are so hot in that dress.*

I do believe I'm getting some tonight.

About the Author

Annette Mori

Annette is a health care executive living in the beautiful Pacific Northwest with her new wife (got to love Washington state) and their three furry kids. Well actually, it might be more than three, but they do not count the ones they only feed. Annette is fifty-five years old and believes it is not too late to try something new. As an avid reader, she is pleased there are thousands of good books to choose from, and hopes that one day hers will be one of the many for readers to consider. She reads at least three to four books a week, so please keep them coming. She has a habit to feed after all.

No matter if you loved it or hated it, I would love your comments. Feel free to e-mail me at annettemori0859@gmail.com. I will always be a WIP (work in progress—just learned that) so feedback is a gift.

Love Forever, Live Forever

Other Books from Affinity eBook Press

Possessing Morgan—Erica Lawson   New York City, in the height of summer. Crime seems to have taken a holiday, and Detective Morgan O'Callaghan is bored, bored, bored. Paperwork is mating and multiplying on her desk, and even a jaywalker is starting to look good. Anything to get her out from behind her desk! Enter Andrea Worthington, Charleston socialite and all-around rich girl, right down to the wealthy fiancé. She's also the new Assistant District Attorney assigned to Morgan's precinct. Their first meeting is like two freight trains crashing head on. Then a high profile, career make-or-break murder case throws them together again. The investigation has barely begun when Andrea becomes the target of a nearly fatal hit-and-run. But was it really aimed at her? Can she and Morgan find the common ground they need to solve the case and stop the attacks, or are the gaps just too wide to bridge?

Twenty-three Miles—Renee MacKenzie   Talia Lisher has a long family history of lying, about anything and everything. With her father dead, and her mom gone on a quest to start a new life, Talia struggles to keep in touch with her only remaining family, her incarcerated brother. When Talia sets her sights on Officer Shay Eliot, she vows to stop lying. She starts watching Shay, waiting for just the right circumstances and amount of courage to talk to her. Talia might be watching Shay, but someone in a dark van is watching Talia. Is the mystery driver a dangerous part of her family's past, or is it all just a coincidence? Shay Eliot has left the

233

police force because of what she perceives as a hostile work environment. When a brutal double-murder on the 23-mile-long Colonial Parkway puts the FBI's magnifying glass squarely on her, her alibi comes from an unlikely source – a young woman who has been stalking her. Shay wants to keep her distance from Talia, but once she gets to know the younger woman she can't keep feelings from developing. This is a story about community, and how it comes together in dangerous and devastating times. When you don't know who to trust, you better have friends who will rally around you. Will Talia and Shay find the answers they need to the mystery of the murders on the parkway, or will justice be elusive? Will they survive their quest for the truth?

Confined Spaces—Renee MacKenzie Andie Waters spends her days pulling waste samples for environmental testing and at night, she tends bar at The Cave, a popular hangout for straights in a small Georgia town. Serial monogamy has grown stale for her, so she's content working to pay off her debts and hanging out with her old hound dog. Or so she thinks, until a beautiful lesbian drops by The Cave. Andie suspects her involvement with the woman will be only temporary. Little does she know no part of her life will be left untouched. Kara Travis likewise anticipates nothing more than a brief fling upon meeting Andie, especially given her reputation as both a personal ice princess and a corporate hatchet wielder for Royal Environmental. What luck to find a hot lesbian bartender in nowhere rural Georgia. Andie and Kara spend a passionate weekend together and find that their notions of no strings attached are far from accurate. Their supposed short-term ideal diversion of a commitment-free romp hits a major complication when they come face-to-face with one another at Royal Environmental's offices Monday morning. While carrying out her duties, Kara discovers crimes being committed by and against Royal Environmental employees. Will Kara be forced to shut down the Georgia Division of the company? If she does, Andie will lose her job. Worse yet, Kara may lose Andie before she's really even sure she's got her. Corporate politics, complicated romance, and long distances conspire to keep Andie and Kara all boxed in. Can love triumph despite the Confined Spaces?

Reece's Star—TJ Vertigo Reece Corbett watches over the dancers in her gentleman's club with the blue, razor sharp eyes of The Animal. Few know that resting comfortably in her office is her newest love, a tiny MinPin named Smudge. What happened to The Animal, known for her rapacious appetite for women and danger? Faith Ashford is what happened to The Animal. Faith and Reece have been together a while now and they have settled into something resembling domestic bliss. This bliss alarms Reece. It's one thing for Faith to see her softer side, that's vulnerability enough, but to let her friends see it...no. Not the best plan. Under Faith's guiding, loving hand, will Reece successfully traverse the rocky road of emotion and embrace the positive changes in her life? Or will she panic and be unable to control that Animal part of herself? Will she take that next step to declare herself fully capable of love and devotion? This third installment in the popular series that began with *Private Dancer* continues the passionate and often hilarious romance of Reece and Faith as they both grow in love and in trust.

Flight—Renee Mackenzie It's 1983 and Kate Hunter is a student at a small, private college in Virginia. When Lana coaxes her onto the back of her beat-up scooter one night, Kate's education starts to encompass more than just her pre-vet studies. Kate has always done as expected of her, so when she starts staying away from home on weekends to spend time with her new lover it's way out of character for her. Lana is secretive, but Kate accepts things as they are and gives Lana her space. When she feels the sting of betrayal, will she be able to continue giving Lana her privacy? Kate's sister April is a high school student playing with fire as she parties with her older boyfriend, Boyd. After finding someone overdosed the morning after a big party, April grows weary of all the drugs and alcohol. Will she be able to convince Boyd that they should slow down? Will she be able to pull it together before it's too late? Kate and April are forced to face up to events from their younger years, their mother's desertion, and their long-deteriorating relationship with one another. Some lives will be lost and others changed forever when the sisters' lives intersect. Will they be consumed by the wreckage, or will they be able to pick themselves up and take flight?

Reflected Passion—Erica Lawson Where passion, reality, and destiny combine.

Dale Wincott is a 27-year-old woman born into Bostonian wealth and groomed to marry into the social hierarchy. Her mother is a hard-hearted society matriarch, but her father feels for his daughter and helps Dale find a life on her own as a furniture restorer. Françoise Marie Aurélie de Villerey is a 28-year-old Countess, born into the French aristocracy and forced to marry a count much older than herself. For ten years, she was his trophy wife, forced to endure his perverted desires, until the day he finally died. He had broken her emotionally and she no longer cared for what life had to offer, slipping from one sexual partner to another as often as she changed her clothes. Until... that one night when Françoise looked up during a sexual encounter and saw Dale watching her from the mirror. A veritable angel, full of innocence and curiosity, who touched her very soul. Through the mirror, Françoise embraces life anew, while for Dale it is a powerful awakening, forcing her to discover not only her sensual nature, but the inner strength she possesses.

The One—JM Dragon Phil (Philomena) Casters loves her work as a pilot, above everything else in her life except Ming, her married lover. Phil needs to enhance her status in the community before asking Ming to leave behind her wealthy husband. Rosa Moran a teacher, raised by missionaries in China after the death of her parents. She loves the country of her birth and the people. Her English grandfather desperately wants her to live with him to atone for the guilt he feels about the death of her parents. He sends her a letter requesting her to come home. When Phil flies to the mission to deliver the letter to Rosa, neither can envisage the chain of events about to take place. It starts as a collaboration to save four children, leading them to the surreal private paradise of Langshow. Could this be the perfect place for the children and Rosa to settle? Phil is not so sure. Chang, an old friend from Rosa's childhood lives in Langshow and makes no bones about the fact that he wants Rosa. All thoughts of Ming disappear as Phil tries to fight her attraction to Rosa. However there is the little matter of an innocent misunderstanding—Rosa thinks Phil is a man. *The One* is a romance with everything, love, intrigue, misunderstandings with a happy conclusion—the only question—who gets the girl?

The Chronicles of Ratha: Book 2 A Lion Among the Lambs—Erica Lawson It has been three years since Jordana Laren's path first crossed the Noorthi's - three years since she's had a drink, had sex and a life of her own. Her only excitement has been spent keeping up with her two year-old daughter, Rice, who is definitely a chip off the old block. All has been peaceful until one of the colonists becomes sick. Bad news shifts to worse news when the disease spreads through their community. Unable to get proper medicine, Jordana is forced to rely on the Noorthi healers to come up with a cure. Soon the herbs run out, leaving her with no choice but to search for more on the Noorthi home planet. What is supposed to be a simple pick-up flight turns into a nightmare. Can Jordana believe in herself like her Noorthi sisters do? Only then can she fulfill her destiny as The Chosen One. Follow the colorful cast of characters in this action-packed adventure sequel as they traverse the galaxy. Of course, nothing ever goes smoothly when Jordana is involved.

Cowgirl Up—Ali Spooner When the new ranch hand, Coal Bryan, arrives at the MC2, the last thing she's looking for is love. Her co-workers are surprised when Coal turns out to be female. Coal, used to the reaction, quickly earns the respect of the crew with her work ethic and skill with horses. Coal uses the strenuous work and friendship of the ranch hands to try and forget her broken past. Melissa Conway, owner of MC2, offers Coal a place to live in her home. They both are shocked to find they are linked in a way neither of them imagined. Mary Leah, Melissa's sister, arrives at the ranch to recover from a recent tragedy. The attraction between Mary Leah and Coal is instant and mutual. Can the three women survive their personal dilemmas? The love and friendship they develop certainly helps but will it be enough to bring them together. Ride along with the MC2, for boot scootin', butt kickin', dirt eatin', rodeo adventures, with a love story thrown into the mix.

If I Were a Boy—Erin O'Reilly Katie McGuire appears to have it all. A devoted husband, a job she loved, and a comfortable lifestyle. Helen Swenson is a successful financial director of a prominent investment firm, with an unfaithful husband, and few friends. Their husbands' annual trip to Padre Island National Seashore to reunite with their air force pilot squad becomes a pivotal point for the two women. Their lives take on a completely new meaning when an undeniable magnetism between them draws them together. Passion and secrecy becomes the norm, as they have no choice but to succumb to their attraction. Can the vacation love affair continue? When they leave for their respective homes, will they regret what happened? Life is not that easy to change and the people around them are the hardest to convince. There is no more powerful motivation than love. Except hate and there are plenty of people who want to see their relationship destroyed. Will Katie and Helen be able to make a life together work or succumb to doubts and the pressures of family? This story will fill you with the thrill of passion and the tenderness of love.

The Chronicles of Ratha: Book 1 Children of the Noorthi— Erica Lawson Jordana Laren is a hard-drinking, hard-fighting womanizer, who works as a freighter pilot in her spare time. Her latest customer drugs her, steals her ship, and abandons her on a desert hellhole called Rigeus, infamous penal planet for the worst women criminals. Her chances of survival aren't looking good. She has no food, water, or weapons, and the nearest bar is a million miles away. Just when she's ready to write her last will and testament, Jordana is rescued by a group of barely-clad women. Has she found nirvana? Her own personal harem seems like a possibility, until the intercession of their enemy, the Velkren. Their leader, Vel, remembers Jordana well, and not fondly. But why is Vel on this planet, surrounded by murderers, thieves, and bad-tempered bitches? Jordana knows Vel isn't a prisoner, so why is her nemesis on Rigeus mining mud, of all things? Jordana knows only one thing. She has to get off the planet before Vel kills her. Unfortunately, the women who saved her reveal themselves to be holy. They are the Noorthi, and Jordana's dream of endless debauchery becomes a nightmare of eternal servitude. The Noorthi make her one of them, marking her with a wrist tattoo, and leaving her no choice but to protect them with her life. The last thing Jordana wants is to become involved in galactic politics or heroic actions. But the tattoo ochre in her body is suddenly giving her morals and scruples, not to mention a better vocabulary! And she really can't pass up a chance to outwit Vel, whose megalomaniac plans are endangering not only the Noorthi, but the civilized galaxy itself. But Jordana is torn. Does she stop Vel at all costs, or does she get out from under the thumb of the Noorthi while she can? Some things were never meant to be easy…

Nesting—Renee MacKenzie Macy Stokes, a divorced mother who is struggling with her sexual identity, jumps at a once-in-a-lifetime opportunity to help her friends. She doesn't foresee it will put her in jeopardy of losing her son, Jeremiah. Fresh out of high school, Cam Webber travels to Augusta, Georgia, to reconcile with her aunt. When she learns that's impossible, she determines to gain acceptance from her aunt's partner, Sharon. Meanwhile, Cam sets her sights on Macy, but Macy has other ideas. Kenny Brewer is a good old boy who loves his wife, Dorianne, even when he thinks she's gone totally off her rocker. Dorianne gets it in her head that a local woman is her long-lost half-sister. But soon, her obsession with that is eclipsed by medical problems that involve them all. Set in Augusta, Georgia, *Nesting* explores the age-old issues of guilt, regret, and redemption, and the part they play in driving people to create and protect family-at any cost.

Reece's Faith—TJ Vertigo In the return of the main characters from the bestselling novel *Private Dancer*, we see the blossoming relationship of bar owner, Reece Corbett and actress, Faith Ashford. The two women explore new, uncertain territory together, using sexual intimacy as a glue of comfort, helping them become strong and whole. A trusting Reece shares with Faith the sordid tale of how she became *The Animal* and Faith finds herself newly empowered by Reece's ongoing trust and support. Jealousy arises when Faith has to kiss a man on her TV show and two amorous women stalk Reece. When Faith is outed on her television show, things get crazy. With the arrival of her parents on the scene, the craziness escalates. As Faith tries to justify her lifestyle and defend her love for Reece, she discovers that nothing about her parents is as she once believed. This, not to be missed passionate and erotic romance, will have you begging for more.

Starting Over—Jen Silver Ellie Winters, a successful potter, is living on a remote hilltop farm inherited from her parents. Her well-ordered life is shaken apart when her past meets her present. Robin Fanshawe, Ellie's philandering long-term lover, has a fragile truce with Ellie. The arrival of women from Robin's present threatens to break that tentative pact. Charming Dr. Kathryn Moss, an archaeologist and an old lover of Ellie's, arrives on the farm searching for a new site to dig. When she discovers a previously unknown Roman settlement and ancient burial site on Ellie's farm, Ellie allows her to start an archaeological dig of the area. Will Ellie also allow the rekindling of an old romance or will she stay with Robin? Can that long term relationship, albeit tentative, recover from this collision or will an old romance trump everything she knows? Will Robin, seeing the interaction between Ellie and Kathryn, leave her womanising ways behind? Will she take a chance on giving herself wholly to the woman she loves?

240

These questions and the mystery of whose royal resting place is disturbed at Starling Hill are answered in this classic romance of simmering passions, anguished loss, and the wonder of love.

Twisted Lives—Ali Spooner A twist of fate leaves Bet and her daughter Kylie stranded at the entrance of the home of Alex Graves, as she flees the control of an abusive husband. When custom–homebuilder Alex arrives to find steam boiling from Bet's car and a beautiful child asleep in the passenger seat, her heart goes out to them. Alex offers shelter to the pair setting off a chain of events that bring both mother and daughter close to her heart and danger to her door. A heartwarming story of true love that will keep you smiling long after you've finished the book.

Malodorous—Del Robertson   Sequel to My Fair Maiden Something in Fairhaven stinks. Other than the mutton stew, that is. Gwen thought life after being a virgin sacrifice would be a bed of roses. Bodhi was just looking for a wench to bed. Neither less-than-dashing hero nor not-quite-so-pure maiden imagined they would meet again, much less be trapped together in a city the likes of the ill-named Fairhaven. There's a killer on the loose. Fairhaven's on lockdown, its citizens fearful for their lives. The local guards are corrupt. And, Bodhi's been accused of murder…

E-Books, Print, Free e-books

Visit our website for more publications available online.

www.affinityebooks.com

Published by Affinity E-Book Press NZ LTD
Canterbury, New Zealand

Registered Company 2517228